"HOW'D YOU LIKE ME TO SQUASH YOUR FACE WORSE THAN IT IS ALREADY?"

Zemo picked him up under the arms and shook him like a rag doll.

"No!" screamed Dolly, covering her face, exposing her cleavage at the same time.

Raider exploded in rage and burst free, then turned and cracked him squarely in the jaw. It was like hitting armor plate. Pain shot through Raider's fist and up to his elbow. But the demonic grin was still stretched across Zemo's face as he threw his body sideways. He pounced on him, pinning his arms away from his body with knees the size of oak stumps, leaning over him, hammering Raider with his fist and knocking him cold.

J. D. HARDIN

THE MAN WHO BIT SNAKES

PLAYBOY PRESS
PAPERBACKS

Published simultaneously in the United States and Canada by Play-boy Press Paperbacks, New York, New York. Printed in the United States of America. Library of Congress Catalog Card Number: 79-92153. First edition.

Books are available at quantity discounts for promotional and industrial use. For further information, write to Premium Sales, Playboy Press, 747 Third Avenue, New York, New York 10017.

ISBN: 0-872-16657-0

First printing May 1980.

1

Raider smoothed his flowing black mustache with his thumb and second finger as he eyed his face in the glass. The swelling under his left eye had taken on the color of a storm cloud; his right eye was beginning to open a trifle, shyly reintroducing itself to the world after hiding behind locked lids for upwards of fifteen hours. The red and raw abrasion strapping his chin stung, so he was moved to splash cold water on it out of the bowl and mutter obscenely.

It had been a rousing good squabble with his fellow Pinkerton operative, Doc Weatherbee, whose own face displayed a similar set of contusions and abrasions, with a bloody nose as the main attraction, awarded him by Raider in payment for the black eye.

The fight had been broken up by two bartenders and a teenaged bull of a boy. The partners had parted company loudly vowing never to speak to each other again, these ultimatums delivered with appropriate vicious threats and accusations. It had all come about over a woman, one Flossie DeRoy, who had proven long on promise, short on delivery, and confused in her timing, scheduling both Raider and Doc for her bed for the hour of ten the previous night. Confusion had led to disappointment, to difference of opinion, to loud argument, to blows. In the midst of the exhibition, Flossie had deserted the field on the arm of a good-looking young stranger and the two Pinkertons had wound up battered, bruised, bitchless, and bound to go their separate ways.

Raider raised the nearly empty bottle of Rookus Juice to his lips and emptied it. Breakfast on the run. He cast about the gloomy little hotel room for the last time, taking in the brass-trimmed iron bed, the chest of drawers, each of which stuck so one would swear someone was hiding inside holding them closed, and the washstand with the thirty-cent plate mirror hanging over it. The glass was a dingy yellow, lending Raider's complexion the sallow look of a victim of jaundice. He buckled on his Peacemaker, hauled on his hand-tooled calfskin Middleton boots, donned his Stetson and, slinging his saddlebags over one shoulder, noting as he did so the four matching bruises on the knuckles of his left hand, started out the door.

Moments later he had paid his bill and was outside in the street unhitching the *grulla,* draping the saddlebags over her back, and climbing on. It was noon, the sun's baleful white eye focused on New Mexico Territory from directly overhead. Noon in Golden, New Mexico, squatting a few miles east of the Rio Grande almost in the shadow of Sandia Peak.

Four years, he mused as he set himself in his saddle and heeled the mare's flanks, wheeling her about toward the south end of the little town. Four years chasing lead, throwing it, catching it, stopping it with various parts of his body—none, thank God and Lady Luck, vital spots; four years eating trail dust up and down the territories, cold beans, rotten meat, bitter coffee, bushwhackings, blizzards, brawls, butchery, and bullshit in a ceaseless flow from Chicago, from Wagner and the Chief, Allan Pinkerton. Short money, long complaining, almost never a pat on the back, groaning, griping, I-told-you-so, and scant rest for the weary. Fuck it. He didn't need it. Never had. What upset him more than anything was his simpleminded reluctance to accept that fact until now. He'd be better off punching steers, railroading, even mining. Maybe the pay wasn't the greatest, but the danger was nil and there'd be no Weatherbee to lock horns with. Four years with that college boy, that cashmered dude with his big mouth, his know-it-all attitude, stickling him to death with his goddamn rules and regulations, Allan Pinkerton's General Principles. . . . As if, for Christ's sakes, you could solve a case with a goddamn book of rules in place of a reliable gun and a fast horse! Face it, he and Weatherbee were just too goddamn opposite to ever get together on anything—rules, regulations, routes, strategy, whores, name it. A boon, a benefit to both if they never laid scowls on one another again. Let the custom-tailored, cologne-covered bastard turn a rock over and find himself a new partner, if he was dumb enough to stay on with the agency. Some green kid who'd cheerfully endure his incessant needling and swallow all his bullshit. He himself had had it up to his mustache.

His hand climbed to his black eye, wincing at the contact. Jesus, it was sore, full of dead blood, no doubt. What he wouldn't give for one last go-round with the grinning prick! Get in two more licks, smash his smile clear out from under his curl-brim derby.

He rode on. He was a mile out of town, loping along the winding road at a leisurely pace, striving to shed all memory of Golden, of his ex-partner, the agency, the past four years, the whole stinking kit-and-boodle when he heard hooves pounding off to his left behind him, a lone horseman galloping over the sagebrush-tufted land, short-cutting to the road. No mistaking those flapping coattails, the gold-and-black checkered vest showing underneath, the hand holding the derby in place.

Doc Weatherbee came pounding up, grabbing Raider's reins and grinning at him fiendishly. His nose was saddled with a two-inch strip of court plaster, and in spite of his grin it was evident he was having difficulty breathing.

"Let go, or I'll bust your hand off at the wrist, so help me!" boomed Raider, fishing out his .44 and raising the grip like a hammer.

"Relax, Rade, take it easy." Doc let go. "We have to talk."

"No thanks, I've done all the talking I'm ever gonna do with you, you mangy bastard, you friend fucker from way back. I need you and that goddamn agency like I need the clap!"

"What are you so hot about? I didn't get to bed her down any more than you." Digging in his pocket, Doc brought out a telegram, waving it. "We've been handed a new assignment. This just came in ten minutes ago."

"Fuck you and it. Count me out. Me and the Pinkerton National Detective Agency are quits, as of now. When you report in, you can tell Wagner I'm finished. I got other things to do with my life. You can also tell him the agency owes me twenty-six dollars and fifty cents in back pay. Which he can wire me in . . ." He paused, realizing that he hadn't really thought about where he would go. Let alone what he'd do when he got there.

"You horse's ass!" exclaimed Doc irritably.

Raider bristled, dropping the reins. "You want to start up again? Do you? Want me to bust every bone in your worthless goddamn body?"

"Don't be ridiculous. You can only see out of one eye; your cheek looks to be fractured. You've no more stomach to start in again than I have. Look at my nose, look . . . The doctor says it's broken in three places."

"Good! Terrific!"

"Which has to make you better than even, doesn't it? Rade, will you wipe that dumb look off your face? You'd think I'd raped your sister. How can you get so burned up over a dollar whore?"

"Fuck her with a dead ox. She's got nothing to do with this. She was just the last straw. I been meaning to quit for months . . ."

"You mean years."

"I'm fed up."

"You're not the least bit curious what's in this telegram?"

"Hell no. Wipe your ass with it for all I care. I'm goin' and you'd best not try to stop me. Grab my reins again, they'll be the last thing you'll ever grab!"

"Boy, are you tough as hell!"

"Try me."

Doc snatched the reins, this time with both hands, crumpling the telegram in his left. Raider cursed, jerked one foot out of its stirrup, and heeled him full in the ribs, knocking him out of saddle, landing heavily on the ground, groaning and rolling over. Down like a flash, Raider ran to him.

"For Christ's sakes, what'd you make me do that for? You bastard. SON OF A BITCH! Hey, are you okay?"

"I think my shoulder's busted," said Doc tightly, screwing up his face and stroking his shoulder gingerly.

"Bullshit! You landed soft as a feather. Lemme look." Raider examined him, flexing the shoulder, Doc wincing, protesting. "It's okay."

"You shouldn't have done that, Rade, I could have landed on my nose."

"I warned you fair. Twice. You got no right grabbing my horse like that."

Raider picked up the telegram fallen to one side. The "kya kya" of a golden eagle sounded high over their heads, its great wings spread and its tail fanned outward, lending it the appearance of a domino mask. Both men eyed it briefly; then, realizing what he was doing, Raider flung the paper from him in disgust. Doc rose tiredly to his feet, retrieving first his derby, then the telegram, uncrumpling it.

"You wouldn't be able to decipher it anyway. What it says is . . ."

"I DON'T GIVE A GOOD GODDAMN WHAT IT SAYS!"

Raider was back up on the *grulla* and away, dusting down the road toward Edgewood.

"It says," said Doc quietly, "that a counterfeiting ring operating in the Territory of New Mexico has been giving the Secret Service fits and at the personal behest of Governor Sheldon, President Hayes has granted permission to call in the Pinkertons." Raising his eyes from the yellow paper Doc followed Raider until he was only a speck under a vertical column of red dust shimmering behind waves of heat between the hills. The eagle too had shrunk to a tiny dot, carrying its quest for food to the west into the mountains.

Doc mounted. He would follow Raider at a distance,

unseen, and when darkness enshrouded the earth, close
to nine hours ahead, he would close the gap.

It was less than twenty miles to Edgewood; Raider
passed straight through the sleepy little farming community without so much as a tug on the reins to slow
the *grulla*. Putting the ramshackle buildings behind
him, he followed the narrow road, veering sharply to
the southeast toward Moriority, which to his pursuing
ex-partner meant that he was heading for Texas, well
over two hundred miles distant. Doc had no pressing
urge to follow him all the way to the border; he didn't
enjoy horseback. It was, in fact, far down on his list
of modes of travel. His preference would have been
the driver's seat of his apothecary wagon, comfortably
cheeked on his new rubber cushion, Judith his mule's
reins in one fist. But she and the wagon were stabled
in Albuquerque following the wind-up of the two Pinkertons' last assignment.

Nine hours was a long time, possibly half the distance to Texas, counting stops for rest, for food and
water. Better he put a stop to his partner's asinine
behavior sooner than later. This decided, he cut away
from the road just beyond Edgewood, bypassing Moriority and pushing his mount to inspired effort, pulling
up alongside the Laguna del Perro, the only water he
knew of between Moriority and Duran to the southeast.
Watering his horse and tying it in a grove of peach-leaf
willows, out of sight of anyone coming down to the
water, he then hid himself behind the thick, black-
barked trunk of a tree and waited. And waited well into
late afternoon. Gradually second thoughts began to
assail him.

Was Raider heading for Texas after all? Had he deserted the road this side of Moriority, or worse, before
then, just beyond Edgewood? To head where, east,
west? Had he stopped in Moriority and climbed aboard
a New Mexico–Central train? Heading south, it would
pick up the El Paso and Rock Island line, which headed
down to the El Paso and Northeastern line to the
border. Such a course of action certainly made sense.

A ride on any of the three lines would be free, thanks to his agency railroad pass. He could even bring his horse along.

"Damn!"

He was on the verge of remounting and heading for Ancho at full gallop to catch the first train through, heading for El Paso, when the sound of a horse easy-gaiting reached his ears. His stallion, standing in the willows, whinnied.

"Sssssh, don't." He eased a branch aside, peering between the light green and gray leaves.

Raider dismounted and, removing his Stetson, whipped the dust out of his denims with the brim. The *grulla* ambled down to the water and drank greedily. He pulled her head back, letting what she'd swallowed get down into her stomach and spread itself before he let her have more. Down on his knees he splashed water against his face with both hands, undoing his neckerchief, soaking it, and patting his neck with it. It was so insufferably hot and he was so sweaty he was half tempted to strip to the skin and go for a swim. But better a plunge bath with a sponge and a bar of yellow soap wherever he stopped for the night.

This was more like it, he thought, freedom of choice, swim or don't, ride or not, stop or move on. No more orders from Chicago, no more you will, you must, you are hereby ordered to. . . . An irreversible end to his career of mopping up crime like puke off a barroom floor, stomping out little fires that had sprung up three and four in number for every one you managed to put out. Sitting in their comfortable chairs in Chicago, Allan Pinkerton and Wagner hadn't the remotest idea of what conditions really were, what law and order were like out here, or what it took to bring them to bear. It was like running around the African jungles trying to keep the lions and tigers from killing the monkeys and zebras and each other, seeking out one needle after another in the haystack. What really hurt every lawman was the vast distances. A killer or thief could hit and then run five hundred miles, lose himself in the mountains or the desert or go over the line into Mexico. And everybody wore a gun, all types, all ages. And knew how to use it. Three quarters of the population from the Mississippi to the coast comprised half the riffraff of the world. Half . . .

The thought coursing through his mind was stopped abruptly by a silent explosion, bringing with it sudden, intense pain and a great bursting of crimson flashes.

2

The tar pit into which Raider had plunged, pain and all, seemed to lighten somewhat, the blackness graying perceptibly. But then the pain in his head swiftly returned, pushing him down once more to the bottom of the pit, restoring the blackness. He was dimly, distantly aware of additional pain, not nearly as intense as that afflicting his head, duller, more like a soreness slowly worsening. His stomach. And his wrists and ankles felt as if steel bands were locked around them. Until his return to the pit bottom wiped away all sensation.

When the gray came back a second time, it softened from slate to pearl to an ethereal whiteness, a deathly pallor that prompted the conviction that he was dead. But to his relief he found that he could move his lips and breathe and even groan, a sound barely above a whisper. His head throbbed mightily and his wrists and ankles were sore, as was his gut. His mouth felt as if it were stuffed with dirty waste. And a new sensation joined the lot. An unusually pleasant, familiar feeling that seemed to be moving upward in his crotch, a delicious, tingling, welcome warmth surging in his balls. Slowly, tentatively, he parted the lids of his unafflicted eye. He was lying in a bed, his head against a straw pillow, his body fully clothed stretching down to the foot, his fly unbuttoned, his cock out and standing tall, a pink face with a mop of coal-black hair poised above it, a wet mouth roping him, sliding slowly up and down, up and down, down, down, holding, her lust-loaded tongue punishing him, his tool halfway down her throat. Then her mop of hair resumed bobbing as once again she began stripping the life out of him, sucking ravenously, gluttonously.

He came, groaning loudly, lifting his body braced on

13

his hands. Droplets sneaked out of the near corner of her mouth, plopping like tears down upon his pubic hairs, glistening in the warm yellow light of the lamp. Her mouth released his cock, letting it sag limply. Turning her face, she smiled at him. She was slightly cross-eyed and her beauty mark plastered against one cheek had somehow slipped down to the opposite corner of her mouth, giving her a ridiculous appearance. A square jaw and a nose resembling a flattened mushroom did little to improve her looks.

"Who . . ." he began.

"You can call me Angel." She tittered and straightened up, setting her little tits jogging, threatening to jump free of the confines of her low-cut blue satin dress. Around her neck was a black ribbon with a brooch fixed at the front of it against her throat. She began undressing.

"What are you doing?" he asked.

"What does it look like?" She paused in unbuttoning the back of her dress. "You do want a ride, don't you? I mean it's all paid for."

Raider sighed wearily. The son of a bitch. He sneaked one hand around to the back of his head and winced as he found first one bump, then another. His wrists were red and sore where he had been tied, as red and sore as his ankles felt. Belly down over his saddle all the way to . . .

"Where am I? What town?"

She had resumed undressing, finishing undoing her dress, letting it fall, stepping out of it with affected daintiness. Her breasts were not that small, he noted, and the nipples were lusciously round and pink. Once more she stopped and stared at him.

"Are you funning me? This is Albuquerque, the Wallace Hotel, Room Two-B. Your friend brought you in about ten minutes ago. You've been sleeping like a baby."

"Where is the son of a bitch?"

"He . . ."

A knock rattled the door. "Mr. O'Toole, sir, are you decent? Can I come in?"

"Go away, you deceitful prick!"

"Tsk, tsk, tsk, such language. And with ladies present . . ."

Angel smiled demurely. "Shall I let him in?"

"Like hell, just hurry up with what you were doing there. Time's wasting."

Doc gave it up moments later. Even before he did so, Angel was down to the liberally powdered and perfumed buff, hauling Raider's pants off, unbuttoning his shirt, and climbing in alongside him. Grabbing his cock she began jerking it back to hardness, rolling it between both palms like a ball of clay being rounded and lengthened, getting it semi-hard before burying it in her face to bring it to full erection. Releasing it from her lip grip, she grinned at him.

"How do you like it? Upsy-daisy? Loop-the-loop? Back door, doggie, sitting, standing, chair, floor, wall, round the horn, whistle deep, pinwheel?"

Raider made no response. To him fucking was serious business, not an experience to be ventured into lightly. Lifting himself up and over her he slid his throbbing tool between her thighs and into her quim. Slowly, gradually, until he was halfway home. Then ramming all the way. She squealed and bounced and began rocking her hips, bucking like a fly-bitten pony. He let her do the work, the sweat bursting from him, his breath coming in short pants, his knees drilling into the mattress as he hung on to her upper arms for dear life.

Unlike many a fast fuck he had known, the lady was no actress. She obviously thoroughly enjoyed her work. She screamed when she came, her shrill cry assaulting his eardrums, all but piercing them. Coming the first time charitably delayed his coming now, but at length his balls built up to full hardness and up came his juice, splattering her walls, drenching them gloriously.

Letting himself fall slowly down on top of her, he rolled over to the side on his back and lay perfectly still. Raising herself on one elbow she once again reached for his cock.

"Hey, no . . ."

"Relax, this one's on me. No charge."

"Lady, you are flogging a dead horse. Let it loose, please."

"Suit yourself."

She was up and dressed and heading toward the door, humming gaily; catching sight of her shifted beauty mark in the glass over the commode on the way, she restored it to its proper position without breaking stride.

"I'm free later tonight if the dead horse comes back to life. Angel's the name. I'll be downstairs in the bar. Remember, first come, first served."

And she was gone, her place in the doorway quickly filled by Doc who, Raider imagined, must have been standing outside in the hall all the while.

"You're the next worse thing to a goddamn peeping Tom, you know that?" snapped Raider. "You ought to be fuckin' ashamed o' yourself, sneaking up behind me, bustin' me on the scalp fit to crack my skull. Not once but twice. You damn near broke my spine from the front slingin' me over my saddle that way." Drawing his knees up tightly, Raider rocked and pushed himself forward onto the floor. "I'm gonna fix you permanent!"

Doc brought up both hands with surprising quickness, pushing him back down, the iron springs squeaking resentfully. His .38 Diamondback appeared in his hand.

"Lie down, shut up, and listen, ingrate."

"Fuck you, go ahead, shoot . . ."

"Rade, will you please listen? I know how you feel, I know you're fed up. You've every right to be. They pile it on us, we work like dogs, we barely have time to breathe; so quit if you want to. Retire to the farm, hang up your six-gun and your .94, peddle your gear to the first passerby and start working sugar beets or corn, whatever you please. I don't blame you and I'm not about to try and talk you out of it."

This speech was so entirely unexpected, so discouragingly sincere Raider found himself at a loss to respond, giving his partner the chance to resume.

"You quit, so will I. I wouldn't work with anyone else, how could I? Old dog new tricks, I guess that's it."

"I ain't asking you to quit. I muchly prefer you go to hell."

"Whatever you say."

"Oh, cut the horseshit, will you, Doc? I mean what are you trying to do, make me feel guilty? This is a free country, isn't it? Ain't I got every damn right to quit?"

"Of course. There's just one thing."

"Here we go . . ."

"Please." Doc restored the .38 to his shoulder holster. "We've just finished up a pretty messy case, wouldn't you say?"

Raider shrugged, doing his best to feign disinterest. "I suppose."

"Too much blood. You yourself killed three of those renegades. For what? For Wells and Fargo and their forty thousand dollars and to add a new star to Allan Pinkerton's crown?"

"You can say that again."

"To have to kill people for stealing lousy money . . . A messy case." Out came the crumpled and since flattened and folded telegram Doc had produced earlier.

"Now, as usual, the agency wants us to take on a new case."

"To hell with 'em—Allan Pinkerton, Wagner, the lot. You take it on, count me out. And don't make me keep sayin' it over and over. Out. O U T!"

"Right." Doc got up from the side of the bed. "I'll take charge of it myself."

"Do that. Now kindly get out and let me get my drawers on."

"Counterfeiters."

"Don't tell me, I don't want to know. Just git."

"It looks like a dandy. I have a thought. You're going to retire, right?"

"Not going to, have."

"It comes to every man."

"Oh, for Christ's sakes . . ."

"But answer me this, wouldn't you prefer to go out feeling good, feeling proud, satisfied? Not like both of us feel after Sante Fe and that Wells-Fargo go-round.

What do we get out of this job, Rade, but satisfaction? We're certainly not in it for the money. We've got to be masochists to be in it for the danger, the thrill of the chase, as it were. What do we have to show for it but that warm feeling surging up inside when everything's buttoned up and the case journal is closed? How about this? How about one more assignment before you hang them up?"

"You go to hell. One more, sure, and one more after that. Then one more. Until somebody's shotgun retires me to a hole in the sod. No thanks."

Doc sighed. "Maybe you're right. What's the point." He waved the paper. "Though this one really is a dandy. With the President's permission, the governor has hired the agency. I know for a fact that Allan Pinkerton is a long-time friend of Governor Sheldon. What's stumped the Secret Service so far is that this group appears to be no ordinary koniackers. In the first place they deal in banknotes exclusively."

Raider sighed and eyed the ceiling, avoided his partner's eyes, hummed out of tune, even turned his face back into his pillow pretending sleep. But he did not cut Doc off. The banknotes were paper periodically issued by bankers against increasing assets. It was a system that had been much in vogue up until the war's end. Then the U.S. government began to issue a national currency. In 1866 Congress imposed a ten percent tax on all currency still being issued by state and territorial banks, which drove other notes out of circulation almost completely, except for the private banks in the as yet uncommercialized West.

Someone was taking advantage of these holdouts. Virtually every bank printing its own banknotes did so in the identical manner. The president, his cashier, and a guard would carry the plates and special banknote paper to a local printer and watch the pressman closely while he inserted the plates and ran off the required quantity of banknotes.

"The problem that's cropped up in Deming and now here in Albuquerque is that more than twice as many banknotes as were legally printed are showing up at the banks' windows to be exchanged for silver or currency," Doc added.

"Which bank here?"

"T. D. Morgan's Territorial."

Doc proceeded to explain that the agency's information was that the phonies were works of art printed on authentic stock and signed in both Deming and Albuquerque by the individual banks' presidents and cashiers.

Raider scoffed. "That's bullshit. How can it be? They musta' miscounted their goddamn assets."

Doc had cast his net and caught the fish. Just inside the edge, he mused, forcibly suppressing a smile of satisfaction. Close enough to the edge to permit it to flip free and scoot off into the dark waters of Stubborn Refusal from whence it had swum.

"Rade, we've got to give this one a shot. We've got to nail down the lid before this bunch papers the whole Southwest. They're good, bright, resourceful, and clever as the devil. Are we better? Can we lick them?"

Raider glared at him venomously without speaking. Had his eyes been fire he would have shriveled him to a cinder. But slowly, almost indiscernibly, his features softened to a degree threatening a genuine grin.

"You son of a bitch!"

In his mind's eye Doc saw the net close tightly, the fish slung inside it. Into the creel, clamp the lid shut.

"Get dressed," he said. "And shake it up. We've got a meeting with T. D. Morgan himself in . . . He pulled out his new seventeen-jewel "Special Railway" Hampden watch with the hunting case and frowned. "Five minutes."

Before he was even aware of what he was doing, Raider had his legs over the side of the bed and was pulling on his denims, pausing before lifting his butt to fit the seat and close his belt buckle.

"What in red hell am I doing?"

"Four and a half minutes."

"I must be stark staring crazy!"

"Think of it this way, Rade, the last case of your brilliant career."

"Oh shut up." He stood and buckled on his Peace-maker. "It really is, Doc, I swear to God and all the angels. We wrap this up and I'm climbing on the first train to Chicago. I'm handing in my resignation personal, signed and sealed. That way I'll be sure to get my twenty-six dollars and fifty cents."

"Peanuts, Rade. We crack this case and we could be in for a bonus."

"Don't hold your goddamn breath. The day that penny-pinching Scotch bastard ever lets extra cash slip through his hand into either one o' ours is the day you walk through hell barefoot. Stark staring crazy, that's me, stupider than a damned ore-cart jackass. . . ."

He continued to seethe and fume and fuss out the door, into the hall, and down the stairs to the street, his partner bringing up the rear, one hand clamped tightly over his mouth to keep from laughing out loud.

3

T. D. Morgan was a grizzly bear of a man, everything his physique carried outsized, impressive, including the enormous mustache flowing across his face matching the white thatch atop his head and the snowy brows nestling above his eyes that sent wild hairs an inch long thrusting forth in every direction. It was his eyebrows rather than his eyes that lent him his wild look, for his eyes were a pale, almost watery blue. He sat at his desk in his private office with the parts of a belltop clock spread about the blotter. It was late in the evening, nearly eleven, and the bank was in darkness save for the small office illuminated by a single brass perfection student lamp, its shade directing its glow over the desktop, leaving T. D. Morgan's face in semidarkness. The office smelled of furniture polish. A bottle of Farquard's Rye stood at the banker's elbow, a wet glass beside it. Introductions over, he had gestured both Pinkertons to chairs and offered them clean glasses from out of a bottom drawer in the desk. All three drank briefly; T. D. Morgan rolled his sleeves up one more turn and, picking up a screwdriver and adjusting a loupe to his left eye, began tightening a screw.

"Either o' you boys interested in timepieces?" he asked in a voice resembling a well-controlled rumbling funneling upward from an active volcano. They confessed to no such interest. "Pity, it's the most relaxing hobby a man can have."

"Do you know where all those parts go?" inquired Raider.

"I sure enough better." Morgan laughed, lowering his work from the loupe, letting it fall from his eye and reaching for a drawer at his left. "You boys really got to excuse me. I get so involved I forget my manners.

21

Happens all the time." Bringing out a large cloth he draped it carefully over the blotter. "Got to keep the dust off. Dust, dirt, neglect are any timepiece's worst enemies. Keep your clock or watch clean and cared for and it'll outlast you and your son and his son. But there I go again, you didn't come here to talk about timepieces. Though I confess this clock is helping me keep my nerves from jumping outa my skin at this sorry business." He glanced from one to the other, his broad brow crinkling. "Only sent two o' you, eh?"

"Hopefully we'll be enough," said Doc dryly.

"It appears to be the sorta case best played close to the vest," added Raider.

"Too many cooks, eh?" Morgan scratched one cheek and drank a little. "I expect you're right." He cleared his throat, sending the clearings flying accurately through the gloom and rattling into a spittoon in the corner. He then began recounting everything Doc had earlier told Raider. Both operatives let him ramble on without interrupting, until he began describing the banknotes.

"Could you show us some samples?" asked Doc.

"Sure." The banker produced four five-dollar banknotes from his billfold, pushing aside the cloth and the parts under it, making space enough to lay the notes down in a neat rectangle, edges joining. They looked identical, each one an artistically wrought collection of multiple swirls and geometric designs. The coloring of all four was consistent and excellent, the designs clearly reproduced, and the lettering accurate. The ink and stock appeared to be the same.

Doc studied each note in turn closely. Morgan watched him just as closely.

"You can't see any difference at all, can you?" said the banker.

"The signatures . . ."

"Ahhh, good, excellent. You've a sharp eye, Mr. Weatherbee." Morgan indicated the top left note. "There's my signature and my cashier's, authentic." His finger moved on clockwise to the others in turn. "This one and this one are forgeries, just a hair off, you might say. But any man can spot his own signature forged. This last one is an out-and-out botch."

Raider bent close to examine it. "The 'g' in Morgan . . ."

The banker nodded and produced a magnifying glass. "You notice how cramped it is compared to those in the other three? And the tail end coming out of the second hill of the final 'n' cuts off; it isn't brought up high enough into what you might call a semi-flourish. The problem is, gentlemen, these notes are so legitimate-looking in every other respect the bearers don't look closely enough, or don't bother making comparisons with other specimens."

"Why should they?" asked Doc.

"Why indeed. What they don't know won't hurt 'em, eh?"

Doc finished his liquor and Morgan wet the bottom of his glass for him. "When was this last batch printed?"

The banker thought a moment. "Less than two weeks ago. Ten thousand dollars' worth, and we, Dawson Harder my cashier and I, estimate that at least fifteen thousand have already shown up at the windows. To be blunt it's threatening to ruin us. If it keeps up, it will."

"The paper and the ink look to be the same," said Raider.

Morgan made a face and shook his head. "They are. But there's nothing unusual about that. Anybody can get his hands on both. If he's clever, if he does his homework. It happens we get our paper from the Pierce-Atherton Paper Company in Waltham, Massachusetts. You boys, anybody can buy the same."

Doc continued, engrossed in the banknotes, having borrowed the magnifying glass from Morgan and examining one after the other over and over again.

"Do you keep your plates in your vault?" he asked.

"In a strongbox in a safe in the vault." Morgan fished in his watch pocket, brought up a small brass key. "This is the only key in existence to the box. I lost the other one."

"Who manufactures your plates?"

"Masterson Engraving in St. Louis, a highly reputable outfit."

"It's possible somebody working there isn't quite as reputable as the company is," ventured Raider.

Morgan shook his head. "We thought about that, Dawson and I, but look here, these plates are seven years old; why should anybody duplicate them, then wait seven years to put them to work?"

"Maybe they fell into other hands?" Raider shrugged.

"It's possible," said Doc, "but I'd have guessed as you do, Mr. Morgan, Masterson's on the up-and-up. They have to be; they've too much at stake. All the same, these notes, this one with the cramped 'g' and the cut-off 'n,' had to have been made from your plates. Apart from the signatures I can't see one iota of difference."

"Nor can I," said Morgan in a defeated tone. His huge body sagged as he exhaled. "Which is what scares the life outa me."

"If we rule out duplicates, then there's only one explanation," continued Doc. "Somebody 'borrowed' your plates."

"I tell you it's impossible. I took them out of the box, handed them to the guard, and walked with him and Dawson to the printers. Just down the street and around the corner. Moody's. I never took my eyes off the guard's hands, not for a step, not for a split second. We walked in, the plates were handed to the printer, locked into the press, and inked. The printing was started, two samples run off, examined, declared flawless and kept, and the rest of the run went on. It was completed, Dawson counted the money twice, I counted it twice, the plates were removed from the press, cleaned, and handed back to the guard. Back we came to the bank, back went the plates into the strongbox, into the safe in the vault and the door closed and locked. You two tell me how they do it."

Raider and Doc exchanged glances.

"I wish we could," said Doc quietly. "And I'm sure we'll be able to, once we've conducted a thorough investigation."

"Which will take time. Time that could ruin me."

"I doubt that." Morgan tried to cut in, but Doc gestured for his indulgence. "Whoever is doing this to you is obviously out to make a bundle. They intend to make as much as they can, but without ruining you completely. Think about it; if they forced you to close your doors they'd lose out too. On the face of it, I have to give them credit for more intelligence than that."

"What he means is there ain't no sense milking a dry cow," said Raider.

"Perhaps," said Morgan. "Be that as it may, this thing has been a nightmare. When in God's name will it end?"

Doc pointed out one thing Morgan could do—specifically hang up the cramped "g" forgery and alert his people to be on the lookout for similar discrepancies. Morgan was way ahead of him. The bank had been doing precisely that for a week.

"Every day we have half a dozen near riots. Unfortunately I have to believe that most of the fakes are almost perfect, that this note and any others like it"— he tapped the lower left note in the quartet—"are rarities. It stands to reason; if I were grinding out identical specimens and only had to forge the signatures, having accomplished the hard part I'd be goddamned careful to take my time on the easy part, I mean signing them."

"They're using your plates," said Doc solemnly.

Morgan groaned. "How? How is it possible?"

"I don't know."

"Then how do you know they are?" asked Raider.

Doc glowered at his partner. "Rade, don't mess things up; they are and that's that. You'd have to be half blind not to see it." He handed the magnifying glass to him. "Look."

"How do you propose to upset their applecart?" asked Morgan.

Again the two operatives exchanged glances. Raider turned away and Doc consciously suppressed a shrug. "I wish I could answer that. You've got to give us some time . . ."

"Yeah. Not too much time, hopefully. Every day goes

by is sinking me another thousand or so deeper into the red. The people who patronize this bank are beginning to take a long hard look at us. To their way o' thinking there is no counterfeiting. The way they look at it, we're just not willing to back up our own paper. Who can blame them for thinking that?"

Reminding himself of his dilemma was obviously having a telling effect on the man's nerves. His frustration was getting his face redder by the moment, his lower lip was trembling, and tiny beads of sweat were setting his brow gleaming. Whipping the cloth off the clock parts he sat down, finished his drink, restored his four banknotes to his billfold, screwed his loupe into his eye, and, picking up his screwdriver, resumed working.

"We'll see you tomorrow noon," said Doc quietly. "We'll solve this thing, I promise you."

"I hope to heaven you do."

Raider and Doc left. Outside in the street the night lights of the town glowed feebly against the blackness, the moon and stars obscured by a thick blanket of clouds. Raider sighed in exasperation.

"You got a big mouth, mister."

Doc extracted an Old Virginia cheroot from his inside pocket, lit it, and sent the match hissing into a nearby horse trough. "Sure . . ."

"I mean it. You got no right promising him we can beat this thing. Christ Almighty, it looks to be tougher than pulling nails with your teeth!"

"I had to say something, Rade. The poor man's breaking up into little pieces. You saw him."

"That's no reason to make promises you can't keep. Jesus Christ, why in red hell did I let you talk me into jumping into this in the first place?"

"Oh for God's sakes, we're not going to start in on that again, are we?"

"I will if I want to. That's the whole fuckin' point. We get ourselves locked into a case, all of a sudden I'm not supposed to gripe or question anything or let out my feelings or nothing! Which happens to be the bullshit part o' this whole shebang that gripes my ass purple! And the main reason I'm quittin'."

"Then quit, goddamn it. Stop talking about it and do it! Climb on your horse and leave." Raider stared at him, his jaw slack, his dark eyes wide in wonderment. "I'm serious. I'll clear this thing up alone. I don't need you, Rade. I don't need anybody who's not interested. Good night, old friend, I'll see you around. Maybe."

Tossing away the one-puffed cheroot in disgust he stalked away, muttering.

Raider snorted. "You son of a bitch. Come back here, goddamnit! YOU HEAR ME?" He ran after his partner, grabbing him by the shoulder. "I'm talking to you . . ."

"Hands off, Rade. That's the shoulder you pushed me down on. It's sore. Don't touch it." Doc flattened both hands against his chest and pushed him away hard, bitter resentment twisting his handsome features. "Just beat it."

Raider pushed him back. Doc spun around, seething, and started away a second time. Once again Raider caught up with him. Once again he grabbed hold of his bruised shoulder, turning him toward him, but this time Doc brought around his right hand, cocked and ready, and ramming hard into his partner's rib cage, doubled him over with a roar.

"You son of a bitch!"

At it they went, hot and ponderously heavy, driving fists into each other's midsections, missing wild round-houses, Raider catching Doc flush on the jaw, sending him staggering back, Doc lowering his head and bulling forward, knocking Raider flat. Doc landed on him, astride his belly, clipping him alongside the head left, right; left, right. Raider bucked him off, brought his own left up from the street, and smashed him so hard in the temple the other side of his head hammered to rest.

Both were bleeding now from various cuts, Raider's black eye re-blackened, Doc's nose catching knuckles, the bandage straddling it loosened on one side and hanging down limply, both nostrils gushing fresh blood.

He brought up the palm of his hand, cupping it gingerly against his nose and yowling in pain.

"Damn you, you clumsy bastard!"

He'd had enough; any further damage to his nose would mark him for life, if it hadn't already. Turning from Raider he walked off. His partner was down on one knee catching his breath, exploring his own face with the tips of his fingers.

"That's it; quit, you yellow polecat."

Doc stopped abruptly and turned back, trying unsuccessfully to restick the court plaster against the upper edge of his cheekbone, giving it up, ripping the plaster away entirely and flinging it from him.

"All right, all right, all right, what are we picking on each other for? Only because we're exhausted and hurting and boxed into one heckuva bind."

"You, not me."

"You really mean you'd desert me, you'd leave me holding the bag?"

Few people were in the street at such a late hour, but those that were, and others drawn from inside a nearby saloon by the two combatants' yelling, had gathered to watch. Aware that they were being stared at, Raider retrieved his Stetson, picked up Doc's derby alongside it, slamming it into his hands, snorted, donned his hat, threw up his hands, and stomped off. Doc legged it after him, trailing blood as he ran. Their audience followed them with their eyes, quizzical looks on everyone's faces, low-voiced comments, a titter or two.

Raider headed for the saloon, the Yucca House, pounding through the batwing doors and up to the bar. He spied himself in the mirror behind it and gasped. His bad eye was closing fast, his good eye threatening to follow suit; his face was beet-red, as if strong hands had been massaging it for fully an hour. Blood curled down out of the left-hand corner of his mouth and, investigating with thumb and forefinger, he discovered his first and second molars sitting loosely in their bloodied sockets. He was amazed his jaw wasn't broken, or at least dislocated; it was sore as blazes. Shock waves of pain shot clear up to the top of his head as he moved it slightly from side to side to test its solidity.

The bartender's brown eyes were baleful. Without even asking, he poured and shoved a glass toward him.

"Drink up, it's on the house. We don't want any trouble in here."

"Mister, do I look like I do?" Raider dug out a coin and slapped it on the bar. The man behind the apron and the handlebar mustache turned, taking the coin and the bottle with him, but Raider's hand shot out, snatching hold of the latter.

"Leave that . . ."

"You look as if you been fighting all week."

"Yeah."

The whiskey rolled into his mouth, hitting his two loosened teeth like twin branding irons, white-hot, and shoved home. He groaned so loudly the piano player behind him stopped and everyone turned to stare. For two seconds. Then festivities resumed. Laying a greenback on the bar, he drifted to the nearest empty table, sitting down hard. Taking off his Stetson he set it alongside the bottle. Which, he mused, he didn't really need. Not if it meant branding his teeth every time he took a swig. What he really needed was a bed. Ten hours' sleep, a telegram of resignation off to Wagner in Chicago, mount up and ride out. His horse left tied up in front of the hotel would be all right for the night. As for Weatherbee, screw him. They shouldn't have had at it. It was dumb, unnecessary; they ought to have known better. They should have just parted company, even shaken hands and wished each other well. You just don't wind up four years shoulder to shoulder flailing away at one another like two hotheaded kids half smashed on pulque. It wasn't civilized; it wasn't right. But that was how it had turned out and what was done was done.

He hoped he hadn't hurt the son of a bitch. At least no more than the son of a bitch had hurt him. As far as the case was concerned he didn't even want to think about that. Why should he? His mind had been made up to quit before they'd even sat down with Morgan, before Doc had heard from Chicago, actually. Oh, Doc had tried to talk him out of quitting, but he hadn't really succeeded. All that was was what you might call a little lapse in resolve. Yes, that's exactly what it was, the last smidgen of uncertainty, the here-and-gone second thought that every man bumps up against in such a circumstance.

His burning molars notwithstanding, he resumed drinking, determined to get drunk, gradually building a soft wall around him to cushion away the noise and distraction, then setting it reeling slowly, igniting his aching frame in the process, inspiring a warm glow. And getting sicker to his stomach by the sip. He was a brother in that distinctive lodge, hard men, rugged men with weak stomachs. Imbibing invariably made him sick, which in no way deterred him. Long experience had proven that he could put up with nausea, even with the grisly pastime of heaving his guts out in payment for the numerous other benefits offered by a drunken stupor, the balm, the enforced detachment from reality, forgetfulness, sweet solitude, and all the rest.

Getting drunk was, of course, more fun than being drunk, anesthetizing his body, feeling the pain in his mouth and the other oases of affliction dull, the overall effect downright soothing. He was, however, getting sicker to his stomach by the minute, not yet sufficiently besotted to be oblivious of it. He longed to lie down; he was surveying the floor with this in mind when a pair of breasts the size of Imperial Valley muskmelons hove into view. Perched above them was a rigorously rouged round face, inch-long lashes beating down upon wide blue eyes, hair pitch-black, and a mouth provocative, voluptuous, and semen-stirring.

"Hello, friend."

He passed out, his head thudding against the table, upsetting the bottle, sending what was left of its contents spewing about.

* * *

Doc stood before the mirror painstakingly strapping a new two inches of court plaster across his injured nose. He had gently stuffed both nostrils with cotton to stop the bleeding and noticed, to add to his chagrin, that his lapels and vest and shirt front were thoroughly spattered with blood. It felt as if somebody had smashed the center of his face with a Spalling hammer as hard as they could. Once the bleeding stopped, before the bone and septal cartilage began to knit, it would have to be properly set by a skilled surgeon. He suspected too that the perpendicular plate of ethmoid and the vomeronasal cartilage were likewise shattered. Indeed, it felt as if everything was in ruins all the way back to his brain!

Lying on the bed he stared at the ceiling for a long time. The pain, initially excruciating, was now slowly dulling, but gave no indication of releasing him from its grip. Little sleep would be in store this night, next to none without a bottle of something.

He didn't need this, two battles with Raider in two days, not even time for the old hurts to begin healing before new ones were added. They'd fought before, of course, but no more than once or twice a year on average and generally then only when both were drunk. And they'd always made peace shortly afterward. This time, both times, in spite of his wounds it hadn't been him Raider had attacked, rather the man's own frustration. Clearly he was torn between going and staying. That was the job, a love-hate situation, and his giving in, agreeing to tackle one last case before quitting only to come up against T. D. Morgan's problem, was burning him up.

For the first time in four years Doc was forced to acknowledge to himself that this was it; the final breakup. The case was his alone to solve.

Rising, he sat on the edge of the bed and began divesting himself of his jacket, vest, and shirt, laying each in turn, stains and all, neatly at the foot. Then using the towel draped over the wash basin, he set about sponging the stains with cold water. His nose was beginning to close his eyes. He glanced at his watch. Almost midnight. Much too late to go looking for a doctor. First thing in the morning, even before coffee, he would see to having his nose restored to something resembling its original shape. If this were possible. When a teacup breaks into a hundred pieces, can it be put back together again, even with Diamond Glue, "mends anything, strong as a rock"?

He would have to see to Judith and his apothecary wagon as well. She was in good hands at the stable but by now had to be getting lonesome for him, for his voice in her ear, his hand stroking her neck, patting her rump.

Sponging the bloodstains, he thought about the case. T. D. Morgan was no man's fool. You don't organize and run your own personal bank without something in the way of intelligence to guide you. Intelligence, resourcefulness, and conduct becoming a bank officer and a gentleman. When he'd insisted that he'd never taken his eyes off the plates to and from the printer's and that nobody but he had access to the strongbox wherein they were kept, Doc had to believe him. Just as believable, unfortunately, was the evidence of his own eyes. The forged banknotes Morgan had shown them hours earlier had to have been printed on the authentic plates, front and back.

Which could mean that somebody, his cashier, Dawson Harder, or another employee, was engineering the scheme. Or at least provided the plates needed to do so. Morgan had shown them the key to his strongbox, the only key, so he claimed. The only key he knew of? It was certainly far easier to duplicate a brass key than steel plates as intricately engraved as the five-dollar banknote plates.

He made a mental note to consult with Morgan, request his permission to question his people individually. Read their eyes as they responded to his questions, judge who was telling the truth, who was not, if he were lucky enough to find such a person. A strange case, the case of the roving plates, plates that jumped out of a locked box, locked safe, locked vault, printed up thousands in extra, unbacked notes, and jumped back in again.

Most counterfeit cases involved either homemade plates, usually palpably phony in spite of the hours of labor and unquestioned talent that went into their creation, or authentic banknotes whose denominations had been skillfully raised using pen and ink. Counterfeiting coins was an altogether different matter, one he'd had little experience with, few law enforcement people had any experience with, so very little of it went on nowadays. Why work like a dog to duplicate a fifty-cent piece when the same amount of labor could result in five, ten, or twenty dollars? There was, though, the Joshua Tatum case. When the first Liberty head nickels were put into circulation, Tatum had gotten his nefarious hands on one and noticed two things immediately, that the coin was about the size of a five-dollar gold piece, and that the designer had neglected to place the word "cents" on it. The only indication of denomination was a large V on the reverse. Whereupon Tatum and a Boston jeweler friend invested in a thousand Libertys; the jeweler set about reeding the edges and gold-plating the coins. Tatum then set forth, going from store to store buying five-cent merchandise, offering his gilded nickels in payment and getting four dollars and ninety-five cents in change. He went through the initial thousand and an additional five thousand before being caught.

At his trial the prosecution had scores of witnesses prepared to swear that Tatum was the man who had bilked them out of four dollars and ninety-five cents. Tatum's attorney asked each witness one question only, "Did the defendant ever ask you for change?" The answer was always "No." It was the only honest answer possible—Tatum was a deaf mute. It being no crime to take four dollars and ninety-five cents when somebody offers it to you, the prosecution found itself with no case. Tatum went free. The Mint hastened to rectify its oversight by adding the word "cents" to the reverse of their new nickel. And the government passed a law making it a crime to deface American coins.

Doc went downstairs for a quart of Taos Lightning and took it to bed with him. But even emptying three quarters of it into him failed to bring sleep. The case of the roving plates was too firmly rooted in mind.

4

Her name was Dolly Dee; she was from Middle Water, Hartley County, Texas, she'd had five husbands, she was twenty-three-years old. In the privacy of her fragrant and absurdly overfurnished bedroom she nursed Raider back to sobriety and started him down the road to recovery from his wounds with an epsom salts bath, a compound of oregano, salt, and vinegar for his bruises, one of basil, marjoram, and rosemary for his hangover, one of catnip, red pepper, and savory for his aching teeth, and care as tender and loving as a mother lavishes on a baby.

She sucked him, she fucked him, and in between he enjoyed the warm and formidably fondlable proximity of one massive dug, it being more than enough for any grown man to handle. She also fetched him breakfast—four fried eggs, practically half a side of bacon, and a quart tin filled with Peaberry Santos Coffee sweetened with honey.

The more she did for him, the less attractive appeared thoughts of leaving Albuquerque. After all, his quitting the agency certainly didn't oblige him to get out. He could settle down and live here the next fifty years if he wanted to. He had no need to run and hide from Allan Pinkerton's wrath. To be sure, there was the twenty-six dollars and fifty cents owed him, bonafide expenses, vouchered and entered in the office books. They couldn't hold that back merely because he was walking out. He saw no need to worry about it, a telegram would fetch it promptly. The Chief may have been tighter than a javelina's asshole in winter, but he was honorable. Thinking about Allan Pinkerton brought back a memory of his lecture on counterfeiting: "Counterfeiting at the present day is literally one of the advanced arts. . . . It is no longer the common 'shover of the queer,' as he is called in police circles, who is the worst and most dangerous pirate on the monetary seas, for behind these vulgar fellows, who are merely brazen and dexterous, and who are daily being apprehended, there stands an organization composed of men of actual genius and unbounded resources. These men take the lead and utilize the skill of unscrupulous artists and engravers of the highest order of merit and, when fully prepared, make their assaults upon the Commonwealth with all the combined subtlety of a Gorchakov and concentrated energy of a Bismarck."

"What you thinkin' about, O'Toole?" twanged Dolly Dee nasally.

"What? Oh, nothing. Nothing important."

She had gotten up from the bed and was dressing, strapping on her garterbelt, hauling on mesh stockings, and depositing her mother lode of breastworks into the oversized cups of a heavily flossed French coutel corset featuring red sateen stripes trimmed with handsome silk embroidery.

"You feeling better?"

"Yeah."

"Feel up to a little walk?"

"Where to?"

"A couple blocks over. To San Pedro and down to the fairgrounds."

"What's there?"

"The carnival. I work there days, mornings, afternoons, and the early evening show."

"What doing?"

She winked and grinned mischievously. Then sobered. "You know you look fairly peaked. Still sick to your stomach?"

"I'm okay."

She helped him into his boots, straightened his hair with a German Silver comb half the size of a barber's strop, playfully sprayed some Sears and Roebuck Meadow Blossom perfume on him, which he failed to duck completely, finished dressing herself in a demure-looking fancy-figured shirtwaist with ankle-length skirt, touched up her hair to her satisfaction, assaulted her mouth with a lipstick the color of a fresh wound, and together they set forth for San Pedro Street, which headed south into the fairgrounds. Despite the earliness of the hour the carnival was open and doing business, a ferris wheel grinding away, gaily pennoned tents collecting streams of people, various games of chance, including nickel-on-the-number-and-spin-the-wheel, the baseball dodger, topple the bottles in full swing, a carousel whirled, and popcorn, cotton candy, candied apples, and lemonade and dozens of other digestibles being spiritedly hawked.

A towheaded farm boy with arms like railroad ties wielded a huge sledge, sending the weight up to the bell so hard it all but knocked it loose, and won his girl a kewpie doll.

"Isn't it exciting?" asked Dolly Dee, releasing Raider's arm and sweeping her own wide, taking in the extravaganza.

"Yeah." A broad banner was suspended over the entrance to the grounds proclaiming "Colonel J. P. B. Hardy's World's Greatest Carnival." Raider lifted his face to it. "Who's the colonel?"

"Oh, he's dead. Zemo just keeps the name, on account it impresses folks. It's Zemo's show right down to the tent pegs. Look . . ." She pointed ahead to a stage, behind it a large banner: "The Great Zemo, World's Most Fearless and Strongest Man."

Both, mused Raider? He must be some fine specimen.

He was. Parting the tent flaps at the rear of the stage the Great Zemo appeared—two-hundred and fifty pounds of solid muscle standing six-foot-six with a waist on him steel-belted around no more than thirty inches and shoulders that made the towhead, who had all but destroyed the bell, look puny. His physique was gathered inside a fake leopardskin, one strap over his shoulder, steel wristbands and legs strapped like a gladiator's. Across his face stretched a seven-inch mustache as black as the pit, and the muscles of his neck looked like steel rods implanted under the skin to support his massive head. He was wiped down with bear grease, which set his sinews glistening in the morning sun, and his green eyes burned into whomever he stared at like fire arrows into clapboard siding.

Dolly Dee waggled her fingers at Raider and started off into the crowd.

"Hey, where you going?"

"Got to get ready for my act. Last tent down the line. Show goes on in ten minutes. Right after Zemo. Watch him, he's something, then come and see me. I'll leave you a pass with Franklin, the ticket taker. See you."

"But . . ."

She waved again and vanished. The crowd surged forward, milling about the stage apron. Three men had brought out a collection of weights marked from one-hundred to five-hundred pounds. A barker, attired in a checkered jacket so loud Raider almost blinked, stepped forward, twirling his cane, doffing his derby, waving to the crowd, urging everyone in closer.

"Ladies and gentlemen, introducing the Great Zemo, the world's most fearless, the world's strongest man."

The introduction went on, suitably exaggerated, and the performance that followed was predictable. Weight after weight, each a hundred pounds heavier than the previous one, was elevated to shoulder height. Then a two-inch steel bar was slipped through the grip holes of all five weights and, after considerable preparation— deep breathing, stretching, and meticulous attention to proper positioning, was elevated two full inches off the stage, then dropped with a thud that all but set Albuquerque quaking.

Strong, that he was, allowed Raider. But fearless? How so?

At once the Great Zemo set about living up to the other half of his claim. A pair of full-grown Prairie rattlers were brought out in a wire cage with a wooden top fixed in place by hinges and a single sliding bolt. Following a second speech pompously delivered by the man with the derby, the cane, and the jacket, the cage was set upon a small table in front of Zemo. The snakes writhed restlessly. Raising his powerful arms in triumph, he stepped forward, whipped open the cage, pulled out one of the snakes, and held it wriggling furiously, over his head, while he slid the bolt back into place with his free hand. He then stepped back a second time. Holding the rattler's tail firmly in his left hand and its neck in his right he stretched it full length over his head, turning slowly around.

"Ladies and gentlemen, one bite from those deadly fangs you see displayed before your very eyes and the Great Zemo would be a corpse inside of three minutes. Snake bites man is a story as old as time; you've heard it a thousand times. But here and now before your very eyes you are about to witness a phenomenon calculated to reduce such a happenstance to the realm of the trivial. Ladies and gentlemen, watch closely."

Out of nowhere came a drum roll, loud, louder into the crash of a cymbal. The Great Zemo slid the hand holding the rattler's tail up to meet the other hand clutching its neck, which released it, sliding forward to grip the creature's jaws firmly, leaving the three inches of neck exposed. Bringing the neck up to his mouth, the Great Zemo promptly bit the snake, forcing his jaws together, snapping the bone with an ominous crack. The crowd gasped, a woman screamed, two others joined her, and a few more fainted. The band struck up "The Jolly March," Zemo dropped the twitching, doomed snake at his feet and, raising his arms in victory, backed between the tent flaps out of sight, bowing as he vanished. The applause was tumultuous.

"Jesus Christ," whispered Raider quietly. "Now I've seen everything . . ."

Preoccupied by the exhibition, somewhat upset where his breakfast was seated, and with scant attention to where he was heading, he wandered down the line to the tent Dolly Dee had earlier pointed out to him. Out popped the barker to wave the crowd in around him and introduce: "Semena, Queen of the Nile, the most beautiful ecdysiast in the world!"

The tent flaps were drawn and there stood Dolly Dee under a ponderously huge orange wig attired in a round dozen satin veils of varying colors, wearing sequined bracelets and anklets, her face thick with theatrical makeup. A concealed four-piece ensemble struck up an undulating strain of dervish dance music and she began twisting and writhing to it, her Imperial Valley wonders bobbing seductively in their hammocks. The women in the crowd reacted in disgust and disdain and, pulling back their children, deserted their men, who forged themselves into a tight ball of humanity, ah-ing, grinning, and ogling the sight.

It was purely a tease, two minutes of sensuous gyrating without the loss of a single veil. The music built to a crescendo and cut off sharply, the barker reappeared and announced that for the sum of one dollar, paper or silver, aficionados of the dance, admirers of female shapeliness, and lovers of music of the mysterious East were invited to step inside and enjoy a performance "that, once viewed, no red-blooded man in his right mind will forget."

Franklin, the ticket taker, hawk-eyed each man entering, pouncing on his dollar with avaricious alacrity. Raider came up to him, cleared his throat, mumbled his name, and was ushered inside with a nod. And a look on Franklin's face that plainly betrayed his disappointment at the loss of the one dollar.

Nearly seventy men were assembled inside the hot, airless little inner tent to be greeted by sight of a crudely constructed stage, five planks laid across four sawhorses with the pole set directly in front of it supporting the roof of the tent. Crates had been piled up for stairs in the rear. The music on the other side of the back wall started up and "Semena, Queen of the Nile, the most beautiful ecdysiast in the world" reappeared. Mounting the makeshift stairs she again went into her dance, but this time every eight bars was punctuated by the dexterous disposal of one of her veils until the stage was littered with them. Now all that covered her were her bracelets, anklets and a blue-and-silver sequined corset between. Applause started up in time with the music, and voices loudly encouraged her to divest herself of the corset. She did so, bringing cheers and exuberant applause. Raider gulped; God Almighty, she was huge, they seem to have added three pounds apiece since the previous night. They jounced and bounced and rocked and rolled about her chest as she strutted about, her black beaver completely exposed. The onlookers' enthusiasm and the band's gradually increasing loudness stimulated her to a wild frenzy, bringing beads of sweat to every part of her. She arced her body backwards, and supporting herself on all fours, opened her beaver, revealing the pink chasm of her cunt in all its wet and wondrous glory. A wag in the crowd tossed a coin at it and presently pennies, nickles, and dimes were flying toward it from all directions, striking and falling, rattling to rest on the stage.

Nimbly shooting to her feet, bringing her massive dugs up with her, she attacked the tent pole, grabbing it firmly with both hands and rubbing her beaver up and down slowly and sensuously in time with the music. Her face took on a languid look, her eyes blazing with lust, her tongue lolling carelessly out one side of her crimson mouth. Accompanied by the rhythmic clapping she fucked the pole for all she was worth, so enthusiastically, so vigorously Raider half expected it would start smoking, catch fire, and bring the entire steaming tent down on their heads.

Appropriate sounds escaped her throat as she abraded the pole, shaking the tent, setting it quivering all about them—grunting, groaning, oohing, ahhing until she pretended to come, practically swooning in ecstasy, closing her eyes, reeling in her tongue, moaning loudly, then slowly stopping. The unseen band wound up in a drum roll wherein she ground down everyone's eyes, gyrating her cunt at a furious pace, grinding and bumping to rest at last. Then gathering up her veils, her sequined corset, and her money, she fled, loudly cheered and applauded.

"He bothering you?" Zemo had come inside, his frown deepening, his fingers fisting, the muscles of his jaw tightening as he set it pugnaciously. He brought his face up to within inches of Raider's. "Are you?"

"You heard her," rumbled Raider, "Beat it."

The words were no sooner out then he regretted them. He shouldn't have uttered a sound; there was no need. It was between the two of them, no need to stick his oar in. It was what Zemo had hoped he'd do and like an idiot he'd played right into the big lummox's hands. His own hand started for his .44 but stopped. It wasn't the spot for gunplay; better he back off and get out.

Zemo glowered at him, twin storms coming up in his eyes as they narrowed and appraised him. Out shot his hands, one grabbing Raider by the shirt front, tearing the cloth, the other lifting his weapon and flinging it aside.

"Hey!" burst Raider. "Do you mind?"

Zemo shoved him away, sending him sprawling, the back of his head narrowly missing the pole.

"Zemo, stop!" He had started after Raider; she moved to intercede; he swept her to one side effortlessly with one shovel hand. Closing in on the Pinkerton, picking him up under the arms, he shook him like a rag doll.

"How'd you like me to squash your face worse than it is already?"

Raider swallowed hard. "Take it easy, take it easy . . ."

Holding him three feet off the ground, Zemo grinned demonically and began to shake him again, dislodging his Stetson, dropping one boot off. Raider colored, squirming to free himself, burning with embarrassment. And losing his temper, hauling off and smacking his tormentor squarely in the jaw.

"NO!" shrilled Dolly Dee.

It was like hitting plate steel. Pain shot through Raider's knuckles, through his fist up to his elbow. It felt as if he had fractured all twenty-seven bones—

and failed to break Zemo's grin with so much as a split-second wince.

Jesus, he thought, what am I doing? How did I get into this? Struggling mightily, he was finally able to wriggle free and, twisting agilely, duck under a badly aimed right cross and get in two well-timed shots to the big man's belly. Again plate steel, again pain shooting up to his elbow. Both elbows. The grin seemed to be stamped on Zemo's face. Raider backed off, shaking the hurt out of first one hand, then the other. Zemo laughed and, bowing his great head, lunged forward. Raider sidestepped him easily, letting him bull through and ram pate first against the tent wall, all but bringing the tent down around them. Dolly Dee screamed, covered her face, and, as she backed away let her robe gape, revealing her charms. Back came Zemo, flailing the air, a wild left glancing off Raider's shoulder. Like many outsized men he was slow, cumbersome, unskilled and, goaded by mounting frustration, hurrying his blows, neglecting to set his body, to balance himself properly. Simply by continuing to sidestep him he could tire him out, Raider thought.

He could, he might have, had Zemo persisted in rushing at him, swinging blindly.

He did not. Instead he threw his body sideways, bringing both legs hard against Raider's and knocking him flat. Zemo pounced on him, pinning his arms away from his body with knees the size of timber oak stumps. And leaning over, his devilish grin restored, he hammered Raider with the side of his fist, the blow traveling less than four inches to the center of his forehead, knocking him cold.

6

Doc sat as stiffly as a cadaver on a tall four-legged stool while the doctor fixed the ludicrous-looking wire frame over his reset nose and around the sides of his head. The "doctor" was Roy P. Simpkins, M.D., according to the legend arcing across his street-front window in six-inch cloister text lettering. The cramped, dusty little office smelled of formaldehyde with a half dozen other odors submerged beneath its sharp, unpleasant presence. The only object in the entire office that wasn't well past its prime, including Roy P. Simpkins, M.D., was a Yost typewriter standing on the solid oak curtain-top desk. The window announcing Simpkins's presence to the world of Albuquerque badly wanted washing, the floor sweeping, the furniture dusting, the doctor a bath. His boiled shirt looked as if he'd slept in it for a week, as did his vest and trousers. Clamped between his teeth was the Chinese amber stem of an English Bulldog briar pipe, its contents half smoked and gone out, the smoker seemingly oblivious of this.

"You keep this contraption on for at least a week; you're even to wear it to bed," intoned the doctor in a voice heavy with gravel. "Especially in bed, on account you could roll over in your sleep and . . ."

"I understand. How will my nose come out of it, do you think? How will it look?"

"Good as ever. But it'll be sore as blazes for a good six months or more. Whatever you do, don't lay a finger on it. No bandage, no scratching an itch, nothing. And see you don't let anybody else touch it. It's taken just about all it can. You were smart to look me up before the bones began to knit."

"I'm very grateful, doctor. How much do I owe you?"

"Five dollars for the job, thirty cents for the Pearl-man protective frame."

Doctor Simpkins stepped back to study his handiwork, nodded approvingly, and gestured Doc to his feet. He counted out the fee, thanked Simpkins, and left. Outside in the street, as he expected, people turned to stare at the simplified version of a birdcage covering the upper half of his face. Children tittered and an elderly man riding by in a buckboard called out: "Hey, you lookin' for a ball game?"

Doc ignored one and all and, setting his course for the saloon into which Raider had vanished following their disagreement the night before, went inside and approached the bar. The place was empty, not even a bartender was visible, until one straightened up behind the mahogany.

"Morning, friend. What's your preference?"

He was trying hard not to smile at the sight before his eyes. Doc looked past him into the mirror. He looked ridiculous.

"Ever see anything so funny-looking in your life?"

"If it holds it together, what do you care how you look? Besides, it's only temporary."

"Thank the Lord."

Doc described Raider. The bartender tried to be helpful, planting one elbow on the bar, resting his bearded chin in his palm, screwing up his forehead, and listening attentively. He had not seen Raider, which wasn't altogether surprising, he hastened to add, since he hadn't been on duty the night before. A second man came in from the back as they stood talking, a younger fellow with a belly like a barrel rounding his clean white apron, his string tie awry, a hangover lurking in his sallow cheeks and bloodshot eyes. The first bartender described Raider to him.

"Dolly Dee took him upstairs," he said. "Two-B."

"Mind if I go up and have a word with her?" asked Doc.

"Go ahead," said the first bartender. "If she's up there."

"She coulda not come down already from last night,"

added the other. "Either that or did and goed back up the backstairs."

Doc thanked both, threw a last glance at his new acquisition in the mirror, and headed for the stairs. He found 2B down the hallway from the second flight up and addressed the door with his knuckles.

"Who is it?"

"Good afternoon. I'd like a word with Mr. O'Toole, if you don't mind. My name is Smith."

"Beat it!" snapped a familiar voice. "Go away, don't bother me."

"Come now, John," said Doc mildly, suppressing a grin in fear that broadening his face would stretch his nostrils and induce pain.

She opened the door over Raider's protests. He was sitting up in bed, stripped to the waist, a large bruise forming in the center of his forehead. He looked terrible, as if he he'd been set upon by a mob and had barely escaped with his life. A tin basin of water was set on the bed and she was standing over him, wringing out a cold towel, preparing to lay it across his forehead. Her jaw dropped, as did his. Both laughed.

"You look like a damned ball-game umpire," piped Raider.

"Thanks to you."

"What do you want? Oh, this is my ladyfriend, Miss Dee. Dolly, this is Mr. Smith, a what-you-call old acquaintance. Ex–old acquaintance. We got nothin' to talk about," he said, glaring at Doc.

"Would you mind terribly if we had a word in private?" asked Doc. "Just a few minutes. I'd be very grateful, Miss Dee."

She glanced questioningly at Raider. He sniffed and rolled his eyes. "If that's all it'll take to get rid o' him for good, give us a few minutes. Okay?" he muttered.

"I have to get back for the afternoon show, anyway." She set the cloth across his forehead and withdrew, stopping in the doorway as Doc moved into the room. "If you go out, John, lock the door. You really shouldn't, though. You need bed rest."

"Yeah."

She closed the door. Doc sat down wearily at the foot of the bed, hanging his derby on the post.

"What hit you?" he asked.

Raider explained.

"So you're not leaving town after all. Good."

Raider bristled. "I never said that."

His partner tilted his head toward the door. "She looks to be reason enough to stick around. Seriously, Rade, I stayed up three quarters of the night deep-thinking this thing and all I came up with are blank walls."

"Doc . . ."

"Hear me out." He ticked off his fingers. "We know what's being done, we've seen the forgeries, we know the operation'll keep up until Morgan's bank is on the verge of collapse and then they'll move on, as they moved up here from Deming. What we've got to come up with is who and how."

" 'We' your ass . . ."

"Oh, come on, Rade, are you trying to tell me you haven't had second thoughts about quitting? You always do the morning after."

"Not this time."

"Be serious."

"You think I'm not? You know, that's really your whole trouble, Weatherbee. You're too goddamn cocksure o' yourself. You get everything all figured out to a T. Well, this time you're all fucked up, and the only reason I let you in here was to tell you so. You know, underline what you already know."

"This case hasn't crossed your mind . . ."

"Not for half a second."

"You're a liar."

Raider snatched the towel down from his forehead and tossed it aside. Then he got up, all but spilling the water in the basin all over the covers as he threw his legs over the side.

"You stick here and talk to the fucking walls, wise-ass. I'm leaving."

"Where to?"

"None o' your goddamn business."

"Have you wired your resignation to the home office?"

"Screw the home office, I can't be bothered."

"So how do you expect to get the money you're supposed to be reimbursed?"

"I can get that anytime." Raider buttoned on his shirt, tucked it in, and put on his Stetson; he grimaced as the lining closed on his bruised forehead and he elevated the brim slightly to relieve the pressure.

"I'll tag along, Rade."

"Why bother, for Christ's sakes? We'll just wind up sluggin' it out again. Neither one o' us wants to, but we will. We just about always do."

"You're going back to the carnival; I can't let you go alone. That big ox gets ahold of you again he'll probably break you in half."

"I can handle him. I won't open my mouth to him, and if he starts up again, I'll just turn around and walk away."

Doc threw up his hands. "You're impossible. I give up, I really do!"

"That's good news."

"To hell with you."

Rising from the bed, he restored his derby to his head and stalked out, slamming the door behind him as hard as he could.

7

Doc did not give up. He very well might have, he told himself, had his partner picked him up bodily and tossed him down the stairs at the end of the hallway, but he did not. On the contrary, Raider didn't even bother protesting when Doc followed him down into the street and across town to the carnival. Albuquerqueans of all ages were continuing to enjoy the show, but the crowd had thinned somewhat since morning. Now more people were coming in as the Great Zemo, Semena, the Queen of the Nile, and other performers launched in turn their second performances of the day.

Raider headed straight for Dolly Dee's tent to wait for her to finish with the pole, retrieve her veils, corset, and small change. Doc came in after him. On the way over, not a single word had passed between the two, but now that they were inside the tent Doc put aside his indignation, supplanting it with an appeal to reason.

"Look at it this way, Rade. Are you going to be able to look at yourself in the mirror next week, next month, knowing you quit your last case because it was too tough to crack? Are you?"

"I quit before I ever started."

"No you didn't."

"I'm not gonna argue with you."

Raider had plumped down on the crate in front of the dressing table; Doc began pacing up and down in front of him, digging out an Old Virginia cheroot, jamming it between his teeth, and searching his pockets for a match.

"Have you got a match?"

"No. When did I ever? When she comes back, you beat it. Okay? We want to be alone." Doc bent over

52

the dressing table and began pulling open drawers. "Hey, what are you doing?"

"Looking for a match."

"Leave off that. There's none in there. She doesn't smoke."

"Oh?"

Smiling in spite of his infirmity, Doc reached into a drawer and brought out a box of Pollock's Crown Stogies. Before Raider could comment he opened the box.

"Oh boy . . ." Removing his unlit cheroot, Doc whistled softly.

"What?"

"Three guesses. On second thought, don't bother." Tilting the box, Doc displayed its contents. Raider reached in, taking out a wad of banknotes with a rubber band around them.

"T. D. Morgan Territorial Bank," he read, his voice as hollow as a reed, his good eye staring fixedly. "What in hell . . ."

"Rade, she's in on it. She's a passer, she's got to be."

"Does she?" she snapped venomously. "Give me that!" Striding straight to Raider, her Chinese dragon dressing gown trailing after her, she snatched the box from him, slammed down the lid, tossed the box into the drawer, and kneed it shut. "Out, the two o' you! And you, O'Toole or Rade, whatever your name is, stay away from me. I mean don't come near unless you want me to sic Zemo on you. Out! Zemo!"

"Take it easy," said Doc. "You can do yourself a great deal of good by telling us what this is all—"

"HELP! ZEMOOOOOOOOO! HELP!"

Doc flashed a glance at Raider and they started for the flap, only to come upon two men blocking the entrance, burly-looking roustabouts, both scowling, both carrying twelve-inch pipes. Zemo pushed between them. Raider and Doc exchanged looks, the latter swallowing hard, both hands sneaking to his nose cage protectingly. The three behemoths in the entrance started forward, but Raider grabbed Doc by his bad shoulder and jerked him back.

"Ow . . ."

Raider spun around, pushing Doc ahead of him. Passing the pole, he kicked it hard, collapsing the tent. He dived to the ground behind the dressing table and squirmed out from under, Doc following.

They jumped to their feet. Zemo, Dolly Dee, and the two roustabouts struggled under the canvas, roaring, screaming, cursing.

"The notes . . ." began Doc as they started off at a trot.

"To hell with 'em."

"We've got to get them, Rade."

"What are you? Stupid? We got out with our backbones in one piece, let's keep it that way. Move!"

Discretion being the better part of raw courage, they decided not to return to the Yucca House. Instead they made their way to the stable where Raider's horse and Judith and the apothecary wagon were being kept. Out in back by the wagon they discussed the situation. To Doc's unbounded relief Raider appeared to have given up all thoughts of quitting. Dolly Dee having played him for a fool, he was determined to get even.

"I swear to Jesus," he grumbled, "every time I get my hands on a halfway decent lay, up jumps the fuckin' devil."

"Don't knock her, Rade." Doc had climbed into his wagon, availing himself of a hand mirror, and was studying his nose cage, reassuring himself that their hasty flight from the tent had not loosened or even slightly dislodged it. "She's the first break we've had. It occurs to me that your friend Zemo's carnival is nothing but a front for the whole operation."

"What a great way to paper the whole territory. Move from town to town . . ."

"Did she happen to mention what their last stop was before Albuquerque?"

"Deming, it's got to be."

"Probably. But did she say?"

"Doc, she's not permanent. Her job's over to the

saloon. According to her, she just fell into this business o' taking off her clothes and showing her quim."

"Unless I'm mistaken she's got herself a whole new career. When that carnival moves on, she'll be going along. She'll have to after that business with the cigar box."

"It won't be very healthy around here for any of 'em, now the cat's outta the sack."

Doc stared at the ground, deep in thought. Fully half a minute went by before he commented. Raider eyed him, waiting patiently.

"Is it?"

"What?"

"The cat out of the sack? Think about it, Rade, if— I say if—we had managed to get hold of that cigar box, what would we have? A stack of banknotes, the signatures forged, perhaps, but not counterfeit, not exactly. There's no law that says she or anybody else can't have a bunch of Morgan's banknotes. She doesn't have to account for them. Because there aren't any missing."

"Mmmm . . ."

"That's just one of the things that's complicating this whole case so."

"I bet you a silver dollar they pack up and move on," said Raider.

"That would make sense to him, Zemo. And that'll be the break we need."

"How do you figure?"

"Wherever they head, they'll have to start over again. Zero in on a local bank and get to printing. Like they did here, like they did in Deming."

They sat down with T. D. Morgan in his office behind the closed door and filled him in on what had transpired since last they'd gotten together. He heard Doc out, but even the optimistic aspects of the situation failed to dispel his gloominess.

"I hope, like you say, they do move out and you catch 'em before they get into business at the next stop," he observed quietly, "but even if you do get lucky, it won't do us any good." Reaching for his bottle drawer he brought out what was left of the Farquard and glasses.

"Have you been able to turn down any banknotes on the basis of suspicious-looking signatures?" asked Doc.

"A few. And every time I raise holy hell doing it. Understand one thing, the people who come up to our windows aren't passers. They're the victims of the passers. And the losers just as much as we are if they show a phony signature." He poured and shoved glasses at each in turn. "The worst of it is, they've practically got to take my word for it. It gets a little bit sticky. A lot sticky. Do you two mind explaining to me just exactly why I can't whistle for the law and have that bunch arrested?"

"On what charge?" asked Doc.

"Possession o' my goddamn banknotes!"

"Mr. Morgan, practically everybody in this town has at least one or two of your banknotes."

"You said she had a cigar box full . . ."

"You can bet it's not that full now," said Raider dryly.

"How about we get a search warrant, cordon off the entire fairgrounds, and turn every mother's son o' those carnival people upside down?"

Doc patiently pointed out that the notes he and Raider had both seen in the cigar box could very well have been the banker's own. There was simply no foolproof method of distinguishing the thieves' paper from his, other than to isolate an occasional sloppily signed specimen. In a sense, it was as if Zemo and his confederates had marched into the bank and held it up for ten thousand, or whatever amount they had seen fit to print up. Unfortunately, whether Morgan liked the idea or not, he was obliged to swallow his loss. The only hope Doc held out was that he and Raider might catch the thieves before they were able to implement their scheme a third time.

"So the satisfaction of knowing the bastards are behind bars is gonna wind up costing me at least ten grand, is that it?" As the conversation flew back and forth over his desk the gloomy look on the banker's face deepened into a look that strongly suggested he was dying. Raider drank up and turned his eyes from the sight, pity welling in his chest.

"I'm afraid so," said Doc quietly.

"Well . . ." The big man shrugged, bottoms-upped, and hammered his empty glass down onto the desk. "That's life."

8

It came as no surprise to either Raider or Doc when the carnival packed up and departed Albuquerque two hours before sun-up. The caravan headed southeast in the direction of Estancia. The two operatives followed at a discreet distance, Raider's *grulla* tied to the tailgate of the apothecary wagon.

Zemo's flight, though not unanticipated, created a knotty problem for Raider and Doc, in particular for the latter. To stay close to the counterfeiters would be easy; to move about in their midst at their destination, however, should it come to that, would necessitate donning disguises. And Doc's cage-covered nose would be undisguisable, in line with Doctor Simpkins' injunction, for a full week at least.

"Like it or not, I'm going to have to take it off," Doc mused aloud, gloomily.

"What'll happen when you do? Will your nose fall off?"

"Ssssh, I'm thinking . . ."

Judith moved slowly, easily through the darkness, the wagon showing no lanterns. Half a mile ahead the likewise lanternless carnival train rounded a bend, temporarily vanishing from sight. The wind was up, rolling down from the peaks of the Sacarmentos to the south, flapping the canvas bonnet, ruffling Judith's mane, and standing up the brim of Raider's Stetson.

Doc nodded, ostensibly agreeing with the thought that snaked through his mind.

"You, Rade, I'm going to age, white hair, white eyebrows, white mustache with two inches lopped off either end. Vigorous old age, no gimping, no deep furrows in your ugly face, but enough makeup to cover your wounds and your eye. I'll have you looking like a skinny version of old T.D."

"And what do you plan to look like?"

"I've changed my mind. What good is a doctor if you don't heed his advice? I'm not going to look like anything for the next six days. I'll just stay in the background with my cage on."

"So I get to handle the whole shooting match all by my lonesome, is that it?"

"Not at all; I'll be close by if you need me."

"What do you mean, 'if'?"

They began to argue the point, though far from heatedly. Both were too worn out from the events of the day, deriving scant benefit from their four hours' sleep, necessarily shortened by a pre-departure get-together with T. D. Morgan at his home. They would, Doc had assured him, be in touch.

Raider continued curious about many aspects of the situation, not the least of which being what lay ahead.

"How can we depend on their stopping off somewheres and the local banker they mean to snooker automatically going to work and printing up a new batch o' his banknotes? How can Zemo plan such a thing?"

"That should be plain. He has somebody out ahead of them scouting the territory. He has to have. Why else would they jump all the way from Deming to Albuquerque, bypassing Silver City, Hillsboro, Socorro? Somebody's picking their spots for them."

"I see what you mean." Raider crinkled his chin, plunging deep into thought, framed another question, and fired it at his partner. Back came the answer.

"Good point. Once we fill in the banker on what's in store for him he very well may hesitate to go ahead with the printing."

"In which case Zemo'll just move on to the next stop, right? And the same thing'll happen again. And again . . ."

An impish gleam came into Doc's eyes. "Ahhhh, but what if we don't tell the banker?"

"You're sayin' set him up, don't let him in on it? Great. But if something goes wrong, if we don't happen to nip the thing in the bud, he could wind up as bad off as Morgan. And if he was to find out we held out on him . . ."

"Come now, Rade, we can't discount the element of risk."

"I don't believe I'm hearing straight. You're always the one who's all for keeping things on the up-and-up."

"If we don't tell him and do catch Zemo with the goods, we'll all come out of it with clean hands."

"If." There was a long pause. Doc dug out an Old Virginia and was about to strike a match when Raider reached over and stayed his hand. "Don't. Anybody up ahead lookin' around could see it for better'n half a mile."

"Right." Doc put away the cheroot. "Tell me something, Rade, just to satisfy my curiosity. You were so dead set on quitting, how come you decided to stick?"

"No special reason. Like you said, finish up the last case clean."

"I see."

Doc resisted the temptation to press the point. There was nothing to be gained by getting Raider's dander up. Reason for his change of heart was all too obvious. As sensitive as he was, he could not begin to abide Dolly Dee's duplicity. She had used him, and he deeply resented being used by anybody. Thinking along that particular line, it occurred to Doc that perhaps Zemo had set her onto Raider deliberately, to keep an eye on him. Though how the snakebiter had gotten word of their arrival in town and been able to identify them was a trifle difficult to understand. On the other hand, from the time he himself had brought Raider in unconscious, up to their discovery of the banknotes in the cigar box, neither one had had the slightest inkling that the carnival people were involved. What it came down to was that Zemo and his crowd would naturally be on the lookout for any strangers arriving in town. And might be expected to go on to the offensive if they spotted two such newcomers, especially if they saw them entering Morgan's bank late in the evening.

Spotting Raider as a threat could have been behind Zemo's overreaction to his presence in the girl's dressing tent. Rather than practically brain Raider, he could have just as easily booted him out.

His partner climbed back into the wagon and, setting his blanket roll on a case of Donald McKay's Indian Worm Eradicator, covered himself with his poncho and went to sleep. He dreamed of breasts as big as bedrooms, discovering himself negotiating the valley between two of them, passing, glancing up at the pink peaks. They were so soft, so smooth, so warm and comforting. Even smelled good. Like Sears and Roebuck Meadow Blossom perfume.

Doc jolted him rudely out of this paradise of the unconscious shortly after sunrise. Sitting up, yawning, his fists going to his eyes, the left fist hitting his extremely sore and swollen left one before he realized what he was doing, causing raw pain, Raider cursed and climbed forward, fuming, to take his place alongside Doc. Doc had pulled Judith over to the side and was getting down, his Mexican Rice Root brush in hand to work the dust out of her hide and mane. He pointed ahead, The caravan was nowhere in sight.

"Jesus!" snapped Raider worriedly.

"Relax, they're just around that outcropping up ahead. I almost bumped into them; they got out of sight and it never dawned on me that they might be stopping. Not at this hour."

Raider yawned and stretched. "What time is it?"

Doc produced his watch. "Six-o-two." Winding it, he restored it to his pocket. "My nose is starting to hurt."

"Don't start bitching on me. My everything hurts!"

"Not like my nose. This cage feels like it weighs a ton. I'll see if I can scare us up something to eat, then

I'm going back inside and sleep. Where do you think they're taking us, Rade?"

Raider shrugged. "Estancia, Carrizozo. Could be maybe Roswell." He shaded his eyes. Up ahead the slopes were covered with piñon, scrub oak, and juniper. And all around them in the immediate vicinity the sagebrush and greenwood were yielding their dominance of the land to white bloom-topped yucca and cactus. Climbing down, Raider started forward.

"Where do you think you're going?" inquired Doc in a low tone.

"Have a look up ahead."

"Please. That walk, that outfit, he or she or somebody would spot you a mile away. Give them another half hour or so. They'll be moving on."

"Don't worry none. I'm just gonna climb up that ledge and sneak a peek."

"Have it your way." Doc set about brushing Judith. "Only leave your hat here, and for God's sake be careful."

Raider tossed off this cautionary advice with a wave and made his way to the outcropping; climbing it, he flattened and sneaked a look around a boulder set with others along the top of it. The carnival people were making breakfast; the odor of bacon carried back to him, wafting its way up his nostrils, releasing his saliva and setting his stomach juices gurgling.

Damn, it smelled good! He could not see Dolly Dee, but Zemo was strutting about. He wore Levi's and a plain cotton shirt that threatened to split under the pressure of his muscles. He looked like a man without a care, moving from fire to fire, letting small bunches of his people bask briefly in the glow of his personality.

Raider's left hand stole toward his Peacemaker, the tips of his fingers touching the grip. He'd love to put a hole in the bastard, but what would that solve? Belly down, he watched for fully five minutes, then, driven off by the smell of the bacon, he scrambled back down the outcropping and rejoined Doc. He had started a small fire in the ditch and, while it was heating up, busied himself strapping Judith's oat bag onto her.

They ate—beans, biscuits as hard as green planking, in Raider's opinion "and one helluva lot drier," and coffee. The coffee smelled delicious, but try as he might, he could not get the odor of the bacon out of his head.

"When we get to wherever we're headin', this old boy's sitting down to four pounds o' steak and a bottle o' the best booze in town."

"Why not. But after we meet with the local banker."

"You meet with the local banker, I'll meet with a steak and spuds."

The carnival and its pursuers traveled all day through the mountains, past Estancia, around the Laguna de Perro into Lincoln County, down to the lazy, dirty waters of the Fifteen-mile Arroyo. On and on down the territory.

Three days later found them some two hundred miles from Albuquerque within sight of Roswell. Roswell, the trade center for the fertile farmlands and profitable cattle ranches surrounding it. Not a particularly lively settlement, in Raider's opinion, save on Saturday night, but well-to-do. With a well-to-do bank, the Farmers and Merchants Bank, presided over by one Horace F. Catterbury, his name and title emblazoned in gold letters eight inches high over the entrance.

The carnival train made its way slowly through the town, drawing the stares of the curious, lighting up the youngsters' eyes, and headed for a large open field on the east side, Roswell's fairgrounds, half the size of Albuquerque's but adequate.

Raider and Doc entered the bank undisguised. On the way down, they had eventually decided that subterfuge in dealing with Mr. Horace F. Catterbury or any other banker targeted by Zemo was not only unwise strategy but impossible to put into practice, inasmuch as one or both had to be present when the banknotes were printed up.

As Roswell was new, so was the Farmers and Merchants Bank, polished mahogany from end to end, pristine white walls, spotless windows, gleaming spittoons,

and an air of sober gentility. A bank guard in full uniform approached them, successfully suppressing a smirk
at the sight of Doc's facial contraption. Touching the
bill of his kepi in greeting, he inquired as to their business.

"We'd like a word with Mr. Catterbury," said Doc,
and he showed his Pinkerton Operative identification
card.

"May I, sir?" asked the guard. Doc nodded; the man
took the card from him and heading for an office in the
rear, knocked on the glass door; being admitted, he reappeared shortly and motioned them to approach.

All but one of the handful of patrons in the bank took
no notice of any of this. That one was a middle-aged
man somewhat shorter than Doc but as fashionably
attired, even to a diamond stickpin flashing in the center
of his silk brocade puff scarf. His dark eyes narrowed
under the brim of his stiff black fur hat and, turning,
he strode swiftly out of the bank. Neither Raider nor
Doc noticed him or his departure.

Mr. Catterbury's office proved considerably more
luxurious than T. D. Morgan's, larger, more expen-
sively appointed, surprisingly impressive, down to the
Persian rug obscuring most of the hardwood floor. Mr.
Catterbury himself was somewhat less prepossessing in
appearance. His was a gaunt, lived-in face with pink-
rimmed, rheumy eyes and an aquiline nose that put
Raider in mind of a bald eagle. Bald was Mr. Catterbury, as hairless as an old bone all the way down to his
temples where wispy gray sideburns sprouted to life and
descended to his deeply hollowed cheeks. Except for his
white shirt fixed around his painfully thin neck with a
string tie he was dressed entirely in black, making him
look more like a professional mourner than a successful
banker. Raising one slender hand with Doc's card in it
he motioned both Pinkertons to chairs and nodded the
guard away; the guard closed the door behind him and
set the shadow of his back against the glass protectingly.
Doc accepted his card. Like liquid filling a bottle, worry
rose in Catterbury's face, tightening his neck muscles,

turning down the corners of his absurdly thin-lipped mouth, coming to light in his eyes and creasing his brow.

"Pinkertons . . . Is something going on I don't know about? Of course there is. Well, what is it?"

Doc crossed his legs, setting his derby on his topmost knee. "We're here to prevent 'something's going on,' Mr. Catterbury. Something very big and very destructive. Which we can stop with your cooperation."

"Yes, yes, get to the point."

Catterbury had been standing; now he sat, slowly, almost as if invisible hands were setting him down. He did not relax in his chair, however, leaning forward instead in anticipation, his body tense. Doc related the recent experience of T. D. Morgan and his Territorial Bank, adding to it an explanation of the progress that he and Raider had managed to make toward solving the case. Curiously, even before he reached that stage, the man behind the desk began to unwind. He did not interrupt, but when Doc finished with a repeated appeal for cooperation, he took up the cudgel of rationalization and began wielding it.

"Really, gentlemen, from what you say, it's clear to me and should be to you where and how this Morgan chap slipped up. He claims his plates were never out of his sight, then proceeds to admit that he handed them over to his guard. Obviously the guard pulled a switch. Very careless. I myself don't let my plates out of my hands for a second. I take them out of the vault, carry them over to the printer's, place them in the press . . ."

"Mr. Catterbury," Doc cut in wearily, "my partner and I have investigated that situation thoroughly and we're convinced there was no switch. Number one, the plates are too large to conceal upon one's person, number two . . ."

"Then the switch was made at the printer's. Did this Morgan chap place them in the press like I do? You haven't said he did. You see, gentlemen, it's all a matter of setting out the necessary precautionary measures and observing every one, allowing for no exceptions, no oversights. Thoroughness, gentlemen, that's the key."

"When are you planning to print your new notes?" asked Doc.

"Day after tomorrow. But now, of course, I'll just call it off. That is, postpone it until that bunch leaves Roswell. I can't tell you how much I appreciate your warning me—"

"Mr. Catterbury," interrupted Raider, "you can't do that."

"What?"

"Please, Rade." Doc settled one hand on his partner's arm and continued in a mild tone. "Mr. Catterbury, for the sake of practically every banker in New Mexico Territory we'd very much appreciate your going through with your printing as planned."

"I'd be crazy to."

"Sir . . ."

"You want me to walk into the same trap this chap Morgan's gotten himself into? With my eyes wide open?"

Raider was tired and hungry and aching and no less disillusioned with his career as a Pinkerton than he had been earlier. The color began rising in his cheeks as Catterbury's obstinacy took root and flourished. But Doc appeared unruffled by the banker's reaction and set about appealing to his intelligence and common sense. He took pains to point out that Zemo and his crowd could not be expected to discontinue their activities of their own accord; they had to be stopped. In order to stop them, they had to be caught with sufficient evidence to prove their crime in a court of law. In his view it was reasonable to assume that the carnival had arrived in Roswell without duplicates of the Farmers and Merchants Bank's ten-dollar plates. This Catterbury was quick to agree with. His plates, he explained, happened to be almost twenty years old and no one had ever attempted to counterfeit them before.

"I'll accept your word for that, sir," said Doc. "Unfortunately, what Zemo will use will be the real thing."

"Preposterous!"

"That's pretty much what T. D. Morgan said," said

Raider airily. "It couldn't happen. Only it did and it's winding up costing him at least ten thousand."

"Simply because he wasn't as thorough as he thought he was," said Catterbury. "As he should have been." He shook his head. "I tell you, these days any fool with a dollar in his pocket can open a bank . . ."

"Let me ask you something, sir," said Doc. "You insist you never let the plates out of your hands and that they're the only ones of their kind."

"Absolutely."

"If you're so certain of that, why are you worried about printing up a new batch?"

"I'm just playing safe, extra safe. As long as they're around . . ."

"What makes you think you'll ever be able to? Just because the carnival leaves town is no guarantee the heat is off. What's to prevent their leaving people behind?"

"What are you trying to do, scare me? See here, I'm not printing up a new batch for the fun of it. We need those notes to cover increased assets. I can postpone printing for a few days, possibly even a week or so, but . . ."

"If you don't print up a new batch you'll be in trouble," said Doc quietly. "Luckily, there's a way to protect yourself."

Catterbury's wet and woefully weak eyes widened. "How?"

"Change your stock. Not drastically, a new paper close to the original in appearance, but just enough off so that anyone looking very closely can see the difference."

"That way," chimed in Raider, "you could check every note that comes across your counter and pull out the phonies."

"That'd raise the roof," said Catterbury worriedly. "We could wind up with hell to pay."

Doc shook his head. "It'll never get that far. We throw them the bait, they grab it and we grab them."

"What if you don't? What if something goes wrong?"

"What can?"

Doc patiently went over the entire plan for the printing; Catterbury heard him out. Confronted by the necessity to deal with the situation "head on" as Raider termed it, the banker's resistance crumbled.

He reluctantly agreed to proceed with the printing, five thousand dollars in ten-dollar banknotes.

9

Raider and Doc left the bank and left Roswell, much to Raider's annoyance. He was still "starving for a steak and spuds." They followed Judith two miles out of town to a stretch of cottonwoods along the bank of the Rio Hondo. The river was carrying a sheen of sunlight atop its muddy waters, moving slowly eastward to the Pecos River. There Doc entered the details of their visit with Catterbury in the case journal and then set about disguising Raider, and announcing his intention to disguise himself. Raider protested.

"You've had that thing over your nose for less than four days," he sputtered. "You got three to go before you're even supposed to touch it."

"Rade, take my word, I don't want to touch it. I'll do so with trembling hands. But this is an emergency. Calling for emergency measures." Studying himself in the hand mirror hanging by its string from a tree branch he gingerly removed the cage and gently flexed his nostrils.

"OW! Boy, that's sore. Oh boy oh boy . . ."

"You better hope and pray you don't run it up against somebody's fist. It could come down to that, you know. The two o' us against sixteen roustabouts and that overgrown ape. Christ Almighty, I'm in no shape to take on a crippled drunk. I woulda done better to gun down all three back in that goddamn tent o' hers."

"Nonsense, you're in shape. Your eye is practically all cleared up. You look good, distinguished. We'll get you some bankers' clothes, one of those four-dollar black cheviot suits with the small flap pockets above the bigger ones, a nice Danbury beaver hat . . ."

"To hell with that, I'm stickin' with my Stets."

"Be reasonable, bankers don't wear Stetsons."

"I've seen a few, anybody in any line can wear one. I'm wearin' mine, Doc, and that's that. I'll give in to you on everything else, but not my damned hat!"

Doc sighed. "Have it your way."

A bobwhite's "whic-whic-ic" came drifting up from the river and up the bank he came, emerging from the weeds, his dark eyes spotting them, measuring them, disapproving of them, his head plume high and haughty. Off he marched.

Doc went to work with patience and the care one would accord a rare and fragile Chinese porcelain. Using his makeup kit he altered the color of his hair and eyebrows and added a mustache and beard. Then he deepened the lines in his face, shadowing them artistically, giving himself the appearance of a seventy-year-old.

Raider looked on with unconcealable admiration. "I got to hand it to you, you got some eye for makin' up a face."

"It's a gift, Rade, one very close to artistic genius."

"Oh shit!" There was a trenchant and overly long lull in the conversation as Doc finished his face to his satisfaction, examined it one last time in the glass, and began putting away his materials. "There's still one thing about this business has got me completely stumped," murmured Raider.

"Only one?" Doc asked, turning and grinning, then feeling it in the bridge of his nose and wincing.

"Nobody has his plates stolen. Only used. How can that figure?"

"Whatever it is, it's done during the actual printing. Something is substituted, sleight-of-hand . . ."

"Aw, come on."

"Who knows what? All the same, that's the critical phase. I'd bet my life on it."

"Old Man Morgan didn't see a damned thing. He swore up and down."

"That doesn't mean something didn't take place. I just used the term 'sleight-of-hand' groping for words. But that could be it, Rade. You know how a magician forces your eye away from a move he has to make, one you're not supposed to see? Maybe dropping something, forcing your eyes down to his feet while his hand presses a spring in his sleeve. Or something."

"Or something, yeah."

"Somebody during T. D.'s visit to Moody's, his printer, did something like that."

"To give 'em time to switch the plates? They couldn't have. He claimed the plates he took back were his, the same ones he brought over."

"I know what he claimed."

"They'd have to have the genuine plates for as long as it took 'em to print up what they did print up, isn't that so?"

Doc's hands went to the sides of his head. He shook it back and forth slowly. "It's all a muddle up here, Rade. We've just got to go to Catterbury's printing session and see for ourselves what goes on."

"Yeah. You done it again, you know."

"What?"

"Promised him he wouldn't get into the fix Morgan's in, thousands o' bucks in the hole."

"How can he if he changes his stock?"

"All the same you oughtn't to make rash promises like that."

"I had to do something. We had to talk him into going through with it. That is, I had to. You never do have much to say when I need backing up, do you?"

"Oh shit. This face you gimme is starting to itch with the heat already. Am I gonna be able to eat without it falling off?"

"Let's go, let's find out."

10

Joshua Overstone—Printer was conveniently situated almost directly across the street from the Farmers and Merchants Bank. The shop was two small rooms, the larger front one looking out on the street. The back room was reserved for supplies and equipment, and in one corner was a cubbyhole office filled with a small desk and chair. In the center of the workroom, in full view of passersby, stood a Carmody Jobber Platen Printing Press. The machine was worked by foot pressure, noted Raider, upon entering in the company of his partner, Horace Catterbury, and the guard who had greeted the Pinkertons at the bank on the morning of their arrival in Roswell. In the trade, according to Joshua Overstone, the Carmody was known as a perfecting machine, so termed because it produced sheets printed on both sides or, in technical language, "perfect." It was self-inking and easily driven, the average output approximately one thousand copies of anything from wedding invitations to wanted dodgers to ten-dollar banknotes inscribed with the name of the Farmers and Merchants Bank of Roswell. The machine required only one operator.

This information was proclaimed in a halting, tinderdry tone for the "Jones brothers'" edification, following Raider and Doc's introduction to Mr. Overstone by Horace Chatterbury. The room smelled strongly of ink and creosote and grease and, noted Raider, if a body was not alert and careful where he backed or swung an elbow or knee he could easily acquire a pungently scented stain. Overstone introduced his printer, one Joe Gilbertson, then apologized for leaving, and withdrew to keep a dentist's appointment.

"Aren't you new around here?" asked Catterbury, a

72

trace of suspicion in his voice and his eye as the printer made final adjustments to his press and ran a handful of clean waste over the plates carefully set in place by the banker.

Joe Gilbertson, a gangling, round-shouldered boy wearing a leather apron, denim shirt, and flannel yacht cap, grinned. "I done your last four printings, Mr. Catterbury sir. I been here almost two years. Don't you recall me?"

Catterbury was squinting at him close up; gradually recognition filled his face, dispelling his suspicion. "Oh, yes . . ."

The guard had already unwrapped the supply of stock he had carried over from the bank, setting it on a near-by stool. It was to be fed sheet by sheet under the platen.

Raider eyed Joe Gilbertson. He had half suspected that Overstone's regular printer would be out for the day, for the job, his place taken by a stranger, but that would have been a bit too obvious. All the same, he would watch this boy like a Cooper's hawk, before, during, and after the printing. Throughout the rest of the day. Until doomsday, if need be. Money could buy anything, even printers who had printed up banknotes four times previously without anything nefarious resulting.

Everyone gathered about as Gilbertson inked up and fed the press, footing the pedal and taking out a wet, stamped ten-dollar banknote, holding it up for Catterbury to examine. The banker studied one side, then the other through a pocket magnifying glass and pronounced both perfect.

Again Joe Gilbertson grinned. He took off his cap, hanging it on a peg, wiping his brow with a handful of clean waste, and nodding to Mr. Catterbury. Raider and Doc exchanged glances at the sight of the cap being hung up, but neither said a word. Nor did they look out in the street in time to catch sight of the well-dressed man with the diamond stickpin in his silk brocade puff scarf standing on the opposite side with an excellent view of the press and those gathered around it. He too removed his hat.

The run was begun. Out on the sidewalk people passing by glanced in curiously, some watching for a time, then continuing on their way. The notes rolled off the press with rhythmic precision, Catterbury counting them with pad and pencil in hand. He had taken off his own hat and coat against the sultry closeness of the room and stood staring at the moving press. The cylinder was "stopped" by a cam motion as the bed traveled backward; in went the sheet, set against the "marks," down came the gripper closing on it, the cylinder was released, and the impressions made. Then the sheet was seized by a second set of fingers and transferred to a second and smaller cylinder positioned over the larger one which delivered the sheet to the "flyer," which in turn deposited it into a catch tray.

Any distraction, any occurrence, any sound, any disruption of the norm which may draw one's attention from what one is looking at comes with suddenness. Outside the window on the wooden sidewalk the citizens of Roswell continued to pass back and forth like actors traversing a stage. Traffic in the street beyond them, buckboards, men on horseback, and the stage coming in from Fort Sumner moved slowly by, like figures in a dream.

Until the distraction. A blue-black mustang came galloping up the street pell-mell carrying a rider with a neckerchief tied over his face. Turning in his saddle as he passed, he began emptying his six-gun at a pursuer. Man and horse passed out of sight.

A second rider appeared, following closely, booting his roan to catch up, firing two guns at the fleeing man. The suddenness of their appearance, the sounds of shooting, the screams of female onlookers, the men passing by outside ducking for cover, the almost instantaneous pandemonium drew all eyes in the room to the window. Instinctively.

Save two.

Doc's.

At the first shot and first sight of the man with his

face covered he started to look away from the press, but something clicked, a voice lodged in a corner of his mind shouting warning. Back flew his eyes to the press.

He saw nothing done to it. Nothing out of the ordinary. Joe Gilbertson continued to feed in the paper, the printed notes dropping one after another into the catch tray. Doc saw nothing in the press, no break in the steady rhythm of the operation. What he did see was the boy's left hand dart around the other side of the machine to the tray, lift out the last note, examine it closely, then restore it to the tray. Positioned where he was, Doc could only see the upper third of his body, the bib of his apron and above.

Why pick that note, he thought, why then, when the distraction he had signaled for by taking off his cap had occurred?

The job was completed, five hundred and one shiny new ten-dollar banknotes run off, the extra one destroyed on the spot by Catterbury, the others recounted for the sixth time and banded in stacks of fifty. The plates were cleaned, removed from the press, wrapped in a piece of clean muslin, and handed back to the banker.

Joe Gilbertson, for all his tender years, was a cool one, decided Doc. Awaiting the action in the street, getting it, using it to do what he had to do, he hadn't batted an eyelash. It was as if he'd run it through in practice a hundred times and had it down pat. Run what through? Reaching around the far side of the machine and examining one banknote, bringing it close enough to read front and back, then putting it back in the tray? What had he accomplished with that?

Parading back to the bank with Catterbury and the guard, Doc and Raider said their good-byes, left the banker ebullient, brimming with confidence, and walked off down the street to the nearest alley, slipping inside and fixing their sights on the window of the print shop. Joe Gilbertson was still at work, clearly seen through the window.

"He's a cool one," remarked Raider.

"I was thinking the same thing. Did you see what he did?"

"He put something in the press while he fed in the sheets. A plate o' some kind under one. When it landed in the tray, he picked it up with the printed note covering it, made believe he was examining the note, and slipped whatever he had under it down behind that wide arm that comes up from the base o' the press to support the works."

"You actually saw a plate?"

"No, but I could see something was under the sheet and it shook in his hands when he was looking it over, like something heavier was sliding off it down outta sight. I'm just puttin' common sense together, Doc."

"Could be, Rade."

Raider shook his head.

"What?" asked Doc.

"Catterbury. He's so goddamn cocksure o' himself. We warned him to keep his eyes peeled. He slams T. D. Morgan for bein' careless, sloppy, blows off about the pains *he* takes and he still falls ass over teakettle for that bullshit in the street, taking his eyes off the printing to gape out the goddamn window!"

"What were you watching *him* for, Rade? How come you didn't keep your eyes on the printer?"

"I did, goddamnit! How else could I tell you what he done, chapter and verse? All I saw Catterbury do was look back; him and his dumb guard with the funny cap."

"I don't think we should say anything to old Horace. Not yet."

"Amen. What he don't know won't hurt him."

"Hopefully." Doc thought a moment, his eyes glued to the window across the street, but unseeing, totally rapt as he was in pondering the situation.

"What, Doc?"

"You know what you saw, that is, what you *didn't see* shake that banknote our friend over there took out of the tray. . . . A plate of some kind, probably lead. To catch the impressions of both plates." Warming to this intelligence rapidly, Doc turned to his partner and smiled, daring his nose to hurt him. It obliged him. "That's it! It has to be. How else could their banknotes come out exact duplicates? They don't steal the plates, they don't have to. All they do is get impressions of them."

"On lead."

"Better than clay, better than anything. Soft enough to take an imprint, hard enough to retain it perfectly."

"How in red hell could they print from that? Without squashing it flat?"

"Ah, they don't."

Raider twisted up his face, glaring, then staring blankly. "Doc . . ."

"Hear me out. They have to transfer the designs on both sides of the lead sheet to more durable plates, probably copper."

"How?"

"That I can't say, but I'll bet my last dollar it can be done. Then all they need do is run off the notes and forge the signatures. Which gives us plenty of time."

"Maybe not that much. Look . . ."

Across the street Joshua Overstone had returned from the dentist's and entered his shop. Through the window they could see owner and employee in conversation, Joe Gilbertson, his apron removed, putting on his cap, grinning, talking animatedly.

"You follow him, Rade. He's going out to lunch."

"Out to deliver that plate, you mean."

"Of course. Pinpoint who he gives it to. They'll be the ones working on it. If you can't get a look at who it is without arousing suspicions, at least establish where he delivers it."

"Don't worry about me, I'll do my job. Where are you goin'?"

"Back to the bank."

"What for?"

"I think Catterbury ought to hold off putting his signature on those new notes. Just until we break up Zemo's operation."

"Yeah, that makes sense."

Joe Gilbertson had left the shop and was heading up the street toward the Baptist Church.

"Get after him, Rade, I'll meet you in an hour at the hotel."

Raider "got after him"; Doc walked slowly back to the bank. Unseen by either was a well-dressed man who was emerging from the Roswell House Hotel, down the way from the print shop. Well-dressed and sporting a diamond stickpin in his silk brocade puff scarf. He did not look at Doc, nor at Raider, but at Joe Gilbertson ambling up the street toward the church.

11

The year had snailed forward into the heart of the dry season, the sun increasing in ferocity with each passing day, broiling the territory and everything set upon it, reducing the creeks to muddy sloughs, the mud drying and cracking, lowering the rivers to creek size and smaller, bringing an aridity which wasted and wilted and withered every living thing. The kangaroo rat escaped the heat by remaining in its burrow, the ground squirrel similarly retired underground, its body temperature falling as it entered a state of lethargy, its heartbeat, its breathing, and all other bodily functions slowing to a rate barely capable of sustaining its life. The creosote bush dropped its leaves as did the ocotillo. Only man failed to effect any radical adjustment in his mode of life to ease his uncomfortableness. In line with custom he shed hat and jacket, took to drinking to excess, liquids hard, liquids soft, and perspiring. And complaining.

"This blasted heat is enough to collapse a body's lungs," grumbled Horace F. Catterbury, sitting in his shirtsleeves behind his deck, pushing the sultry air back and forth in front of his frown with a plain black Japanese folding fan.

Doc nodded. And in measured tones, calculated to keep from shocking his listener out of his wet red skin, proceeded to detail what he and Raider had observed during the printing. Unhappily he failed abysmally.

"GREAT CAESAR'S GHOST, YOU DON'T MEAN IT! YOU CAN'T!"

Catterbury rose unsteadily from his chair, his fan slipping from his hand, his eyes straining at their sockets, his jaw trembling.

"Now there's no cause for alarm . . ."

79

"No cause for alarm? You tell me those thieving devils have pulled it off right under all our noses and . . ."

"They've pulled off nothing, yet. Other than to enlighten us as to their modus operandi. At this very moment my partner is following the printer with that plate he made."

"He'll apprehend him, of course. I want to see that plate!"

Doc shook his head. "I'm afraid he can't apprehend anybody, not at this stage. Sit, please, compose yourself. I tell you there's nothing to worry about. They'll never print up a single note. You have my solemn word on it."

"That's very generous of you, but it's not good enough." Clasping his hands, Catterbury began swinging them up and down in front of him in the manner of a man appealing to the Almighty. Back and forth he paced, head up, head down, clasped hands up and down. "This is unbelievable! It can't be happening!" Stopping short, he glared at Doc. "I knew I shouldn't have listened to you two, I felt it in my bones." Lurching to the door he wrenched it wide. "Leland! LELAND!"

A young man in vest and absurdly baggy trousers, his shirt two sizes too large for him, his elastic band armlets concealed by billowing folds of material, came rushing in, wide-eyed and visibly paling.

"Sir?"

"Leland, that new batch of banknotes. I want you to destroy them."

Doc shot up from his chair. "Now just a minute . . ."

"Every blessed one. Take them out back to the incinerator and burn them. Then get over to Overstone's Print Shop and tell Joshua to print me up five hundred flyers announcing that all brand-new ten-dollar banknotes on issue from this bank bearing forged signatures and printed on the old Elliot Number Forty-one stock are worthless. No, illegal. Illegal and worthless. Not worth the paper they're printed on."

"Yes sir, Mr. Catterbury, sir. Right away, sir."

"Stay where you are, son!" snapped Doc. "Mr. Catterbury, you can't do this, you'll wreck everything."

"Mr. Pinkerton, don't you tell me what I can and can't do in my bank!"

Doc cringed. At the word "Pinkerton" Leland had turned his cow eyes on him in fear and wonderment. The balloon was going up fast, Doc decided, taking the whole case with it. Moving with unaccustomed alacrity he gained the door, jerked the knob out of Leland's hand, and closed and locked the door.

"WHAT IN HELL DO YOU THINK YOU'RE DOING?" Catterbury burst out.

Doc held up both hands. "Please listen. You can't destroy that batch of banknotes. You can hold them back unsigned for forty-eight hours, but then they have to go out. Otherwise the whole shooting match goes down the drain. You're overlooking one very important thing, all-important. We have two different stocks here; theirs is nothing like yours."

"It's close enough. I must have been out of my head to listen to you two. Con men, that's what you are—"

Doc cut in, pouring forth soothing words, placating the man, persuasively countering his fears with logic. Gradually Catterbury began to calm down, eventually to the point of dismissing Leland, who departed more confused than he'd been when he'd arrived. Catterbury then accepted an Old Virginia from Doc, and both sat and puffed away.

"What it comes down to is disarmingly simple," said the Pinkerton. "Our moves govern theirs. If the bank doesn't begin distributing, they'll likely hold off until you do. They're clever, they're experienced; they don't take unnecessary chances, at least they haven't so far."

"I'm nothing more than bait for your trap," responded the banker, eying Doc with a skeptical look, still far from convinced that cooperation was in anything like his best interests.

"You can't lose a red cent."

"That chap Morgan up in Albuquerque lost his shirt!"

"Before we arrived on the scene. Your paper is different, that's still your protection. If Raider and I dropped dead and they succeeded in flooding the area with their forgeries, you'd still be able to stop them at your windows."

"Which could turn this bank into a madhouse, the whole town . . ."

"It won't come to that, I give you my solemn word."

Catterbury puffed on the cheroot, hauled it from his mouth and aimed it at Doc. He opened his mouth to speak, changed his mind, reached into his belly drawer, brought out a piece of paper, scribbled a few words down on it in pen and ink, hesitated, added more, restored his pen to its holder, blew on the paper, turned it around and shoved it under Doc's eyes.

To whom it may concern:

We do hereby accept full and complete responsibility for the consequences, whatever they may be, of the strategy we have devised and are employing to foil those parties who are attempting to counterfeit the ten-dollar banknotes of the Farmers and Merchants Bank of Roswell.

In the event the thieves succeed in their effort, any monetary loss incurred by the bank will be reimbursed in toto by the Pinkerton National Detective Agency.

Attested to this date, the 9th of July, 1880, by the agents whose signatures appear below.

X's below indicated where both were to sign. Taking his pen from its holder, Catterbury dipped it and proferred it.

"Sign it. And when your sidekick comes back, get him in here to sign it, too."

Doc hesitated, then nodded and accepted the pen. He hated doing this. He shouldn't do it. He had no right to; there was no need to. It was ridiculous, preposterous, capitulating to the whim of a frightened man. Allan Pinkerton would hand his and Raider's heads to them if he ever found out. It wasn't the two of them they'd be entrapping, it was the agency. It could wind up costing Chicago five thousand dollars. Five thousand—five million, it might just as well be!

Catterbury stared at him steadily. The fear was long gone from his face, supplanted by a patent self-assurance that verged on smugness. He was testing the courage of the man who had pushed him into a corner. He had reversed their roles. Not alone cleverly but effectively. *Put your money where your mouth is, Mr. Pinkerton. Are your words just words, or is this the voice of sincere belief?* He wouldn't accept excuses like "I'm sorry, I'm not authorized," "This will have to be forwarded to the main office for Chief Pinkerton's consideration," "We're not dealing in concrete certainties here; this is not a mathematical problem."

"Well?"

Catterbury almost smiled, but there was no humor in the situation, no warmth, nothing to inspire such a display. The man still had to be tipped over the edge into unqualified acceptance of the scheme. It was now or probably never.

Doc nodded, redipped the pen, and signed. "Raider will sign as soon as he gets back," he said, striving for a jaunty tone.

It came out nothing like jaunty.

12

Raider followed Joe Gilbertson at a safe distance, crossing to the other side of the street, putting the man with the stickpin parallel to him. The printer passed the church, running his hand aimlessly down the fence pickets and turning right at the corner. A short way down the side street he stopped in front of a dismal-looking unpainted three-story house with trellises covered with scraggly-looking yellow roses decorating the otherwise undistinguished front of it. In went Joe, the man with the stickpin following him. Raider remained across the street, withdrawing into the shadow of the roof of Maltby's Feed and Grain, his eyes fixed on the doorway, his wheels whirling. Presently boy and man appeared in the third-floor window in the center of the front. The upward angle permitted only their heads and shoulders to show. Just long enough to allow Raider to identify them before a third party, whom he also recognized, approached the window and pulled the shade.

Franklin, the man who had taken his ticket outside Semena the Queen of the Nile's show in Albuquerque. Which figured. Everybody associated with the carnival had to be in on the act. How else could secrecy be preserved?

He waited in the shadow, glancing out from under the overhang, when the bell atop the Baptist Church came to life to toll the hour of noon, sending the sound rolling out over the little town. Moments later the stickpin and the printer came out the door and walked back, side by side, the way they had come. Still Raider waited. Suddenly he was seized by an urge to enter the house, climb the stairs to the third floor, and get a look inside the room. He took three steps toward the house before giving in to a spasm of common sense as swift in arriving as his first urge. He started for the hotel. He got to the corner, turned back for a last glance at the house and the third-floor window, jettisoned his common sense and returned.

The landlady was pillowy fat, with a pouchy face, gold teeth, and a smile that crinkled her eyes at the corners behind her spectacles. Raider did his utmost to conform to his disguise, bending slightly with the weight of years, speaking haltingly in a voice he hoped sounded tired. And taking pains to shelve his usual alias, remembering that Zemo and his people were familiar with it.

"Mr. Dearborn you say?" inquired the woman. "I'm Emma Struck." She tendered her hand in friendly fashion. "I got a room first floor rear that's mighty nice. Looks out on the willow."

"Anything on the top floor? I sort of like to be away from things, if you know what I mean. . . ."

"There's a corner room, it's a mite small."

"Size makes no never mind."

"Seventy-five cents the night, that includes breakfast, o' course."

"Sounds fine."

She tilted her head and eyed him sympathetically. "All alone in the world, are you?"

"For goin' on fifteen years."

"Tsk tsk . . . Well, you must be used to it by now. You got a bag?"

"Back at the hotel. I can fetch it later."

"Good. If you'll step this way."

Raider doled out seventy five cents and followed her up the creaking stairs to the third floor, pausing to rest at the top step, leaning against the banister for support.

"Land sakes," she said, "a body'd think you'd prefer the ground floor. Save you all this climbing . . ."

"I climb all I can," said Raider between gasps. "Keeps me fit." Getting his breath, he kept step with her down the hall to a corner room barely big enough to hold a bed and a nightstand. Two hooks fastened to the wall served as a closet and there was no wash-stand.

"Washstand's down the hall, other end," she said, anticipating his question. She handed him the key, then going inside she smoothed the bedcovers and fluffed the pillow. "I hope you won't be cramped."

"Is it quiet?" he asked timidly.

"Oh my yes." She nodded down the hall. "Mr. Hanrahan, he's a blacksmith and quiet as church. Out all day every day. Mr. Patterson next door, he's a drummer, farm tools. He's away for days at a stretch." She indicated the ticket taker's room. "And over there's Mr. Otis, he's just arrived in town. He's a chemist. Only be staying a few days, so he tells me. My others are all permanents."

"Chemist?"

"He mixes things, drugs mostly. Got all sorts o' equipment set out, paraphernalia. Had to fetch the long table up from the back room for him."

"Does he make . . ." began Raider. He lowered his eyes. "Does it smell?"

"Land sakes no. I warned him 'bout that right off the mark. In a polite way, you understand. Said to him this was a rooming house and that the other folks couldn't be expected to put up with well you know, sulfur and that sorta thing. And nothin' dangerous, explosives and all. He gave me his solemn word he wouldn't be fussing with anything that's either. A quiet sort, but pleasant. I'm taking him at his word, but if there's any cause to raise objections, out he'll go."

"I'm sure there won't be. Thank you, Mrs. Struck. If it's all the same to you, I think I'll lie down a spell."

"Go right ahead, bed's paid for."

She laughed and went away. Raider closed the door, then opened it an inch, just enough to be able to see Franklin's door. He waited until the woman's steps died away, below, then venturing forth, he approached the door. One look inside, that's all he wanted, two seconds to sweep the interior. Reaching into his pocket, he fished out a ten-dollar bill, then knocked.

"Yes?" asked a muffled voice.

"Excuse me, I'm just across the hall. Could you change a bill for me, please? I hatè to trouble you, but . . ."

"How much?"

"Ten dollars."

"Just a second." There was a long pause. Raider could hear silver quietly clinking. Then: "Sorry, I ain't got it."

"Oh. Well, thank you all the same."

"You're welcome."

"The name's Dearborn. Frank. I'm just across the hall. If there's anything I can do you you, don't hesitate."

"Thanks."

"You're welcome, I'm sure."

He went back to his room. Son of a bitch! Better he'd asked change for a quarter. Better a look at the man's door key, pretend that there was something wrong with his own. Ask his help in unlocking his door. Anything to get his goddamn door open, even two inches.

What was he doing here anyway? Why bother to go to all this trouble? What did it matter what was in the room; he knew for a fact the lead plate was, which was all that mattered. What he ought to have done was head straight back to the hotel and rejoin Doc as planned. It was getting on toward half-past twelve, most of the hour alloted him was already used up. If he had the brains of a goat he'd head back at once.

But Christ Almighty, being here in a room eight feet away from Franklin's door, with three quarters of an inch of pine separating him from a sight of the room was far too enticing to turn his back on. Sitting at the foot of his bed, he considered his next move. Not toward Franklin, that was for sure. A second approach would raise his suspicions sky high.

His door ajar, Raider continued to ponder when all at once he heard a door open down the hall. Sneaking a look, he saw Franklin come out, lock his door, put on his hat, and leave. His steps faded to silence below as had Mrs. Struck's earlier.

Raider descended the stairs. Mrs. Struck had put on a flowered apron and was bending over the oven. The odor of fresh-baked bread curled up Raider's nostrils, alerting his taste buds.

"Mr. Dearborn . . ."

"Hello again, m'am. I been wondering . . ." he began haltingly, affecting the same sheepish demeanor that had brought the kindly smile to her face when he'd introduced himself. "I hate to trouble you . . ."

"What is it?"

-   "You were right, I'm afraid that room is a trifle small."

"I knew it would be. For a body big as you are."

"Do you have anything bigger on the third floor?"

"I will have, depends on how long you'll be staying. Mr. Otis's . . ."

"That's right, you said. Would it be too much trouble to show me?"

"Not at all." She selected a key from a board beside an Old Sachem Bitters Wigwam Tonic calendar and tucked it in her apron pocket, motioning him to follow her.

There was a one-pound can of Filchock's Beeswax, there was copper sulfate, turpentine, what looked to be sulfuric acid in an open tin, and other bottles and cans. There was a burner and a wooden frame suitable in size for holding a banknote plate. There was, however, no sign of the lead plate. Packed safely away, mused Raider.

"This is better'n twice as big as your corner room," she said, making a grand sweeping gesture with one arm. "It's a dollar a night, though. A bargain at that."

"The street does seem quiet," said Raider, nodding.

"It is." She dug her fist into the mattress. "Good firm tick."

"Put me down for it, if you will please."

"Gladly."

He left the house a few minutes later, returning to the hotel to find Doc waiting impatiently in the lobby; stumping out a cheroot, he broke out of the grasp of a cheap leather easy chair and preceded him up the stairs. Closing the door and bolting it behind him, Doc leaned against it.

"What kept you? What have you been up to?"

As Raider's explanation poured out of him, Doc's scowl became grimmer and grimmer.

"I wish you hadn't done that, I really do."

"Doc, I saw where they work up the plate. Where they're goin' to . . ."

"That's the point, you didn't have to see it. The boy delivers the lead plate there, you'd have to be a moron not to take it for granted the room is set up for the work. I should be happy you didn't spot the plate; you'd probably have lifted it."

"Don't be stupid, will you?"

"All right, forget it, what's done is done. I just think it's chancey for you to be that close to him. You scare him and this whole thing's liable to blow up in our faces."

"I'm not gonna scare him. Christ Almighty, give me credit for a little brain matter, can't you?"

"I do, Rade, darned little." He brought out a piece of yellow paper, unfolding it. "I got a telegram from Wagner. I decoded it. Read it."

REGARDING YOUR INQUIRY THE GREAT ZEMO STOP BE ADVISED OUR INVESTIGATION REVEALS HIS REAL NAME TO BE HEINZ WERNER BRAUCHITZ AMERICAN CITIZEN WITH NO KNOWN RECORD OF ARREST COUNTERFEITING BUT SUSPICION COMPLICITY IN PROCTOR CASE SAINT LOUIS THREE YEARS AGO STOP BRAUCHITZ HAS SERVED FOUR YEARS MANSLAUGH- TER STOP FREQUENTLY ARRESTED ASSAULT AND BATTERY SAINT LOUIS AND ELSEWHERE STOP COL- LEGE GRADUATE STOP CONSIDERED EXTREMELY IN- TELLIGENT BY INFORMANTS STOP IS CURRENTLY SOLE OWNER CARNIVAL STOP PROCEED WITH CAU- TION STOP

"He don't have to tell me that last," said Raider. "Isn't it about time you and me called in the goddamn reserves?"

Doc nodded. "Help is on the way."

"How many bodies?"

Doc shrugged. "Whatever William Pinkerton up in Denver can spare us. We can't pull in anybody from around here. We're the only two operatives in the entire territory."

"Great. How about the local law? We could sit down with the sheriff."

"No, Rade." Doc took out his handkerchief, wiped the inside of his beaver hat, and set it on the bed.

"Jesus Christ, don't you know that's bad luck!"

Doc set it on the washstand. "I was about to say, the quieter we can keep this thing, the better our chances for success."

"Yeah. What do you think about that room?"

"What's to think? It only confirms my original suspicion. They're electrotyping."

"What's that?"

"Electroplating applied to typography. It's a bit complicated for your feeble intelligence . . ."

"You mean you don't know exactly how they do it. You got to go running to the library and look it up before you can show off how fuckin' smart you are."

"Rade, there's something I have to tell you, something that came up while you were gone. Sit down, why don't you, take a load off."

Raider sat. "What did you screw up now?"

"Will you listen?"

He explained about Catterbury's letter. Raider listened, his jaw dropping lower and lower, his good and almost good eye widening, giving him the look of a spooked horse.

"You didn't sign it, you couldn't be that stupid! Course not, nobody's that stupid . . ."

"I had to sign it."

Raider jumped to his feet and began raving, cursing volubly, hauling out every known obscenity and purpling the air with them, dressing his partner down, shrinking him, wilting him.

"Now just a minute, Rade. Let me get a word in. Can I? CAN I?"

"You call my intelligence feeble! Jesus Christ Almighty, feeble is better than none! What kinda stupid goddamn ridiculous fuckin' play is that?"

"It's very simple. If I hadn't signed, if I'd even hesitated to sign, he would have dropped out of the game. And taken his five thousand in banknotes with him. He would have, Rade, he was on the verge. Then he got this bright idea . . ."

"Jesus Christ, I don't believe it."

"The thing is, friend, my signature alone isn't enough for him. He wants yours, too."

"Fuck him!"

"You have to sign, Rade."

"Why, 'cause you did?"

"That's right."

"Shit! I mean SHIT! How come you're all the time gettin' us into the hot fuckin' soup? Gettin' me into it?"

Doc patiently repeated his explanation of the situation, reiterating his fear that Catterbury would junk the scheme if they failed to accept responsibility in the name of the agency for any losses he might sustain.

Raider seethed and fumed, occasionally breaking out in an additional spate of cursing. All the way to the bank. Where, finally persuaded by his partner that doing so was not only in their best interests but the sole choice open to them, he signed. With help from William Pinkerton the rooming house would be surrounded and when the first banknotes were printed up and the signatures of Horace F. Catterbury and his cashier affixed to them, the Pinkertons would close in and seize the evidence and the culprits. A second detachment would capture Zemo and his people at the carnival at the same time.

What could possibly go wrong?

13

It would take at least two more full days before
the counterfeiters would be able to prepare their plates,
print up their banknotes, and forge the necessary signatures. It would be at least two days before Raider and
Doc's promised reinforcements arrived. Upon leaving
the bank, the two Pinkertons headed for the stable to
look in on Judith. They found her being brushed down,
having just consumed a bucket of fresh oats. They were
talking to the stableman, who seemed to have developed
a fondness for her, when a sudden, tremendous explosion rocked the world. Dropping his brush, the man
gaped in awe and pointed toward the north end of
town, Raider and Doc following his hand. A cloud
of black smoke billowed upward about thirty yards to
the right of the Baptist Church steeple.

The stableman gulped and swallowed. "Holy jumpin'
Jehosophat!"

All of Roswell headed for the scene, people pouring out of doorways setting up a chatter and clatter,
charging up the main street. Raider and Doc and the
stableman had covered half the distance to the church
when the rumble of hooves and the insistent clanging
of a fire bell came rushing up behind them. The fire
engine shot ahead, careening around the corner, water
sloshing out of its tank, people and horses fleeing its
path like the Red Sea parting before Moses. Raider and
Doc and the stableman had been running hard, the two
Pinkertons drawing stares from the people they left in
their wake, surprised at the agility and endurance of
men obviously well beyond their primes.

It was Mrs. Struck's house. Had it been any other,
Raider would have been amazed. The front had been
blown away entirely, the smoke still rising, fire licking

the edges of the destruction. By the time they arrived on the scene, the firemen had manned their pump, four of them bobbing up and down at the crosshandles, driving water into the three-inch hose while a fifth man played it on the flames. The crowd quickly gathered, the sheriff and two of his men invading the rubble, braving the heat with forearms upraised and wet bandanas over noses and mouths. The fire was extinguished, but not before most of the building had been destroyed. Only the two ends remained standing, the sections of the roof attached to them leaning inward precariously, threatening to break loose and fall to the ground. From where Raider was standing, it looked as if a tornado had split the house in two, taking away the center third with it.

He could see Mrs. Struck off to one side, sobbing loudly, wringing her hands, an empty bread tin at her feet. Friends and neighbors were comforting her. She was lucky she'd been out, thought Raider, as lucky as her roomers. As near as he could judge, only the cause-of-it-all had been at home. Proof of this assumption came when one of the deputies stumbled upon the grisly remains of Franklin's head and part of one arm. The crowd reacted in horror.

"Jesus Christ," moaned Raider softly, seizing Doc by the elbow and steering him off to one side. "This cuts it, we're dead!"

"Not as dead as he is."

"The whole scheme's blowed."

"Yes and no."

"What do you mean, 'yes and no'?"

"Actually, it doesn't hurt us."

"It sure as hell doesn't help us."

"It ruins Zemo. They'll cross Roswell off their schedule and pack up and leave. Which, if you stop to think about it, gets us off the hook on that paper Catterbury forced us to sign."

"We'll still have to start all over again someplace else."

"Maybe not. Zemo's lost his electrotyping talent; who knows, maybe he'll retire from the field?"

"Goddamn, that's even worse! We'll never nail the son of a bitch with the goods."

"Let's get out of here. Let's go back to the bank and see Catterbury."

"He's standing right over there. See him in front o' the feed and grain store?"

Catterbury hailed them and the three of them drifted away from the crowd.

"I see no reason why I shouldn't put those new tens into the drawers bright and early tomorrow morning," said the banker expansively, in the manner of a man from whose puny shoulders a great weight had been lifted. "Do you two have any objections?"

"It might be wise to wait until the carnival leaves town." said Doc.

"Why bother? Their show's over before it starts. Ha ha, you get that little play on words? Show's over . . ."

Raider and Doc swapped glances. Raider cleared his throat and studied the ground between his feet. "Play it any way you like, mister, just as long as you tear up that paper we signed."

"Oh no . . ."

Raider glared; Doc's brow furrowed apprehensively. "Why not?" he asked.

"Simple. The storm *looks* like it's passed us over, but we won't know for certain until the end of the week. No sense unlocking the shutters till then, is there?" He shook his head, leering at one, then the other. "Not as far as I can see."

"You're a bit of a prick, you know that, Mr. Catterbury?"

"Rade . . ." Doc grabbed his partner's arm, pulling him back a step.

"I'd say I'm a sensible man of business, mister. That piece of paper is my insurance policy. I'm not tearing it up, I'm not giving it back. It stays in the safe. Who knows, it may come in handy at some future date." He doffed his hat. "Have a pleasant day, gentlemen."

14

At midnight that night, having lost the coin toss, Raider climbed wearily out of his bed in his room on the second floor of the Roswell House, pulled on his pants, thrust his arms into his shirt and jacket and his feet into his Middleton boots, washed the stale taste of Taos Lightning out of his mouth with a swig of "fresh" Taos Lightning, and wandered over to the carnival site. Satisfying himself that Zemo was not moving on this night, he returned to the hotel and bed.

At seven in the morning he met Doc by the front door. At such an early hour the easy chairs in the lobby were unoccupied and there was little traffic between the desk and the front door. The two operatives were preparing to go down the street for breakfast when the desk clerk called out to them.

"You gentlemen hear the news?"

"We just got up, young feller," explained Doc, affecting the dry tone of an elderly man that set Raider's eyes rolling toward the ceiling.

"There's been a murder. Down to the print shop."

"Not . . ." began Doc.

"Young Joe Gilbertson. They found his body an hour ago draped over his printing press. Somebody'd busted his neck. And left the whole front o' the shop in a shambles."

"Jesus Christ," whispered Raider.

"Go down and take a look for yourselves, why don't you?" continued the clerk.

"Yeah." Raider nodded. They stepped outside. "Murdered . . ."

Doc wasn't listening; he was thinking. Raider knew that look, eyes unseeing, head nodding slightly, as if he were gently jouncing his brain to get it into gear. He ran a hand over his chin, then used it to shade his eyes from the sun as he looked up the street toward the print shop.

"His neck busted," continued Raider. "Zemo."

"Zemo!" said both.

"But why?"

Doc's face began to light up slowly, understanding seeping into his features, triumph setting his eyes gleaming. He had, one would have thought, just discovered the secret of the philosopher's stone, and was prepared to inform the world.

"Rade, he held out on them . . ."

"What are you talking about?"

"Listen to me, he made the lead plate, right? We, all of us, left the shop. We watched him clean up from across the street. We saw Overstone come back from the dentist. We saw the boy leave. You followed him."

"He took the plate to Zemo's man, Franklin."

"Did he?"

Raider stared. A butterfly sailed by them, basking in flight in the warmth of the sun, lighting on the hitching rail, flexing its black-webbed yellow wings and taking off.

Raider frowned, fighting to repel the suggestion, but unable to. "Are you trying to tell me he had other ideas, like holding out for more money before handing it over? He couldn't have, Doc."

"Why not? Think about it, as if you were he. You're not one of the gang, you're local talent. Zemo approaches you, hires you. He gievs you a hundred dollars, let's say. A lot of money for somebody making eight or ten a week. You practice and practice and pull it off beautifully, slick as can be. Then you get to thinking, Zemo and his people stand to make five, ten thousand dollars. With what? With *your* plate. *Yours,* Rade."

"The whole plan hinges on that plate."

"You decide you want more money. Maybe you're stupid, maybe you threaten to spill the beans. Zemo's got a temper, who knows better than the two of us? He loses it, breaks the boy's neck, then turns the place upside-down looking for the plate."

"It all sounds fairly pat, Doc."

"Does it sound plausible?"

Raider wrinkled his chin and put on a look of grudging agreement. "More than plausible," persisted Doc. "Highly probable."

"I hope to hell you're wrong."

"What do you mean?"

"If you're right, if Zemo did do it and it was him who ransacked the place, what if he found that plate? It puts him back in business; I mean Franklin may be blowed up, but he's not the only talent in the world. Who knows but maybe old Zemo's got two, three, four guys who can . . . can . . ."

"Who have a practical knowledge of electrotypography. Good point. Damn, I wish we'd gotten that paper back from Catterbury!"

"Maybe we can't get it, but we can sure as hell stop him from doling out those tens o' his. Come on."

They were at the door of the bank, breakfastless and biting the bit when Horace F. Catterbury arrived to open. He greeted them airily.

"Isn't it a lovely morning?"

"Yeah," said Raider.

"Makes a man happy he's alive." The banker inhaled, his nostrils quivering, his scrawny chest barely pressing the buttons of his vest as he filled his lungs.

"Heard about Joe Gilbertson?" inquired Doc.

Catterbury's smile vanished. "Oh my, yes, sorry business. I understand the sheriff is holding a prime suspect."

"Is that so?" Raider swept his glance to Doc and back to the banker. "Anybody we know?"

"I don't think so. Carl Haskell, a bank and office equipment salesman. We do business with him. He's well known up and down the territory."

"Mr. Catterbury, we'll make this brief. We'd like

you to hold off distributing those banknotes." Doc cleared his throat, a signal to Raider that his partner was striving for dramatic effect. His words emerged tinged with a solemnity worthy of a preacher at a funeral. "We have every reason to believe that that lead plate was not destroyed in the fire yesterday. It's highly possible that Zemo has gotten his hands on it, in which case . . ."

"He's back in business," said Raider.

"I seriously doubt that, gentlemen. In the first place, the carnival's packing up and leaving Roswell. If it hasn't already. Secondly, your friend Zemo didn't kill Joe Gilbertson for any plate; Sheriff Bundy knows what he's doing or he wouldn't have Carl under lock and key. I seriously doubt if Carl and Zemo have ever laid eyes on one another. In addition, I happen to need those tens in circulation, not lying in the drawers like next year's calendar. The reason we went to printing is because our assets have been rising spectacularly."

"Who told you the carnival's leaving town?" asked Doc.

"I drove my fly past there. I saw them with my own eyes. Less than ten minutes ago."

"And what makes you think that gets you off the hook?" asked Raider. "Just 'cause they're pulling out don't mean they can't print up and pass out their tens. They could do it from a hundred miles away."

"Gentlemen, gentlemen, gentlemen, it's all over. It is for this bank. I suggest you two pack up and follow them to their next stop. With any luck you may be able to catch them in the act there with the evidence you'll need in court. I sincerely hope you do catch them. It's certainly in the best interest of all of us bankers, the public . . ."

"Spare us the fuckin' speech, Catterbury," snapped Raider, bristling. "Just hand over our paper and we'll say good-bye."

Catterbury shook his head. "I'd like to oblige you, gentlemen; I'm not being flint-hearted, nor whimsical, I assure you. But under the circumstances . . ."

"Thanks a lot. Come on, Doc."

Off they walked.

"Have a pleasant day," Catterbury called after them.

"If the son of a bitch laughs," growled Raider, "I'm goin' back and lay him out in the fuckin' horse trough."

15

Sheriff Lamarr Bundy was a good-natured, affable sort, past his prime, perhaps, a trifle slower going for his iron than he'd been ten year earlier, but intelligence lurked behind his ice-blue eyes, and the manner in which he mulled over a question before responding, inspecting its facets, testified to the fact that the man knew what he was doing in his job. Mulled over Doc's questions, as he and Raider sat in the sheriff's outer office, their hats on their knees, Raider sneaking an anxious peek at the Seth Thomas clock over the sheriff's desk, mindful that Zemo and his carnival were on their way out of town.

The two Pinkertons had laid everything out on the table for the lawman, including their suspicion that Zemo himself, not Carl Haskell, had broken Joe Gilbertson's neck and draped him over his press.

"Interesting," ventured Bundy. "Certainly looks to be motive enough. Though what you tell me about the lead plate and Joe's holding it back for more money comes under educated guessing, as opposed to iron-clad fact."

"We'd like to talk to Haskell," said Doc, "if you don't mind."

"You talk to him," said Raider, standing. "I can't hang around. I got to get onto old Zemo's trail. I'll wire you, either when they get where they're heading or whatever settlement I'm near when they stop for the night."

"I'll have to stick here, Rade." Doc's tone was half apologetic. "William's men will be coming in from Denver, I want to pursue this angle with Haskell, there's Catterbury and his notes . . ."

"I know. I'll let you know where I'm heading soon as I find out myself. Then ride back here."

"You might not be able to. You might find yourself all tied up with the next banker they're planning to take. They won't lose much time, Rade. Keep a sharp eye out for any of Catterbury's notes, too. Do you have an old one? You'll want to compare . . ."

"Nope."

Doc fished out his wallet, took out a ten-dollar Farmers & Merchants banknote, and slowly, reluctantly, tendered it.

"I don't suppose you have ten other dollars."

"I do, but I'll be needin' 'em. Take it easy, Doc. Sheriff, thanks for your time."

And he was out the door.

Doc watched him cross the street and turn down the sidewalk, heading for the stable and his waiting *grulla*. He never liked their splitting up; it always seemed to complicate matters. Always seemed to make both their jobs more difficult and dangerous. He himself had long ago decided that fate had not cut him out to be a lone hand, although Raider seemed to revel in it. Mostly, Doc reflected, because it gave him his chance to toss Allan Pinkerton's General Principles out the nearest window.

But his partner's departure did little to relieve the main worry nagging at the front of his mind, that the lead plate had already mothered two new copper ones and very shortly the area would be flooded with forged notes. Catterbury didn't seem in the least worried; why should he be, wasn't he covered by his precious paper? Eighty-nine Washington Street in Chicago would make up for any loss he sustained. Doc groaned inwardly. Sheriff Bundy lifted himself to his feet, his belly jouncing, his .45 slapping against his hip. He took down his keys.

"*I* appreciate your sticking around, Mr. . . ."

"Weatherbee."

"If between us we can get his nibs off the pan fire and this Zemo onto it, it wouldn't make me mad. Carl isn't a bad sort."

Carl Haskell proved to be the well-dressed middle-aged man with the diamond stickpin whom neither Pinkerton had noticed noticing them when they had first walked into Horace F. Catterbury's bank. Raider would have recognized him as the man who had come out of Mrs. Struck's rooming house with Joe Gilbertson. Unfortunately, Raider was on his way to the stable. Just as unfortunately, Doc had never seen Carl Haskell, not in the bank, not across the street from Overstone's Print Shop, lifting his hat to acknowledge Gilbertson's removing his to signal the two Wild West performers, who had provided the late printer with the distraction he'd needed.

He was pale, he was nervous, his hands shaking as he pulled out a pack of Cameo Duke cigarettes, jammed one into his mouth, and asked Doc for a match. He lit him and Sheriff Bundy closed and locked the cell door, leaving them in privacy.

"I never killed anybody, as God is my witness. I got there just after it happened. I went to him, I could see right off he was dead. Then I felt eyes stabbing into me. People outside on the sidewalk."

"What time was this?"

"Before sun-up. It was barely beginning to get light out. I couldn't sleep, I thought the fresh air might help. Damn it to hell, I did what any normal human being would have done, saw there was trouble and walked in to see what I could do! And this is what it gets me! Do you know, I've never been inside a jail cell before in my life? I've never even had words with the law before. How in God's name did I get into this? I'm a respectable businessman."

"Bank and office equipment."

"Right. Western representative for Shotsford Bank and Office Equipment of Knoxville, Tennessee. Seventeen years. Up and down the territories. Horace Catterbury over at the bank can vouch for me. He and I have been thick as fleas for years. By God we are, he'll stick up for me; he knows I'm no murderer."

"Did you know Joe Gilbertson?"

"Sure I knew him. It's a small town. He worked

in the window all day, every day. When I was in town we'd wave to each other, have a word once in a while."

"I see." Bank and office equipment, he mused; seventeen years up and down the territories. Likely friendly with every banker from here to El Paso and north to the border. As friendly as he was with Catterbury. A man that close to bankers could hear a lot of things that have nothing to do with bank and office equipment.

Doc seized his eyes and held them. "Do you know Zemo the Great?"

Haskell shook his head. "Never met the man; heard of him, of course."

He was good, thought Doc, very good. Just not good enough. It wasn't in his delivery, his face, or the movement of his head. It was the eyes; passing fear had touched them, just for an instant, for the wink of either one. He'd caught it. This man knew Zemo, all right.

"I hope to God you're a good lawyer."

"I'm no lawyer. Never said I was."

"Then how come you're asking me all these questions?" Haskell jumped to his feet with surprising quickness for one so depressed, so crushed.

"You'll get one, just ask your friend Catterbury. But no lawyer can help you like I can. What would you say if I told you I can put my finger on the real murderer, that if you cooperate with me you'll never even go to trial?"

The reaction he was looking for, hoping for, was not forthcoming. Quite the contrary, at mention of "the real murderer," Haskell sat down hard, shrinking back against the wall like a cornered animal, his eyes darting about, his hands beginning to shake again. Snatching the cigarette out of his mouth he flung it against the opposite wall.

"Get out. GET OUT!"

Steps outside. The door opened, Bundy filling the doorway. Doc got up from the stool, turning toward him.

"All done, Sheriff."

"Is something the matter?"

"I want to see Horace Catterbury!" Haskell burst out, his tone verging on hysteria. "At once! Get him over here."

"Calm down, Mr. Haskell."

"GET HIM!"

Doc thanked the sheriff and went out, aware that Bundy probably hadn't even heard him, Haskell was making such a racket.

Outside he lit up an Old Virginia and tugged at it thoughtfully, smudging the blinding sun with a slender column of smoke. There was no mistake, Haskell had stoutly resisted relieving his conscience of the truth, the whole truth and nothing but. And the words "the real murderer" had nearly given the man a heart attack. Interesting.

16

The carnival had left Roswell heading down out of
the mountains southeast for Dexter, situated within sight
of the west bank of the Pecos River. At the first fork,
however, the lead wagon turned east, leading the train
across a bridge toward the Mescalaro Valley; beyond
lay the Staked Plains.

In the direction they were heading Lovington would
be the nearest town of any size. Almost a hundred
miles. Too far for one day, even with their early start.
Far too far in this heat. If Zemo were smart he'd pull
them up in the shadow of an escarpment and wait
out nightfall. The valley wasn't bad, but the Staked
Plains was impossible, far better traveled by moon
and stars when welcome coolness crept over the tor-
tured land.

The plains was not the "hell with the fires out" of
the Badlands; the area had its share of natural beauties,
like the gigantic gypsum crystals, jewels of the gods; incredible underground passages sparkling with red-and-
white crystals and cubes of blue salt, splendid, dazzling-
ly bright caverns with chambers half a mile long, their
ceilings ten times as high as Mrs. Struck's ill-fated
rooming house, wells of oil and artesian water, "bottom-
less pits" to awe the eye.

But there was also the brutal heat and dust, the
boundless and boring flats of brush, arroyos, and nondescript elevations that passed for hills, littered with the
bones of beast and man and the vultures who had
cleaned them, and homely, twisted trees battling for
survival, the brittle-stemmed leafy greasewood, home
for grasshopper, katydid, and the shield-bearing moth,
giant yuccas, drooping junipers, and too little water.

The Staked Plains. He wanted no part of their challenge by day. But what he wanted would be dictated by the Great Zemo, who, unfortunately for Raider, appeared bent on getting where he was going as quickly as possible.

Let him run, mused the Pinkerton, watching the last wagon reach the far side of the river and pass on out of sight. He could wait an hour, two, cross the bridge, and easily spot the train traversing the valley following the only road east. He would water his horse and linger in the shade of a willow. And catch up with them before they reached the far side of the valley. That way he would not get to the Staked Plains until the sun had buried itself in the San Andres Mountains behind him. Doc wouldn't be hearing from him this day.

He stretched out under the tree, letting the horse amble down the riverbank and drink. He examined the situation. If Doc was right about Zemo's finally getting his hands on the lead plate, they could be back into deep trouble. Nothing unusual in that. Trouble was the theme of the case journal of their lives.

Like dollar denims ridden too long too hard, it was all coming apart. They'd managed to get it nicely knotted up, now it was coming unraveled. Willy Pinkerton's troops would arrive in Roswell to find the suspects fled; they and Doc would join him in Lovington or Hobbs or wherever Zemo and his people decided to light, and a hundred miles behind them all hell could break loose. All the snakebiter needed was two people, Dolly Dee and a girlfriend, to stay behind and spread around the phonies possibly being printed up somewhere close by at that very moment. Even in Roswell?

Far from far-fetched; Horace F. Catterbury's banknotes, whatever the denomination, had to be highly acceptable legal tender in and around the town. The farther one got from there, the less acceptable they became. Until you reached places where nobody had even heard of Roswell, let alone the Farmers and Merchants Bank. At which point, the value of the notes was reduced to the equivalent of any bill with Confederate States of America bannered across the top.

The white belly of a kingbird showed through the gently swaying branches of the willow. Wings outstretched and unmoving, the bird rode the wind easily, nonchalantly, he thought, studying it. Its belly had to be full of seeds; never had he seen a living thing so relaxed, so contented. When, he reflected, was the last time he was contented? He couldn't recall. Probably in the cradle, if then.

Whistling the *grulla* up the bank, he looped the reins around a branch, rubbing the horse's muzzle gently, playfully, then lay down again under the tree, kicking off his boots, pulling his Stetson down over his eyes, folding his hands across his stomach, and dozing. He slipped into a dream, of her, Dolly Dee, she of the Imperial Valley muskmelons. They were in bed, she pressing close to him, warming his flesh with hers, then turning toward him, pushing both breasts against him. He could feel her nipples harden, studding the lean meat stretched across his rib cage. Oh boy . . . He was getting harder now, fit to shatter his spike like glass when suddenly an anvil or something heavier came down on the point of his head, dispelling the scene, the sensation, the anticipation, bringing blackness.

17

Doc sat outside the sheriff's office, tilting the bow-backed chair against the front of the building under the wanted dodger board. Presently Bundy came out, shaking his head, rolling his eyes, a somewhat resigned look on his face. He hurried up the street, crossing over to the bank. Doc could see Catterbury standing outside, talking to two men, both simlilarly dressed, the clean-fingernail-and-aftershave-lotion crowd, Raider would have labeled them.

He wondered about his partner, what he was up to, hard on Zemo's tail, no doubt, heading for Texas or hell or wherever. Good man, Raider, none better. Bellyache and grumble until he had your ears sore, rarely a smile, never a laugh, the moan, the groan, and the fault to be found found, but a rustic prince among his peers nevertheless. Doc twitched his nose slightly, testing it, and winced. And did he ever pack a wallop in his left hand!

This was a hairy one for the case journal file, muddled, growing more confusing by the hour. Thanks in no small measure to Catterbury's sudden indifference to the realities of the thing. As if that paper they'd signed afforded him any real protection. Fired by the fury that invariably seized his reason when money, his money, was involved, Allan Pinkerton would tear it up and pack the man's nostrils with the pieces, if it came to that. God willing it wouldn't.

Doc watched as Sheriff Bundy reached the trio, touched the brim of his Stetson, and was greeted magnanimously by Catterbury and introduced to the others.

"You know Senator Largemouth and Judge Allmen," mused Doc.

Catterbury excused himself, moving off to one side

with the lawman, out of earshot of the others. Gradually, as Bundy began filling his ear, Catterbury's hail-fellow-well-met demeanor deteriorated into a gloomy look, just as speedily displaced by one of downright distress. He listened politely, looking away back toward the office, through Doc to the cell within, and began shaking his head slowly. Bundy persisted, but Catterbury was not interested. Perceiving the folly of involving himself in Carl Haskell's dilemma, the banker wanted no part of it. Doc could well imagine what he was saying.

"Sorry, Lamarr, genuinely sorry, but I can't see any sense going over there to see him. I mean, what can I do? Oh, not that I don't feel badly for him. The man has my prayers, he does. Rest assured, I'm not judging him. No sir, a man's innocent till proven guilty, when and if. It's just, well, I've got to think of the bank, my reputation, my image . . ."

No, that he wouldn't get into, he'd leave it at "no thank you," but that last had to be the truth of it.

The sheriff shrugged, touched the brim of his hat again, and started back. Catterbury hurriedly rejoined his friends. In a moment they were laughing uproariously. Not over Carl Haskell, to be sure, not over anything that wasn't fit conversation for well-bred gentlemen.

Fine man, Horace Catterbury, salt of the earth, a true and loyal friend, the sort who'd be happy to go to bat for you when the chips were down.

Bundy came sauntering up, his hands jammed into his back pockets.

"You don't happen to have a stray wad o' cotton on you, do you?"

"Not that I know of."

"Shame." He shook his head and smiled wanly. "Only foolin'. I gotta feelin' it's gonna get fairly loud inside."

He went in, closing the door. In deference to passers-by, decided Doc, rising from the chair and turning his steps in the direction of the stable. On the way he passed Mulholland's Funeral Emporium, spying people inside picking out a casket, a grieving woman, her haggard face almost as white as her gloves, her eyes cried out, the man beside her, his arm around her shoulders, solemn-looking, his mind sent miles away by his own bereavement, the mortician appropriately grave and solicitous.

Better a blacksmith in the family than a printer, thought Doc fleetingly, passing the melancholy tableau. Reaching the stable he hailed the stableman, exchanged pleasantries with him, then went to Judith, feeding her a lump of sugar he had pilfered from the bowl at breakfast, talking to her tenderly, setting her ears twitching. Climbing into his wagon he set about entering the events of the past two days in the case journal, bringing it up to date. Not much to write, actually, only in so many words that the case had taken a turn for the complex.

He paused in his writing to stare out the back of the wagon, noticing the steeple of the Baptist Church set against the soft blue sky. It summoned up visions of the fire, the smoking debris, Bundy's deputy stumbling upon what was left of the ticket taker's head, holding it up, the crowd gasping.

Where in God's name had that plate gotten to? He would have loved to believe it had melted into a blob the size of his fist and was lying under a charred timber. But no sooner had his hopes raised the thought than his instincts dismissed it. There looked to be utterly no sense in wasting time poking about the ruins. Zemo had it, unless he'd failed to find out where Joe Gilbertson had hidden it before breaking the boy's neck.

There was, to be sure, one person other than the snakebiter who might know where it was. Probably did. Haskell. Best to let him sweat a little more before approaching him a second time. Let him fret over his friend Catterbury's decision to abandon his cause. At least until word came in from Raider.

Yes, Haskell would know where the plate was.

Hopefully.

He managed to fill nearly two pages in the journal; then, readying his Premo Senior camera, he walked over to what was left of Mrs. Struck's house and took pictures. He already had pictures of Catterbury, though none of Joe Gilbertson. The wake would undoubtedly be held that night. Which, when he thought about that, would be neither the time nor the place to take pictures, not after what he'd just seen through Mulholland's front window. Forget Joe Gilbertson, let him pass into the hereafter with his privacy intact.

Carl Haskell was another matter; he might turn out to be the pivotal character in the entire drama. Given a few more hours to sweat away his last trace of courage, replacing it with maximum fear, who knows what he'd have to say?

Doc stopped at the Western Union office shortly before sundown. Long brown shadows were already slipping between the buildings and carpeting the streets, the day's commerce was winding down, the saloons beginning to fill up, an emaciated and drooping dog, sagging under the weight of gravity from his eyes to the tip of his tail, wandered slowly across the street, slipping under the sidewalk out of sight, and lights, beacons against the beginning gloom, began to show. The clerk behind the counter was cordial but showed his palms and shook his head in response to Doc's: "Any message from Mr. O'Toole for Mr. Smith?"

Not a whisper. The carnival was evidently rolling on into evening, perhaps all night, without any extended layovers, giving Raider no chance to get off a message.

Raider came to, groaning with pain, sitting where he'd sat. Stripped down to socks and skivvies. Everything else vanished—clothes, hat, boots, guns, gear, *grulla*. He tried to get up, slipped back down, tried again, bracing his back against the tree, and this time made it. He gingerly examined the hen's egg-size lump on top of his head.

Good-bye, Zemo. He figured it to be only five miles back to Dexter. Less than thirty to Roswell beyond. Not the longest stroll in the world, but long enough socks only. The sun was starting down, etching the rim ridge of the San Andres Mountains with gold. A breeze sprang up, lifting the loveliness of the willows toward the water, picking up the road dust, stretching it tall here and there and setting it whirling briefly.

Thirty-five miles. Jesus! No hat, no duds, no boots, no iron, no money for anything once he got to Dexter. Not even his damned I.D. card to show the clerk in the Western Union office to induce him to get off a wire to Roswell on credit. Even better, a wire to Wagner in Chicago asking for money.

He started for Dexter, suddenly beset by a fierce thirst, but staunchly refusing to cast even a glance in the direction of the wet mud that was the river water. He walked on, covering the first hundred yards, twice stepping on stones buried in the dust, both times bringing his knee up and yelping in pain. Swearing . . .

He moved into the shin-high grass alongside the road, but that proved no improvement. Twilight came sneaking over the land, dispelling the heat, absorbing the glare. He had walked about a mile without seeing a living thing other than a kingbird following his progress a hundred feet overhead. He wondered briefly if it was the one he'd seen before. It looked to be, the way it floated on the breeze, wings fixed in place.

Behind him Raider heard a faint rumble and, turning, sighted a black mass surrounded by dust coming up the road. Closer and closer it drew, a four-mare heavy-duty wagon, bows in place, but no bonnet. Up on the seat was an old man wearing a disreputable-looking hat, gold tooth flashing, catching a ray of the dying sun. Beside him was a woman, all polka dots, her face shadowed under the brim of her poke bonnet. In her lap she held a fat brown hen. Closer and closer they came. Raider had sat down in the grass and was gingerly massaging his feet, picking a pebble out from between two toes. His soles weren't cut yet, but the bruises would shortly begin to show, and blisters, and blood mixed with dust . . . Already they were sore, achy.

Now the wagon was getting very close, trundling along heavily, the lead pair almost up to him, bringing with them a foul odor, a stink that no horse ever made, even watery loose. The man with the floppy-brimmed hat was dirty-looking, red bumps showing among the smudges on his face, a three-day beard sprouting all over, even up under his eyes, catching the dust, building it into a mask. The woman looked dusty, but her face was clean, her black-rimmed spectacles magnifying her soft brown eyes lighting up as her pan-plain face lit up with a smile.

"Whoa . . . WHOA!" called out the man, half rising from his seat, pulling hard on the reins, bringing the four to a rumbling, dusty stop. Everything stopped, save the stench. Forward it wafted, hitting Raider, sending his left hand halfway up to his nose to pinch it closed. But he caught himself, stopping his hand, deciding to endure the stink, suppressing a grimace.

Pigs. The stinkingest creatures on the face of the earth. Worse than skunk. Worse than javelina or pole-cat. Pig stink was not a now-and-then assault, not something to let go to discourage an enemy; it was constant, unabating. They wallowed in filth mixed with their own urine and excrement and seemed to dote on it in the way a beautiful woman dotes on perfume. Theirs was a stink capable of totally destroying all breathable air for twenty yards around them. Raider knew them— what farmer did not?—although he'd never raised them back home in Arkansas. Never would. Pigs, hogs, boars, swine, sows, shoats, gilts, all stinkers. A stench so rotten it stung the soft, moist membranes of the nostrils, started burning and tears in the eyes, turned over the stomach, made a man want to run for his life. Even one with feet in his condition.

"Howdy, friend," the farmer called down with a wave. Raider got to his feet, dusting off the seat of his pants, and returned the greeting, mustering up the best he could do for a friendly smile.

"Asa Crump's the name. This be my missus, Bertha."

"This be Dulcina," said the woman, with a downward glance at the hen in her lap.

"Hello, all three o' you."

"You look plumb cleaned out," said Asa Crump solicitously, cocking his head and adding sympathy to his smile. "Not even no boots?"

Raider explained, apologizing to Mrs. Crump for his appearance, adding that he had to get back to Roswell. His eyes were watering badly, so much so that husband

and wife began fading into twin blurs. God in heaven what a stink! How in red hell they could sit up there smiling down without so much as a tear on a cheek was beyond him. Positive proof that a human being could get used to anything. The creatures in the back grunted, stirring, moving about.

"This be your lucky day," said Crump.

"Not really."

"I mean to say we're headin' for Roswell. You're more'n welcome to ride along. Less'n, o' course, you prefers to walk." He winked and chuckled. Raider stared at him, then at his wife, then back to him, lowering his eyes to the seat. The two of them filled it so, the hen had to ride on her lap. Better there than back with the load, he reflected.

"The smell won't bother you none, will it?" inquired Mrs. Crump.

"If it do, my darlin', *you* can ride in back and Mr. . . ."

"O'Toole. John O'Toole."

"Mr. John O'Toole can ride up here. Ha ha ha."

Raider was tempted to let the pig wagon pass, then suddenly wanted to badly. Still, it was probably the first and last transportation he'd see this night and trudging into morning would likely chew away his feet halfway up his ankles. Could a man die of smelling a stink, he wondered? Could it keep him from getting enough oxygen into his lungs and stop his helpless heart?

"You comin' or ain'tcha? As it is we won't git to Roswell till long after dark."

"Sure, sure . . . sorry."

Raider hoisted one foot onto a wheel spoke and pulled himself up on top of the side, straddling it for a moment, looking down dejectedly at the contents of the wagon. There were twenty or more of them, packed in, hide to hide, head to hind end. Chester Whites, boars and sows mixed, fat as pigs, healthy, filthy, smelly.

No. Not a smell. Never such a delicate word to describe them. Stink, and whatever went beyond that. One glanced up with its pink eyes and flat snout, grunting at the sight of him, not overly pleased at his intrusion.

He set one foot down between two sows, then the other, inching forward, feeling their sides against his shins and calf muscles, making his way carefully toward the tailgate. Figuring to lift himself upward onto a corner and sit there, hanging on, knees drawn up, enjoying the scenery and the delicate fragrance rising from below.

Crump slapped rumps and the wagon lurched forward; Raider nearly fell, grabbing the side just in time. Getting to the corner, he turned about and hoisted himself up to a sitting position. The plank edges cut into his cheeks, jamming what little meat he wore there hard against the bones. But this he could put up with; at least it was getting him off his feet.

Holding on tightly, he examined first one sole, then the other. No cuts, no blisters, but bruises already starting to blacken. A man's feet really could take it, he mused, two little platforms of flesh and bone and muscle and leatherlike skin on the bottoms to support all six-foot-two inches of one hundred and eighty pounds. Bless feet.

But not pigs. He liked bacon, liked chops, but not that much. This just might cause him to swear off both for the next seven years. He stared down at them in disgust, revolted by their closeness. They sure were fat.

"How you doin' back there?" called Crump.

"Fine."

He was holding up a pint bottle half filled with a brackish-looking liquid. "How's about a little somethin' to chase the dust?"

"Thanks. I . . . I can't reach. Could you toss it back?"

Crump turned and grinned. "Comin' atcha." Recorking the bottle he tossed it playfully over his shoulder. It fell halfway to Raider, disappearing among the pigs, landing with a muffled clunk.

"Oops, sorry. Get that, will you, friend? 'Afore one o' 'em steps on it, smashes it, and cuts a foot. The smell o' blood'll get 'em all upset."

How could they possibly smell blood, wondered Raider? How could they smell anything?

He got down and made his way slowly through them

to where the bottle had fallen, feeling for it, bringing his face down to within inches of the ugliest pig he had ever seen, great, pulsing, pink, hairy nostrils sniffing at him, round stupid-looking eyes gaping. He groped for the bottle, unable to push the creatures away, so ponderously heavy were they. He prayed a sudden lurch, a shifting of their bulk wouldn't fracture his arm. He got lucky, his fingers closing on the bottle, bringing it up, raising it, drinking two healthy swigs, then tossing it back to Crump, thanking him.

It tasted like tar; looked like it, too. But it burned going down like no tar, even hot for pouring, could possibly burn. He gulped and gasped and choked, grabbing his throat, one hand atop the other to hold it in place against his neck, stiffening, struggling to resist the impact while the liquor descended his gullet, dropping into his gut like a small anvil.

"God Almighty!"

"Powerful stuff, eh? I makes it myself. Corn squeezin's an' barley water mostly. With a li'l Sears and Roebuck Tobasco Pepper Sauce throwed in to give it a nip. Like it?"

"Yeah . . ."

Raider sucked in the foul air, starting back to the corner, feeling his stomach rumble ominously. With any luck at all he would throw it up.

18

It was close to midnight when the Crumps' wagon pulled into Roswell. The streets were all but deserted and few lights pierced the blackness, but those yellowing the interiors of the town's two saloons, the noise and piano tinkling coming from within, served notice to the darkness that Roswell was no ghost town. Asa Crump pulled up in front of the hotel to let his passenger off. Raider climbed down wearily, thanking husband and wife, and watched the wagon roll off down the street. Since passing through Dexter he had managed to fall down into the pigs three times, and when the right front wheel dipped six inches down into a hole in the road, heaving the left rear corner skyward, he had narrowly missed being tossed out into a creosote bush.

He made his way slowly up the steps and through the doors. Four men lounged in the lobby, two sleeping in their chairs, one snoring wetly, the third and fourth in spirited conversation, one waving a cigar, the other pointing something out to him in a wrinkled and torn copy of the *Santa Fe Intelligencer*. Both paused in their discussion to look toward him. The one without the cigar screwed up his fat nose in distaste, leaning into a cloud of smoke released by the other, who scowled and, rising from his chair, backed away from Raider, swallowing. One of the sleepers made a face. The desk clerk, dozing on one elbow, came to life, recognized Raider, and smelled him.

"Good God! Mr. O'Toole, you look . . . What happened? My God!" He sniffed and, hand to mouth, held down a gag as Raider closed in on him.

"You got a plunge bath?"

"Yes, sir, brand-new copper tub."

"Bring it, soap, a brush, towels, the works up to my room. No, up to Mr. Smith's. Make it fast, will you?"

"Mr. Smith went up early; he . . ." A pause to stifle a gag. "He's probably asleep."

"Just bring everything up there, please. Quick as you can. Don't forget a couple buckets o' hot water."

"Yes, sir."

Raider climbed the stairs, found Doc's room, and knocked loudly.

"Yes?"

"It's me."

Raider could hear him come running barefoot to the door. He jerked it wide. He was in his underwear.

"Ra—" He stopped, covered his nose and mouth, and, ducking his head, turned away. "Good God Almighty!"

Raider bulled past him into the room. "Lay off, Doc, the clerk's bringin' up a bathtub."

"Get out, please. Go to your own room to take your bath. Take three or four while you're at it. Then come back."

Having walked to the bed, Raider returned to the door, closing it. "We got no time for that."

"Rade, you have no idea, you smell awful! Vicious. I'm getting tears in my eyes. What are you doing here? Where's the carnival? Why aren't you following . . ."

Raider told him what had happened, running on, refusing to permit him to cut in with questions. The clerk appeared at the door with a copper tub. And with everything Raider needed to bathe in the bottom of it. He set it down as an elderly man in shirtsleeves and vest came up behind him carrying two large wooden buckets of hot water. Smelling the smell he set the buckets down and beat a hurried retreat. As did the clerk. Raider lugged in the tub, poured in one of the buckets, and cooled it with the washstand pitcher water. Then, peeling off his clothes, he climbed in, settling slowly.

"Hand me the soap, will you?" Doc came out of his corner and tossed it to him.

"You don't need soap, you need a bucket of Milk Oil

Sheep Dip, something strong enough for scabs and mange!"

"Lay off, will you!"

Doc started toward his clothes on their hangers inside the open armoire door. "I'm going out."

"Where?"

"Into the hall."

"I told you lay off. Stay here, we got to talk."

Resignedly, Doc sat down on the edge of the bed as far removed from the tub as possible.

"Did you talk to that drummer after I left?" asked Raider.

"I did. He knows more than he's telling."

"About what?"

"For one thing, how well he knew Joe Gilbertson. And he tried very hard to make me believe he only knew Zemo by reputation. One thing I'm convinced of, he didn't kill the boy. He's just not the type."

"What is the type?" Raider had lathered his upper body completely and went at it with the brush, scrubbing his flesh raw.

"The man is a bank and office equipment salesman; he doesn't carry a gun, not even a derringer. If he did kill the boy, he wouldn't have broken his neck. It's much too crude. He's not vicious. Besides, I don't think he'd have the strength."

"It doesn't take that much strength."

"He's a gentleman, clean fingernails, barbershop shave, expensive taste in attire. He wears a diamond stickpin in a silk brocade puff scarf."

"What?" Raider stopped soaping the brush, freezing, staring. "Diamond stickpin? Doc, that's him!"

"Who?"

"I told you before. He's the one followed the boy to Mrs. Struck's, went inside after him, come out with him. They're old friends, they got to be. One look shows that. I told you when I got back from there. Diamond stickpin."

"Maybe you did."

"No maybes about it. You never listen to me, Doc. You make believe you do, but you don't really. You just nod like you are, but all the time your mind's on something else. You bet your life he knew the boy. A lot better than he's makin' out."

"When I mentioned putting my finger on the real murderer he got a look in his eyes as if he'd seen a ghost."

"He knew the printer real good he's got to know Zemo just as good."

"He does, he spots his banks for him. I wonder if he could have put Gilbertson up to holding out for more money from Zemo? If he did, his conscience must be finding it fairly rugged going along about now. It seems to me when the two of them went upstairs to see the ticket taker . . ."

"Franklin."

"It was then and there Gilbertson announced he was holding back the plate. That he wanted more money for it. Holding the aces as he was, that would make sense, Rade. And breaking the news to Franklin so *he* could break it to Zemo wasn't a bad idea, either."

"It turned out a rotten idea. They say a busted neck hurts worse than a bullet in the belly."

Doc stood up. Fishing out an Old Virginia he lit it, tugging the smoke into his throat, letting it slowly out of his nostrils, sniffing it a second time before it dissipated.

"Will you cut that out?"

"Better lather up your hair again; what did you do, crawl around the bed of the wagon with them?"

"Shut up. Stir your stumps, why don't you? Go down and get me some tomatoes."

"What for?"

"You won't find no fresh ones this early in the year, but tinned are better. I got to scrub me down with 'em, then take another bath. I'll be okay."

"Are you kidding me?"

"Tomatoes take away stink, Doc. You being a big-city boy you wouldn't know, but they do. It's the acid. There ain't a farm boy from here to Florida don't know you scrub down with tomatoes when a skunk sprays you."

"It's a trifle late to go shopping."

Raider scowled. "Yeah . . . Well, first thing bright and early. And while you're at it, you can think about getting me some gear, a .44, a horse, boots . . . size twelve. Middletons, if you can find any. A Tower Stetson size—"

"Seven and a half, I know." Doc sighed.

Raider went back to work on his hair, soaping it thoroughly, scrubbing it, rinsing it with water from the second bucket.

"Doc, can you get me something to eat; I haven't had a thing since breakfast."

"It's a trifle late for that, too."

"How about a drink?"

"Fresh out."

"Jesus Christ, you're a big goddamn help to come home to!"

Doc puffed and ruminated. "You say the carnival was heading for Lovington?"

"Lovington, Hobbs."

"Haskell will know."

"You going back to talk to him?"

"Not right away. Better I let him stew in his juices a little longer. It could loosen his tongue."

"Not too much longer. They're slow-moving maybe, but you remember the story o' the jackrabbit and the turtle."

"Hare and tortoise. Boy, you've completely ruined your disguise. I'm going to have to start all over practically from scratch."

"To hell with it, I'll leave it off till we get where we're goin'. Till I'm sure I'll need it."

They talked until Raider was finished. After which he washed his socks and skivvies out in the rinse water, Doc taking pains to add the half bottle of eau de cologne he had left, pouring it into the tub. Wringing out his things and balling them against his crotch, Raider sneaked a look up and down the hallway, then ran like a thief to his own room.

*   *   *

They were at breakfast at Mulvey's Café, sitting at a window table, Doc watching Raider shovel eggs down him like a man who hadn't eaten in three weeks, when Sheriff Bundy came in, took a chair from another table, and sat down with his arms over the back. The place was small, but fairly crowded, the food good, the coffee superior. Bundy ordered a cup, then turned his attention to Raider.

"You look different."

"Is that a fact . . ."

"Mr. Weatherbee, our friend Carl is asking to see you."

Doc stirred his coffee, added sugar, stirred some more, and began counting red squares in the tablecloth.

"He threw me out, remember?"

"He's changed his mind. Do you want to talk with him or not?"

"After breakfast."

They finished shortly, Raider belching loudly to Doc's embarrassment and the sheriff's amusement. Raider stood up, stretching, yawning, starting another belch, but muffling this one with his hand.

"Give me some money, I got to go shopping."

Doc counted sixty dollars into his hand. Raider pinched an additional ten out of his billfold and walked off, leaving him to pay the bill. Minutes later Doc was sitting in Carl Haskell's cell. Haskell had put in a far rougher night than had Raider, he decided at first glance. The salesman's eyes were red-rimmed from lack of sleep, stubble was sprouting on his hitherto immaculately smooth face, and the nerves that kept his hands and lower lip trembling without letup were hard at work.

A deeply troubled man, Carl Haskell, left to drown by his friend Catterbury and rapidly losing the strength he needed to save himself. What he really wanted was a rope thrown to him. Whether his visitor would oblige him depended upon what he had to say. Haskell was well aware of this; the moment Doc sat down opposite him, the Pinkerton could see it in his bloodshot eyes.

"You're a Pinkerton, aren't you?" mumured Haskell.

"Did the sheriff tell you that?"

"He doesn't have to, I spotted you and your side-kick the first day you hit town. When you walked into the bank to see Horace, the son of a bitch. You said you could help me. Did you mean it?"

"I think I can; whether I do or not is strictly up to you."

"I know, I know." Haskell got to his feet and began pacing, stopping short as Doc brought out his cheroots. The salesman patted his pockets. "I'm fresh out of cigarettes." Doc offered him an Old Virginia and lit up both. Haskell drew on his savagely, as if it were filled with courage and he was determined to get all he could out of it.

"What do you want to know?"

"What do you think I want to know? The truth, unvarnished. No nonsense about your 'casual acquaintanceship' with the boy, or 'never meeting Zemo, hearing of him, of course.' I'll tell you what you do; you don't tell me, I'll ask you questions, you answer them, okay?" Haskell nodded and sat down. "You are in this business up to your neck, aren't you? Your job is to feed Zemo information as to which banks are planning to go to print. Which means they follow a travel route set up by you."

"Yes." His voice seemed to lose all its timbre, taking on the hollow tone of capitulation.

"They're now heading for either Lovington or Hobbs. Which?"

"Hobbs. But not to overprint."

"Is that what you call it?"

"Well . . ."

"You've even developed your own vocabulary. So why else stop in Hobbs?"

"When Franklin blew up the rooming house all the electrotypographical equipment and materials went up with it. It has to be replaced."

"I see. And what about replacing Franklin?"

"Oh, he didn't do the work alone; there are two or three others."

"So Zemo has the plate with Catterbury's impressions

on it and is holding off until he's back in business."
Haskell nodded. Doc sighed inside. They wouldn't have
to worry about a glut of Catterbury's banknotes after
all. Not for a while. But eventually . . . "What's the
next bank?"

"Heinz'll kill me if I tell you."

"Zemo. He may kill you if you tell me, but you'll
hang if you don't."

Haskell swallowed and blanched. He mumbled two
syllables.

"What?"

"BARSTOW!"

"Arizona?"

"Texas."

"Never heard of it." Doc cocked his head and narrowed his eyes suspiciously.

"It's down in Ward County. Across the river from
Pecos."

"And the bank?"

"The Barstow Bank."

"You'd better be telling the truth."

"As God is my witness I am."

"How far is Barstow?"

"I'd say about one hundred and fifty miles."

"When do they plan to reach there?"

"Soon."

"Stopping in Hobbs, laying over there until they replace what was lost in the explosion, they'll have to
travel night and day to get down to Barstow in, say,
three days."

"They'll get there fast. They won't stop for anything
once they leave Hobbs."

"Mmmmm." Doc stood up, facing the bars, gripping
them, his back to the salesman. "Let's get back to the
murder. Gilbertson was holding out for more money for
his lead plate."

"How did you know that?"

"Why else would Zemo kill him? Though why he'd
found that necessary . . . I suppose the boy wouldn't
tell him, Zemo lost his temper and broke his neck. Then

turned the place upside-down looking for the plate, found it, and ran out."

"Yes, yes . . ."

Doc turned and fixed him with a curious look. "Oh? Were you there? Did you see?"

"NO! I told you before, I walked in off the street when I saw Joe . . ."

"Yes, I remember now." He paused, turning back to the bars. "Off the record, Carl, was it your idea that he, Gilbertson, should hold out for more money?"

"GOD IN HEAVEN, NO!"

"All right, all right, calm down."

"You must be crazy. Matter of fact, I moved heaven and earth trying to talk him out of it. I know Heinz, he's got a temper you wouldn't believe. Holding out on him is playing with dynamite."

"Gilbertson knew that, but he still wouldn't listen, eh?"

"No. Stubborn as a mule."

Again Doc turned to face him. "What you've told me is exactly what happened."

"Exactly."

"Interesting. There's only one thing that bothers me. Of all the people in Roswell, men, women, and children, it was you who just happened to be the first one passing by and saw Gilbertson draped over his press dead."

"I . . . well . . ."

"What?"

"All right, so I was following Heinz."

"Oh? You said before you couldn't sleep, you were up and out getting a breath of fresh air."

"Not exactly."

"Then what exactly?"

"If you must know I was with Heinz all night. We were drinking. He got drunker than I did. He isn't much of a drinker. He got to talking about Joe, complaining. I tried to tell him he'd produce the plate, that he was just stalling, that there was nothing to worry about. He wouldn't listen; he got madder and madder. It was mostly the liquor."

"It was mostly the animal in him."

"Anyway, he stalked out. I went after him; I tried to reason with him, but he wouldn't listen. I thought he was heading back to the carnival grounds, but across the street we could see a light on in the front room in Overstone's shop. The curtains were drawn, but there was a space between."

"Oh, the curtains were drawn? I thought you said when you were inside you saw people out on the sidewalk looking in at you. What did you do, open the curtains to show the world what had happened?"

"I . . . I lied about that."

"Did you? Tsk tsk tsk. All right, see if you can resist the temptation to lie about this. What was Gilbertson doing in the shop at such an ungodly hour?"

"Oh, Lord, he'd spend fifteen, twenty hours a day there. That press was like a woman to him; honestly, it was his whole life. I've never known anybody so head over heels for their job like he was for that press, for printing."

"Zemo . . . Heinz went in after him."

Haskell nodded. Doc had sat back down on the cot opposite him. "I tried to stop him."

"Did you really?"

The salesman hesitated, avoiding Doc's eyes, studying the floor littered with cigarette butts.

"Well . . ."

"Not really."

"He would have killed me as well. He was furious!"

"Why didn't you run and get help?"

"To stop Heinz, me? Are you crazy? Sign my own death warrant?"

Doc got up. "I guess we've covered everything."

"You're not leaving . . ."

"I'll ask Sheriff Bundy for a pencil and paper for you. I want you to write down Zemo's schedule."

"What schedule, there's only one other town after Barstow, Sauer City."

"Ah, the big time."

"You'll talk to Bundy. And to the judge. You

promised, you gave me your word . . ." Haskell sprang to his feet and grabbed him by the front of the shirt.

"What judge? You're moving a little fast, Carl. You're in Roswell, not St. Louis. Relax. I said I'd help, I will. *If* you're telling the truth."

"I am, I swear I am!"

"So get a grip on yourself. Nobody's going to hang you for what Zemo did. The best they'll be able to get you for will be complicity."

"What complicity? I had absolutely nothing to do with it! I was outside, I didn't even see. I couldn't . . ." He sank back down, covering his face with both hands, and began sobbing.

"Oh, God, oh, God, oh, God, oh, God."

"Complicity in the scheme, not the murder. Take it easy, take it easy . . ."

Haskell didn't hear him. Doc laid a comforting hand on the man's shoulder, then called for the sheriff. Bundy came in and let him out.

19

Human nature being what it is, it is not surprising to find certain people strongly attracted to certain others. Or just as strongly repelled by certain others. In some cases so strongly as to be revolted by the mere mention of their name.

While Doc was sitting in Carl Haskell's cell listening to the salesman detail the events leading up to Joe Gilbertson's murder, at the other end of town the nine-forty-five train from Elkins came puffing into the station. It deposited six men on the platform and pulled out again. The six carried valises and, approaching the stationmaster, were directed to the Roswell House Hotel. When Doc walked into the lobby, optimistically hoping to find Raider already returned from shopping, he found instead the six arrivals rising from their chairs and converging on him. To his chagrin, all recognized him in spite of his disguise.

He knew every one. They were the Fanchette brothers, Leon and Paul; Walter Tyndall from Sioux City; Cy Schwartz and Dominic DePaolo out of the New York office, reassigned to Denver; and Major Henderson Turnbull, an impressive-looking man in his forties crowned with long blond hair reminiscent of George Custer's and displaying the profile of a Greek god. William Pinkerton's shock troops had arrived.

Sight of the first five men warmed Doc's heart; sight of Major Turnbull prompted a somewhat different reaction. Even in mufti, with the War Between the States fifteen years behind him and his uniform long since consigned to mothballs, he persisted in playing the major, in his posture, his patronizing expression, the consciously bridled bark of his voice, everything out from under his shining gold mustache sounding like an order. In command of the Second Battalion, 4th Michigan Volunteers, the major had distinguished himself at the fall of Vicksburg. He had emerged a hero from the battle of Chattanooga and had won a presidential citation for his unit at the bloody stalemate at Petersburg shortly before Lee's surrender. No man in his normal mind could deny that the major was a superb soldier. As a civilian, however, he had his flaws of character. Chief among these was his steadfast conviction that he had none, that he was the perfect man. He considered himself brilliant, a decision-maker without peer. One of his other more obnoxious traits was his propensity for taking charge, whether he had been put in charge or not. In addition, he affected the burdensome mantle of prejudice; he looked down his handsomely sculptured nose at everyone whose education, breeding, background, and war record failed to measure up to his own. He husbanded a particular dislike for the masses, the poverty-ridden, the deprived, the downtrodden, regardless of race, creed, or color.

Raider hated Major Henderson Turnbull. Casual reference to the man was enough to set his eyes blazing, ignite his temper, and disrupt entirely any business at hand. In the four years Doc's partner had been with the agency, occasion had demanded that he work with the major only twice. Both collaborations had culminated in disaster. Two years earlier they had actually come to blows in the midst of a bloody shootout against the Leonard gang outside of Fargo. Ten months later, finding themselves thrown together by Robert Pinkerton's carelessness, assigned with Doc and others to ferret out a gang of holdup men preying on the Oregon Short Line, Raider and the major got into a fight which carried them the entire length of a six-car train. Raider denied this, claiming that the train only had four cars and that he and "Turnbullshit," as he had taken to calling the major, had only fisted their way through two of them.

Be that as it was, the sight of Turnbull coming forward with his supercilious smile plastered on his tanned face heeled Doc's heart a good two inches downward in his chest.

The group crowded around. Doc exchanged handshakes and then led them up the stairs to his room.

"You all look a little travel-weary. I know you've come a long way in a short time," he said, flinging his hat on the bed. "But before you relax, I'd better fill you in."

"Where's your friend, the plowboy?" asked Turnbull. The Fanchette brothers' eyes met. Both knew how the major and Raider felt about each other. Everybody in the agency knew.

"Rade's out getting a fresh horse," said Doc quietly. Of all the people for William Pinkerton to send down. Why not Sitting Bull? Why not Butch Cassidy and Longbaugh?

He covered the important points regarding the case, explaining that the suspects were presently on their way to Barstow, Texas, and were expected to reach there within three days.

"That's no problem," said Turnbull. "We'll just climb back on the train and run on down to Pecos. That's the Eastern railhead. We can switch over to the Texas and Pacific there, and it's only what, ten miles to Barstow? I suggest . . ."

"Why don't we talk about that later?" asked Doc.

"He's right, Major," piped Tyndall, a stocky little badger of a man, and the best shot with a rifle Doc had ever seen. The only man Raider was second best to. The discussion continued for another half hour whereupon the meeting broke up with Doc's recommendation that they get back together at the railroad station in one hour.

"We can take the noon train south. If we get to Barstow a day or two ahead of them, so much the better." Doc nodded, agreeing with himself.

"That goes without saying," interposed Turnbull. "We'll set things up with the bank president, sit by and wait for them to walk into the trap. I have a few ideas on strategy."

"Maybe we ought to wait until Raider comes back," said Doc, standing and restoring his hat to his head.

Cy Schwartz, the glib, bull-necked New Yorker, laughed. "That should be interesting. Can I watch?"

The others laughed. Turnbull and Doc did not. Schwartz was right, however, Doc conceded to himself. The hostility between Raider and the major was that bad, so bad that the two locking horns and putting on a show for whoever else happened to be present was too good a possibility to let pass without comment.

As if they didn't have enough troubles already!

While the newcomers cleaned up and then went out to eat, Doc went looking for Raider. He found him at the stable, about to buy a horse, haggling with the stableman over a nondescript mare with one eye that looked suspiciously cloudy. The price, however, was more than reasonable.

"Twelve bucks," said the man. "Take her or leave her."

"Ten and I'll take her. Look at that off eye, will you? She's almost blind."

"Bullfeathers! She can see outta it better'n you can outta either one o' your'n. Look." He clapped his hands lightly off to one side. The horse turned to look, but too far, gaping well past him out of her cloudy eye.

"What'd I tell you!" rasped Raider.

"Rade, hold off," said Doc, coming up to him.

"Eight dollars," said Raider.

"I mean it. We won't be needing horses until we get there. We'll be taking the train."

"Hey, that's a good idea." He waved to the man and off they walked, the stableman clapping his hands again alongside the mare's head, testing the eye a second time, getting the same result, swearing.

"Who thought it up?"

"A good friend of yours."

"Bundy?"

"Rade, how do you feel?"

"Good. Hey, look at my new boots, new Stets, .45. I couldn't get a decent secondhand Peacemaker. Goddamn highway robber wanted thirty bucks."

"Our reinforcements came in, six of them."

"Not bad. Who?"

They had emerged from the alley onto a sidewalk and were passing Overstone's Print Shop, heading toward the hotel.

"The Fanchette brothers, Walt Tyndall, Cy Schwartz, Dom DePaolo."

"Great! Good men." Raider stopped and wrinkled his forehead. "But you said six."

"Oh yes, I forgot old . . ."

"Who?"

"Ah . . . Henderson."

The storm came up in Raider's face so suddenly, his eyes firing, his cheeks paling that Doc thought for a moment that he had been seized by a stroke.

"No!"

Doc nodded, suddenly overcome by a strange weariness.

"Turnbullshit."

"I know you two aren't overly fond of one another. That you don't exactly see eye to eye on some things . . ."

"I'll be a son of a bitch! I always knew Willy Pinkerton was an asshole, but I never knew till now how big a one."

"So he throws Henderson in our laps. So what? Look at it this way, why don't you take advantage of it, wipe the slate clean, start fresh? You could both pretend you'd never even met before, that you've never heard of each other. That way you can get off on the right foot, be nice to each other, understanding, patient, tolerant, bend a little . . ."

"Turnbullshit."

"Rade, for God's sake don't call him that!"

"I will if I want. First time the son of a bitch calls

me plowboy he'll get Turnbullshit thrown back at his teeth. If he wants to make somethin' of it I'm more'n game. I busted him up before, I can bust him up again!"

"You will not!" Doc stopped short and grabbed a handful of his sleeve and holding him fast. Raider tried to pull free but could not. "Listen to me, we've got our work cut out for us winding up Zemo and his crowd. We've already come close and missed out. Barstow could be our last chance. I'm not about to let you wreck everything by forgetting business and resuming your private war with him. Nor will he with you. If you can't put up with one another's company like civilized human beings, then avoid him. If you can't be in the same room with him, in the same railroad car, then keep your distance. Because if you fuck this case up tangling with him, if Zemo manages to wriggle off the hook, you and I are done for! I'll never accept another assignment with you as long as I live."

It was not his partner's ultimatum that suddenly cooled Raider's temper and gave him pause, it was his use of the word "fuck." Doc almost never resorted to such language, and when he did so, it was a signal to Raider that he was deadly serious, that any disagreement with him was totally unacceptable.

"Okay, okay, okay, just make sure you give him the same goddamn speech. And no 'plowboy,' you understand?"

"Then no 'Turnbullshit.' "

"I never call him that unless he starts up with me. That's the gospel truth, Doc. I never start nothin'; he does it all, I just go back at him."

"With your fists."

"I don't like the son of a bitch lookin' down his nose at me. I don't know what the hell he's doin' workin' as an operative anyways, with his silver spoon, his high-falutin' airs and all. Why don't he go home to Michigan and run for the damned legislature? That's where his sort belongs, in with all them stiff-necked assholes, all them Catterbury types."

"Maybe he likes the life; that's his business. You've

got to admit, he's got a good track record. He's made of the right stuff for the job; he doesn't back off, he's cool under fire, he's intelligent . . ."

"He's an idiot tin soldier, that's all he is."

"This is the last time I'll say it: don't start up with him. Don't do it. We've got our hands full as it is, we don't need you two carrying on like a couple of fishwives."

Raider and Major Henderson Turnbull came face to face, but to Doc's relief did not "start up," at least not right away. All eight Pinkertons departed Roswell on the noon train, leaving Carl Haskell languishing in his cell, buoyed by Doc's assurance that he would not be tried and hanged, Horace F. Catterbury happily circulating his new banknotes, and Judith and the apothecary wagon at the stable, along with the fog-eyed mare Raider had almost bought.

The train, originating in Clovis, was crowded with passengers, seven cars all but filled, mostly businessmen heading for Dexter, Hagerman, Artesia, Lakewood, and Eddy. They would cross the border just beyond Red Bluff. From there to Barstow was a run of about sixty miles through the southern reaches of the Staked Plains Raider had taken such pains to avoid crossing in daylight. To his ultimate regret.

He and Doc and the others had assembled in the baggage car, the clerk obligingly leaving them in privacy. Raider was down and quietly seething. Turnbull's arrival had given an otherwise promising day a wrench toward unpromising. Boarding the train and, unable to produce his railroad pass, being confronted by the conductor in full view of a mob of other passengers and practically accused of trying to sneak on board had done little to improve his disposition.

He and the major had yet to have words, but to Doc the situation was a little like searching about in a room full of dynamite with a lit match; at any time the blow-up could come. Coming face to face, each man had nodded and mumbled greeting. Since then they had ignored one another. The Pecos-bound train was now south of Loving, roughly paralleling the river, heading for Red Bluff. It was time for a council of war, suggestions from everybody, the major not excepted.

The match to light Raider's fuse.

They sat about on crates and barrels checking weapons, smoking, and otherwise relaxing while Doc described for the second time the situation they would be coming up against. Raider let him run on without interrupting, his own interest in the case diminishing rapidly.

Domenic DePaolo, a black stogie stuffed into the corner of his mouth, pulled it free and waved it for attention.

"From what you say, Doc, we could be down there and set up a good forty-eight hours before they even show."

"Exactly."

"Before the bank goes to press."

"That I can't say for certain. We have no idea what their schedule is. All the same, if they run true to the others' form they won't begin printing until after the carnival gets to town. That's the way it worked in Albuquerque and in Roswell. Haskell does his job well."

"He gets the exact date and feeds it to Zemo," added Raider. "That way the carnival doesn't have to waste time hangin' around a place waitin'."

The major gesticulated, interrupting him, and stood up. "Why," he asked, "don't we alert the Barstow bank, advise them to postpone their printing indefinitely? The carnival shows up, we grab them and seize that lead plate. It seems to me that's all the evidence we'll need. You've already got the salesman. He'll testify against this Zemo on the murder of the boy."

"We don't know if he will," said Raider evenly.

"Of course he will! He may not want to, may be scared stiff of Zemo, but if he refuses to tell what he knows he'll be the one to be hanged. Isn't that so, Weatherbee?"

"I suppose." Doc glanced at Raider scowling blackly at his nemesis.

"Suppose? As I see it, we've got this snakebiter of yours two ways. Three. We mustn't forget that fracas up in Albuquerque. The printer up there could be made to testify, he's certainly involved. No, gentlemen, we'd be extremely shortsighted to permit the Barstow bank to go ahead and print. Why run the risk? Better we grab . . ."

"No," said Raider flatly. "No sense goin' off half-cocked. That wouldn't work for sour apples. Number one, yes, we could grab them first thing outta the chute and maybe come up with the plate. But if we don't, if he's ditched it someplace or destroyed it, we'll be outta luck."

"Nonsense!" snapped Turnbull. "On second thought, forget the plate. Forget the counterfeiting. Concentrate on the murder of the printer in Roswell. This Zemo killed him, there's a witness sitting back there who can send him to the gallows for it. I say that's the angle we should work on, not the flimflam."

Leon and Paul Fanchette nodded and the others joined in agreement. Again Doc glanced at Raider. Turnbull was right, as he generally was. For all his flaws the man was bright, perceptive. Raider may not have wanted to admit that, but he'd be hard put to convince anybody else present that this wasn't so. Or that the major was wrong in his assessment of the situation.

"Shit . . ." he muttered.

"I beg your pardon?" Turnbull's handsome face was wreathed in triumph.

Raider got up, turning his back on him.

"Handle the damned thing any way you please. It makes no never mind to me. I'm cashing in after this one anyhow."

Domenic DePaolo stared in disbelief. "Quitting?"

"Retirin'."

"Going back to the farm?" asked the major, a hint of snideness in his tone.

"Maybe, maybe I'll join the fuckin' army."

Turnbull laughed. "Which one, the secessionists?"

"What's it to you?"

"Rade," said Doc. "Why don't we go back to the car? All of us. Rade, you and I can sit . . ."

"I asked what's it to you!"

Raider took a step toward the major, who smirked at him, then turned to Walter Tyndall. Doc grabbed his partner's sleeve.

"Easy, easy . . ."

Leon Fanchette brought out his Essbach's French Harp harmonica, tapped it against his palm to clear the holes, and launched into a tune. His brother Paul sang the words:

> *"Jay Gould's daughter said, before she died,*
> *'Papa, fix the beds so the bums can't ride.*
> *If ride they must, they got to ride the rod.*
> *Let 'em put their trust in the hands of God.*
> *In the hands of God.*
> *In the hands of God.*
> *Let 'em put their trust in the hands of God.'*
>
> *Jay Gould's daughter said, before she died,*
> *'There's two more drinks I'd like to try.'*
> *Jay Gould said, 'Daughter, what can they be?'*
> *'They's a glass o' water and a cup o' tea.*
> *A cup o' tea.*
> *A cup . . .' "*

The train had been jouncing along at a steady clip. Moments before Raider and the major's exchange it had begun to slow, the engine starting up a long grade. The only view of the outside was through small barred windows, two on either side. The Guadalupes rising to the west were already beginning to surrender the landscape to the Staked Plains. The grade would be the last the train would have to climb before Pecos.

The engine labored to gain the summit. Raider stood glaring at Turnbull, who determinedly ignored him. Doc was slowly releasing his hold on his partner as the

Fanchette brothers' impromptu recital effectively dissolved the tension. Suddenly a deafening explosion was heard, shaking the Pinkertons like dice in a bird cage. The car shuddered to rest, miraculously still on the rails.

And started back down, gathering speed quickly. In seconds hurtling down . . .

20

Everyone grabbed hold and hung on. A chorus of cursing filled the air above the roar of the swiftly moving car.

"WE'RE GONNA JUMP THE RAILS!" shouted Raider. "STAY CLEAR O' THE WALLS, WHEN WE GO OVER, THEY'LL CAVE IN LIKE GLASS."

There was little to hang on to but the walls, Turnbull was quick to remind him. Faster and faster they plunged toward the flat, threatening to jump the rails any second. But gradually the floor at the far end came easing upward, level ground was gained, and at least two full miles were spun away by the wheels before the car began to slow to safe speed.

Faces were as white as knuckles grabbing bars, the safe, the forward door latch, as the Pinkertons stared at one another, each man suffering through his own private agony, relief and gratitude to God slowly creeping into their minds. Letting go of the door latch, Walter Tyndall climbed onto a crate and was preparing to press his face to a barred window when the car struck something, the train end bouncing clear, the truck coming down, derailing, flinging Tyndall back down, crashing against the Fanchettes, all three settling in a heap.

Turnbull rushed past the pile, moving to take Tyndall's place at the window.

"Stop!" snapped Raider. "Don't do that. Everybody stay clear o' those windows."

"I really don't see . . . ." began the major.

"Damn it, somebody's stopped us, derailed us, somebody out there who wants inside here. We start showin' faces at the windows they'll see we're a bunch."

"The man's right," said Doc. "As far as they know there's only the clerk, two at the most in . . ."

"Okay, open up in there!" bellowed a voice outside. "MAKE IT SNAPPY!"

Turnbull had drawn his gun, prompting the others to the same action.

"Open it up, Weatherbee," he said authoritatively. "We'll blow them back into the river."

"Hold it," said Raider. "How about we do this right?"

"OPEN UP OR WE'LL BUST DOWN THE DOOR AND BLOW YOUR HEAD OFF! OPEN UP, GET YOUR HANDS HIGH, AND YOU WON'T GET HURT NONE! SWEAR TO GOD. WE DON'T GOT A MIND TO HURT NOBODY; WE JUST WANT THE SAFE AND THE POUCHES!"

Raider gestured. "Doc, take off your coat and vest; make yourself look like a clerk, you know?"

"Right." Flinging his hat to one side, Doc began divesting himself of his outer clothing. "Hey, out there, don't shoot, I'm opening up. I'll have my hands high. DON'T SHOOT!"

"Make it quick."

Doc rolled up his sleeves and, bracing his feet, prepared to slide open the door.

"Don't raise nothin'," growled Raider, "just get clear fast."

Raider and the others, four on one side, three on the other, faded back, guns cocked and ready. The door slid wide, revealing ten masked men astride horses, sixguns and Winchesters leveled at the opening. Doc, meanwhile, had gone the way of the door, pushing along behind it, reaching the opposite side and shouldering against it, satisfied to listen to what was going on rather than chance a look. His fellow Pinkertons, likewise unseen by the holdup men, opened up, a withering crossfire catching the enemy completely by surprise, dropping all but three, who somehow managed to spur their mounts out of the line of fire. The noise was deafening, smoke mantling the battleground, the holdup men barely able to get off a shot or two. Raider had never been in such a one-sided shootout. It was, he mused, like picking cans off a rail fence. Striding into view, he and the others held their fire on Turnbull's order, their weapons leveled at the attackers.

"HEEL THOSE HORSES AND YOU'RE DEAD!" Raider shouted to the three still in their saddles. All about on the ground lay the dead and dying, and one man hit in both arms and a hip but able to struggle to his feet and call out.

"We surrender! We surrender!"

Raider almost laughed.

"Dismount!" ordered Turnbull.

Raider turned on him with a sour look. "You mind my asking who in hell died and left you in charge?"

"I might put the same question to you."

"Shut up, you two!" Doc burst out irritably. Dropping to the ground, he set about collecting weapons and tossing them onto the floor of the car, the three mounted men following his example without prompting, then getting down. The other Pinkertons got down out of the car. Not one had been hit. Three of the ten attackers were dead, a fourth died just as Doc crouched to examine him, the rattle of death issuing from the man's throat, his body twitching as if his spine had been turned inside him, his eyes rolling the whites into view.

"Charlie, Charlie, Charlie . . ." sobbed one of the survivors, hands high, face ashen, stumbling up to where he lay. "He's my kid brother," he said to Doc.

"You look after him real good, don'tcha?" growled Raider.

The survivors were rounded up and trussed up with their own lariats. Raider glanced up the line. The train had stopped at the top of the grade, half of it past the summit, the other half ascending to it, a small black caterpillar draped over a rock resting, he thought. Smoke issued from the spark catcher, the engine out of sight over the rise, but the train did not move. At such a distance it was impossible to make out if the rear truck of the last car had been derailed by the charge that had separated the baggage car and sent it plunging back down the grade. Hopefully, it had not; it could only further complicate an already overly complicated mess. The trainman might just be waiting until he was certain there'd be no more shooting.

A pile of old ties had been laid across the rails by the holdup men, enough to derail the baggage car when it plowed into them. How the engineer proposed to get it back onto the tracks was beyond Raider; likely a crane car would have to be sent for.

The train whistled: three short blasts, the sound drifting down the grade on the breeze. Slowly it began backing down, the engine and the diamond stack reappearing, the brakemen up top straining at their wheels, holding the string in check. The trainman held the grab bar of the last car, leaning out, raising and lowering his signal lamp.

Raider called to Charlie's older brother. "You, over here . . ."

The man came toward him; he was badly shaken, his eyes welling, his dirty face, with his bandana removed, streaked with tears. He hadn't shaved in a week nor, decided Raider as he closed the gap between them, bathed in a month.

"Poor Charlie, poor kid. Just a kid, green as grass . . ."

"Yeah. Let's have some answers."

The other Pinkertons came crowding around, Doc with his derby, vest, and jacket back on.

"Ask away," said the man, "I'll tell you anything."

"You better had. First off, when that train gets down here you're gonna point out which one o' the passengers blew the coupling. Who it is in cahoots with you."

"Mister, I wouldn't know who that was iff'n I falled over him. Jake set all that up." He indicated the fattest of the bodies. "Jake Stoddard."

"You're sure . . . I mean you wouldn't lie to me, would you? If you are . . ."

The man crossed his heart and raised his right hand. "May the good Lord strike me dead as I stand here."

"What's so interesting in the safe?"

"The Costigan Ranch payroll, seventy thousand bucks. And whatever else. And the mail pouches. How come you knowed to lay for us'ns like you done? How come you . . ."

"Never mind about that."

"You railroad coppers? You must be. I mean, are you?"

"Didn't I say never mind!"

"Okay, okay."

"You're still gonna look over the passengers, understand? You just might see somebody you know."

"You cooperate with us," interposed Turnbull, "and it won't do you any harm when you get up in front of the judge."

"We ain't promisin' it'll do you any good, either," rasped Raider, flinging the major a look of disgust. "You better just level with us, if you don't wanta swing."

The train was coming closer now, less than two hundred yards between the car ends. And slowing, the brakemen applying the shoes with all the muscle they could muster. The train ground to a stop; passengers and crew poured down the steps. Doc and Turnbull had taken over Charlie's brother, who sat about studying the crowd, looking for a familiar face. Raider joined Walter Tyndall and the Fanchettes at the coupling. It was plain to see that whoever had fixed the charge knew what he was doing. The coupler was a link and pin without side buffers. The draw-bar connected through a spring to the frame of the car, which had a socket at its outboard end. A solid link was inserted into the socket and then secured in place by a pin. Pin, link, and socket had been blown away cleanly, the charge just powerful enough to do the job but not too heavy to risk damage to either car and possibly cause a derailment. The timing had been perfect; any sooner and the engine would not have reached the top of the grade and started down; any later, the whole string would have been over the top and heading down the other side, the baggage car included.

"Whoever did it has done it before," commented Tyndall in an admiring tone.

Raider nodded. "Whoever done it musta used one helluva short fuse. Light up and skedaddle."

Doc called to them and they and the Fanchettes rejoined him, Turnbull, and DePaolo.

"Our grief-stricken friend doesn't recognize anybody," said Doc to Raider. "So he claims."

"That's his funeral," commented Turnbull. Raising his eyes, he swept the train up and down. "And this train looks to be ours. We could be stuck here two or three days."

"Maybe not," said Doc. He called over the engineer, a burly-looking red-faced old man who was sweating furiously, setting the grease on his hands glistening. The conductor, a cadaverous-looking younger man, tagged along. The passengers, having seen everything there was to see, were climbing back onto the train, getting out of the sun.

"There's gonna be holy hell to pay for this when the full report goes in to Clovis," said the conductor worriedly.

"Oh, shit, Ward," sputtered the engineer. "What they got to bitch over? Two-bit derailment? A twenty-dollar coupling? There ain't nothin' stole."

"Can we go without the baggage car?" asked Doc pointedly.

The engineer nodded. "Sure can, if you and the rest o' your bunch is willin' to stick here and stand guard. Mister, they's almost eighty thousand dollars in that safe."

Doc pressed his thought. "What I mean is, go on and take all the valuables with us, the contents of the safe, the mail . . ."

The engineer scratched his head and tumbled this about in his mind. "We could, I suppose."

The conductor screwed up his narrow, homely face into a homelier frown. "Clovis would raise hell if we left this car standing out here."

"We ain't got an awful lotta choice, Ward," said the engineer. "The line don't own but one crane flat and it's all the way down to Pecos. I don't see why we couldn't leave it stripped o' the goods. It ain't no use to nobody thatta way; and it sure ain't goin' no place on its own."

"What we should do is wire back to Clovis and ask the main office."

The engineer snorted. "Old man Potter'll tell you to sit here and cook in the sun, that's what. You know goddamn well he will. We could be stuck here till Sunday . . ."

"Great!" Raider spat, jamming his hands in his back pockets and glaring sparks.

"Now, now, now," said Turnbull, tossing one hand out in a gesture designed to invite everyone's indulgence. "There's little to be gained in upsetting ourselves. Let's show a little patience, shall we?"

"You show a little fuckin' patience!" blurted Raider. "Open your eyes, man; and the rest o' you . . . We got us ten horses here, saddled up and ready to ride. I say we jump on and get on down to Barstow. What do you say, Doc?"

"I doubt seriously if we can do that," cut in Turnbull. "May I remind you, it is specifically stated in the General Principles, chapter three, paragraph four . . ."

"I think it's four and three," said Doc. "Horses captured in the course of apprehending suspects may be utilized by operatives only in emergencies and only after permission is requested and verbally granted by the manager of the nearest office. In the event the horses are needed for evidence against the offenders . . ."

"Doc, drop a blanket over it, will you? I say we mount up and ride out. Leon, Walter, all o' you, does that make sense? Doc?"

"He's got a point, Henderson," said Doc. "We'll certainly be needing horses when we get there. The Chief can hardly object to our saving the agency the expense of renting mounts. It's even possible these were stolen."

Turnbull threw up his hands. "Go ahead! Don't let me stop you. Do it. But you, plowboy, inasmuch as it's your idea, best be prepared to explain to William Pinkerton. Don't ask me to."

"Watch it!"

"You watch it . . ."

Raider was glaring at him, the "plowboy" sinking in, stoking his ire. "You don't call me that."

"All right, all right." Doc waved both back. "Conductor?"

"What?"

"We could leave a man to see that the prisoners get to Pecos and into the hands of the local law, but we're going to need all of us. Would you and your trainman accept responsibility?"

"See here, Weatherbee," began Turnbull.

"They're tied; their weapons are all on the floor of the baggage car there. We'll put them in a sack or box or something and you can keep an eye on them up front. All you'll have to do when you pull in is send someone for the sheriff and explain what happened."

"I don't know," said the conductor quietly, unwilling to look him in the eye. "They're not exactly our responsibility."

"They're not ours. We're only passengers on this train. They tried to rob you, we did you a favor and stopped them. All the same, we'd rather not be burdened with them."

"The man's hundred percent right, Ward," piped up the engineer.

"I suppose," said the conductor. "But you boys got to accept responsibility for their horses and gear."

"We will," Doc said.

The gang's weapons were collected, deposited in a sack, and lugged up to the engine cab; the holdup men themselves were loaded on board, the three corpses packed away in a latrine. With the help of two brakemen, the clerk who had turned over his baggage car to provide a temporary conference room for the Pinkertons began transferring the contents of the safe and everything else of value to the next-to-last car.

Raider, Doc, and the others set about selecting horses. They looked to be a mixed lot. Turnbull unhesitatingly marched straight as string to the best of the ten, a big-boned gray, all muscle, with eyes as clear as mountain pools. It wasn't the horse alone that attracted the major's attention; in addition to the gear it carried, it had a new, artistically studded Mexican saddle displaying a superb set of white Angora pockets, a silver mounted bridle, a fine rawhide riata, and brand-new blanket.

For a moment, Raider watched his nemesis with unconcealed distaste, then glancing about, took the reins of a trimly built sorrel with strong-looking legs and chest and a blazed face. Mounting, he watched Doc carefully climb up on a handsome chestnut with a head and tail that were never still. The horse impressed Raider as only half-broken and, given a gallop through a thick stand of the splintering cedar brakes of the Plains or too close to cactus, it might, he reflected, decide to toss its back burden and scamper off to freedom. Doc was not all that horse-wise and one look at his partner's face confirmed to Raider that he hadn't the least suspicion that he might have mounted future grief.

"Doc, get another horse, will you? That one could turn out a little too feisty. Too much to handle."

"I'm sorry, I like him."

"Her."

"Whatever. I like any horse with spirit."

"Have it your way."

Dominic DePaolo came riding up on a spotted pony that looked to Raider to be faster than a runaway train.

"Rade," said Dominic, "you're the only operative I know who wears a Stetson hat. How come?" He grinned toothily. "I mean, what are you, a Pinkerton or a cowboy?"

"A little of each," said Doc, "and not much of either."

"That hat's got to go," said DePaolo good-naturedly.

Raider took it off and examined it. "What's the matter with it? Let me tell you something, Dom, this happens to be brand spanking new. My old one got itself stole; and the time between losing it and getting this I felt nakeder than a jaybird. Whether you know it or not, this country round about happens to be John B. Stetson country." He pantomimed with the hat. "This here hat is rugged for rugged weather, boiling hot sun, rain coming down like lead, wind, dust, snow. Hell, this can even protect a man from Kansas hail. And that's not all, not close to it. Mister; you can use this hat to fan a campfire to life, to slap a wolf in the face, to put out a grass fire, to carry water or beans or grub for your horse, for tannin' a stubborn horse's flank to get him moving. More'n that, you can put six bullet holes in this here hat and it won't ravel one inch. Show me any other hat made can stand up like that. Hell, you take halfway decent care of it and it'll last you forty years."

"After a while they smell to high heaven," said De-Paolo, leering at him.

"So do you, Dom."

With this, Raider clapped his hat back on his head and bounded away, waving the others to follow.

21

A fierce and determinedly cruel sun seared the landscape, parching everything along the way including the throats of men and horses. Presently, some sixty-odd miles from the site of the train derailment, a collection of black blocks intruded itself on the horizon and, as they neared them, assumed definition and distinctiveness—Barstow, too small to be classified a town, too big for a settlement, merely a cluster of hardy souls gotten together for mutual welfare and protection.

By the time they reached there, the sun had lowered behind the Sierra Diablos, overcasting the sky yellowish-pink. Raider was tired, physically and mentally, ground down to the nub by the concatenation of events he had wanted no part of to begin with. In his heart he could not blame Doc for his decision to stay on the case; he could blame himself only. Losing everything, including the finest horse he'd owned in three years, coming within a razorback's whisper of being killed, suffering the indignities of the ride back to Roswell in Asa Crump's pig wagon, coming up against Turnbullshit, his wise mouth, his infuriating ways, the unnecessary action in the baggage car, which none of them had even anticipated and in which all could have been wounded or even killed, the snakebiter, that double-crossing bitch with the outrageous tits and the morals of a trashcan cat; he'd wanted none of it. But he'd had it, and more, with even more to come.

"What are you looking so grim about?" inquired Doc, coming up alongside him.

"Nothin'."

"Relax, we'll have this thing all wound up in a few hours."

"That's what you said back in Roswell. Hell, back in Albuquerque."

"I did not."

"You did, Doc. You wear the rosiest rose-colored specs anybody ever put on, I swear you do."

"One of us has to be a little optimistic. To you everything is thunder, lightning, and heavy rains."

"Yeah, well the only reason I'm hangin' in here is on account o' you."

"Me? That's a laugh. You think I can't function without you?"

"You know you can't. Without me you'd be as helpless as a one-legged chicken."

"Well, seeing you put it that way, you may have a point. I am grateful to you, Rade, honestly."

"Aw, shut up!"

They rode on, Raider sinking deeper into his gloom, Doc grinning devilishly, unable to hide his amusement. Raider sneaked a glance at him.

"You're an asshole, you know that?"

"Speaking of which, you've nearly started up with his nibs on two occasions already; do you think you might possibly put a damper on your feelings?"

"Shit! You all the time lecture me on him; how about jumpin' on him for a change? It takes two, you know. How about pickin' on him equal to pickin' on me? Maybe keep track o' the time with that bull ball watch o' yours so it works out fair . . ."

"Frankly, Rade, I'd say he's being remarkably patient with you—"

"WELL FUCK ME! I like that, patient with *me!* You really got to be the king o' all assholes, you know that?"

Doc laughed, Raider cursed and whacked his horse with his hat, pulling two lengths ahead. They came thundering into Barstow raising street dust thirty feet in the air, turning heads, bringing people to windows and doors, pulling up in front of the saloon, dismounting wearily and hitching their horses to the rack.

Six, including Raider, made straight for the batwing doors; Doc and Turnbull headed for the barber shop across the street.

"I need a shampoo in the worst way," Raider heard the major say to Doc as they walked away. "And my mustaches waxed and curled."

"Better he get his cock waxed and curled," muttered Raider to Dominic DePaolo.

They bellied up to the bar, ordered whiskey and beer, and carried glasses and bottles to a large table.

"Rade," asked Walter Tyndall as they sat down, "do you think Turnbull is right, I mean about going after this Zemo for that printer's murder, instead of the flim-flam?"

"What are you asking him for?" asked DePaolo, pouring out a tumblerful of rye, dispensing half of it in two gulps, gasping, and fingering a lingering drop from his lower lip. "You know how fond they are of each other."

"Whether I like him or not, he happens to be all wrong," said Raider. "Sure, we'd nail Zemo—that is, we might. But in the meantime his whole crowd would likely fly the coop. We're too close to the border for that. Besides which, all them bankers up the line wouldn't appreciate us turnin' our backs on their troubles."

The dice danced in the birdcage, the piano player flailed away at "The Dying Cowboy," the mournful tones rising into the smoke-filled air, a skinny redhead in an ill-fitting crimson satin frock attempted to dance with a drunk, and the rumble of conversation floated in on Raider from all sides. He was preparing to add to his reasons why the major's strategy was wrong when he stopped abruptly and stood up.

"Hey, you playin' the piano, how's about something more cheerful? This ain't no wake, you know. How about 'Virginia Skedaddle'?" yelled Raider.

"The 'Badger and the Pig'!" yelled somebody at the bar.

The "Badger and the Pig" it was, a rollicking melody

with a lyric picked up by half a dozen drinkers detailing the nuptials of a badger and a sow.

"Do you really mean it, about packing it in after this job?" asked DePaolo.

Raider nodded. "You bet, all the money you got."

"I'll still believe it when I see it."

"Stick around, Dom."

"I don't believe it either," said Leon Fanchette flatly. His brother's dark eyes agreed with him.

"What do you figure for our first move when Doc and the major come back?" asked Walter Tyndall, finishing his third drink in three minutes by the clock on the wall opposite the bar.

"This is it. We sit. Until they show up. Then . . ." Raider's hand flew through the air, trapping a fly in his fist, squeezing it and wiping it on his trouserleg.

Across the street in the barber shop two new Witcomb chairs sat facing the wall-length mirror; in the glass were Doc and Turnbull, side by side, pin-striped sheets snugged around their respective necks. In front of them, duplicated in the mirror, was a parade of bottles, Prince Igor's Luxuriant Hair Restorer, Milbain's Hair Tonic, eau de cologne, Zenithia, Nadjy and Hawthorne colognes, ylang-ylang toilet water, Jockey Club, white heliotrope and lavender toilet waters, twin quart bottles with elongated necks of Mishkin's Celebrated Hair Oil, Aspeth Grecian Urn Bay Rum, talcum powders, and the usual tools of the barber's trade.

The lone practitioner of same was dividing his attention between the major's mustache, already waxed and about to be hot-iron curled, and Doc's hair, which badly wanted trimming.

"I asked you before, Henderson, and if you don't mind I'd like to ask you again," said Doc quietly, striving for friendliness in his tone.

"Go easy on Rade, would you? For all our sakes."

"*Me* go easy on him? Really, old fellow. Any words between us he's the cause. The reason's obvious, being a clodhopper, a prince of the soil, if you will, crude, uneducated, narrow-minded, he's trammeled with a towering inferiority complex. I swear, you look at him and smile and nod and he interprets it as an insult. He's incredible."

"Then don't look at him."

"Please, don't be tiresome."

Doc turned, glaring, momentarily stopping the scissors at his neck.

"Henderson, do you mind my asking you a personal question?"

"If it'll make you feel better. I say, barber, is this pomatum wax you've put on my mustache?"

"Eez Fromard."

"Is it any good? I should have told you I wanted pomatum; oh, well, just as long as this holds the curl and doesn't darken it."

"Do you have any friends?" asked Doc in a subdued voice. It was not said sarcastically; it was uttered in all seriousness. "*A* friend?"

"Of course. What do you take me for, a hermit? Some sort of pariah? I've loads of friends."

"You're a lucky man. By a friend I mean somebody who'd take your grief on his own shoulders, somebody . . ."

"Who'd stick his arm in the fire, take one's place on the rack, Damon and Pythias, eh?"

"Raider, the clodhopper, the prince of the soil, as you call him, happens to be my friend. My only friend. Oh, I don't know about his sticking his arm in the fire for me or the rack; he's risked his life to save mine, many times. But I'm not altogether sure that that sort of thing is a true test of friendship, the caliber of friendship I'm talking about. I know people think that most friendships are based on goodwill, affection arising out of mutual esteem; there's that between us, but there's something else, something intangible. A bond forged by adversity, you might call it."

Turnbull's hand emerged from under his sheet and he held it in front of his mouth, pretending to stifle a yawn. "Interesting."

"I'm serious. These past four years have been anything but dull for us. What's really puzzling is that he and I are just about as different as different can be, opposites in everything. Everything. I wonder if the overcoming of such opposition, unconsciously developing whatever it is that shunts aside all our differences, is what makes us feel as we do about each other. We may be poles apart, but I've never in my life felt closer to anyone than I do to him. And he feels the same way toward me; I know he does."

"Amazing."

"What's amazing?"

"You. How can you, a man of breeding, educated, with your background, intelligent, sophisticated, form a friendship with somebody like that? I'm not saying he's a bad sort, he has his good points, his strengths, it's just that he's . . . he's . . ."

"A clodhopper."

"Tell me something, can you see yourself striking up a friendship with an Eskimo? A Chinese coolie?"

"Why not? Where do I draw the line? Why should I? Why should anyone?"

The barber smiled, the mere trace of a grin; Doc noticed it in the mirror as the man turned to shaping the crescent of hair around his right ear.

"Every man to his own taste," said Turnbull. "Unfortunately, your friend Raider is not to mine."

"Whether he is or not is not important. What is is this assignment; we've got to put our personal feelings aside and deal with it. And, Henderson, we will put our personal feelings aside."

"Mmmm. You don't like me very much, do you? Though I expect that's something else that's not very important. Well, you can relax, old fellow, I promise faithfully to resist all further temptation to poke fun at him. I won't even call him plowboy. Though you must admit, it suits him admirably."

"Just don't say it to his face."

"Come, come, now, are you ordering me?"

"You can take it any way you like."

"I'm sorry. You don't give me orders, old fellow. Not that sort . . ."

"It's settled, let's drop it. What can be more absurd than two people bickering over a third person, don't you agree?"

Turnbull's face softened. He smiled. "Agreed."

22

The Pinkertons' confiscated horses were bedded down in the local livery stable; the Pinkertons, posing as cattle buyers from Abilene, checked into the Stockton Hotel. Raider took a room on the third floor and after dinner the group assembled there to lay final plans. It was suggested by Walter Tyndall that they keep the lowest possible profile and stick close to the hotel until the carnival arrived. According to Doc, Zemo and the others should be coming in from Hobbs the following day, the day after at the latest.

Without looking at Turnbull, without downing his earlier suggestion, Raider raised the problem created were they to seize the snakebiter for the murder of Joe Gilbertson.

"If we forget about the scam, that lead plate and all, the rest of his bunch'll be free to scatter," he said solemnly. "I say we go back to the original plan, Doc's and mine. First thing tomorrow morning we sound out the bank president and work things like in Roswell. Same pattern."

"Hopefully with better success," remarked Turnbull.

Raider talked through his comment. "What we really got to get is their copper plates, solid evidence. I mean before they even start in printing."

"I disagree, Rade," said Doc. "The lead plate'll do." The others nodded. "I don't see that as any problem, whether we move in before they can make their copper plates or after they've printed. The only problem I see is the banker. If he turns out to be another Horace F. Catterbury, things may get sticky."

"You and I can approach him, Weatherbee," said

Turnbull, rising from his chair, the only one in the room, and taken by him when the group came in. He began appraising his newly shaped mustache in the foggy mirror over the cheap, battered washstand. It spiraled neatly at each end, twin coils of gold, an impressive sight, if somewhat fragile, vulnerable. To a fist, even to a sneeze, decided Raider, watching him. Jesus, he thought, he's no man, he's a peacock, strutting, preening, posing. Mr. Beautiful. Him and Crazy Custer!

"I'm curious," piped up DePaolo. "Do you mind telling me how you keep that thing in shape in bed? Aren't you afraid you'll roll over and bend it on the pillow?"

"It springs right back," said Turnbull airily. "The wax gives it suppleness, you see, a sort of elasticity. Gentlemen, at the risk of sounding like a braggart, the ladies, bless 'em, love it."

Not as much as you do, reflected Raider in disgust.

Turnbull did not take it to ego when his suggestion that Zemo be captured for the murder was rejected by the others. He was in much too expansive a mood, a generous mood; and wholly absorbed by his image in the glass. The meeting broke up around ten o'clock, ending with agreement that Doc and the major would approach the president of the Barstow Bank first thing in the morning.

Raider took this decision to heart more than he should have. Had Turnbull and the others never showed up, he and Doc would be doing the approaching, as they had in Roswell and in Albuquerque. The peacock's superseding him, for no other reason but the sake of appearance to more effectively impress the banker, mildly riled him. His interest in the case, already slowly but steadily eroding, had little chance of resurrecting itself as long as Turnbull was around.

Left in privacy he opened both windows overlooking the alley to let out the heat of the day, stripped down to the buff, washed his upper body, brushed his teeth with his finger, got into bed and, blowing out the lamp, pulled the sheet up under his chin. His pillow felt as if it were stuffed with rocks; his mattress, all of two inches thick, was supported by iron springs that squealed and sang every time he moved; but his weariness overcame these minor discomforts and very soon he dropped off to sleep.

He woke up, what seemed hours later to his fog-bound brain, but could have been under one hour. Two cats were squabbling below, howling at each other, scampering about, rattling the empty trashcans. The racket rose upward; he tried to close his ears to it but could not. On and on the two fought. Under even the most peaceful and charming circumstances, a little, two-week-old ball of fur all tangled up in yarn in a pretty little girl's lap, he was not overly fond of cats. Horses he loved, cows he could take or leave, dogs rarely bothered him. But cats he had early on decided were useless, dangerous, and annoying.

Particularly at the moment. Getting up, he strode to the washstand, bumping his knee against it in the darkness, muttering appropriately, groping for and finding the pitcher two-thirds full of water. He carried it to the open window. Leaning out, he peered down; he could see absolutely nothing, the light of the moon completely blocked by the building rising across the alley. Straining his eyes, he couldn't even make out the building, although it was less than ten feet from him. The cats below kept up a furious squalling, as if bent on killing each other. Holding the pitcher with both hands he dumped it. The sound of the water splashing came upward, bringing with it a loud bellowing:

"SON OF A BITCH!"

The window below slammed shut. The cats flew off. All was quiet. Making his way back to the stand, Raider set the pitcher in its bowl and went back to bed. Somebody must have caught some of the water, he mused. Too bad, but whoever it was wouldn't melt. He was almost asleep, his mind tripping along the edge of unconsciousness, when a loud stomping sounded outside. Rising on one elbow he squinted through the blackness. Something like an anvil thumped against his door, ripping it from its hinges, knocking it flat. Framed in the doorway, the hall light outlining his massive figure, was Turnbull. No mistaking his curly hair, even in silhouette. In he came, roaring. Instinctively, Raider threw himself to one side, dragging the sheet with him, dropping onto the floor, hands and knees first. In the nick of time; Turnbull threw himself down on the bed, collapsing it completely with a loud crash. Lurching to his feet, he swung about; Raider by now was up on his feet, mother-naked but ready to go. A wild roundhouse caught him alongside the head, driving him toward the door, staggering him. Shaking out the cobwebs, he ducked under a second swing, and a third, brought his left up into his attacker's gut, finding it hard as block ice. Turnbull grunted, blowing out his lungs, roaring and coming back at him with a right that glanced off his shoulder, but all but dislocated it. Raider caught him full on the jaw and back he tottered, smashing against the washstand, upsetting the pitcher in its bowl, sending it crashing to the floor. But Turnbull righted himself adroitly and they went back at it, toe to toe, slugging hard, solid blows to the body. Raider sidestepped a bruising right and got off a hard left from far back, straight into Turnbull's heart. It turned an even fight into a ten-second fiasco. Following up quickly with a flurry of lefts and rights to the head, Raider sent him reeling out into the hallway, falling backward as his feet tangled, his head crashing hard against the wall. Down he slumped, as if every bone in his body had liquefied. Doc, Dominic DePaolo, and the Fanchette brothers came running up, wide-eyed with wonderment. For the first time, by the light of a wall sconce, Raider was able to see the major's face; his golden hair was soaking wet, his mustache drooping absurdly. He was wearing silk-finish Balbriggen underwear bottoms, no top, no slippers. His eyes were closed; he looked dead.

"You've killed him!" DePaolo burst out. Kneeling, he began examining him.

"You're crazy! I hit him fair, he fell and hit his head . . ."

DePaolo pulled down Turnbull's lower left lid. His pupil was glazed but still in place. Crouching on the other side listening to his heart, Doc raised his eyes to Raider.

"He's alive." An anger mingled with something very much like fear seized his features. "Good job. GOOD JOB!" He snorted. "Would you mind covering yourself?"

Walter Tyndall had gone into the darkened room and, snatching the sheet from the end of the bed, tossed it to Raider, who wrapped it around him as his partner confronted him.

"Whatever possessed you to douse him? Why do you have to antagonize the man?"

"Doc, for Christ's sakes, I didn't do it a-purpose! There was some damned cats down below . . ."

"We heard. Everybody in town could hear. But that doesn't . . ."

"I didn't see him. I couldn't see my hand in front o' me. I dumped the pitcher sure, but I swear to God I didn't *try* to hit *him!*"

DePaolo smiled and lowered his eyes. Leon and Paul Fanchette looked at each other, then looked away.

"Goddamnit, it's the bald truth! I didn't even know the bastard had the room under me."

"Rade, give us a break, can't you?" asked Doc pleadingly. "Haven't we got enough to contend with without . . ."

"You don't believe me! YOU GODDAMNIT DON'T BELIEVE ME!"

"Hold it down."

"You bastard, all o' you! What am I doin' here? What in hell am I doin', with you, with him, in this? I don't belong here, no more than a damned dog in a soup pot! I never belonged. Not since the first. Jesus Christ, I had to be crazy, outta my head. I been the square peg in the round hole for four fuckin' years . . ."

"Rade . . ."

"Don't Rade me, don't nothin' me! Just leave me be, the lot o' you. I don't need you, I don't want you. Get outta my way. I'm gettin' dressed and gettin' out. Somethin' I shoulda done back in Albuquerque. Out? Christ Almighty, I never shoulda got in in the first place!"

23

Within twenty minutes he had dressed and was on his way to the stable, without so much as a backward look. Doc and the others, even Turnbull, who by now had recovered consciousness, if not his aplomb, stood in the window of Doc's room opposite Raider's, watching the Stetson move across the street down the sidewalk into the shadows.

He had to wake up the stableman, who didn't appreciate it, it being almost four in the morning. He paid him, saddled up the blazed-faced sorrel, and rode out of Barstow. He headed east, only because the road did. He had no particular destination in mind, getting out was what he wanted. What he'd got, however long overdue. A hundred yards from the last building on the street, loping along easily, he began to feel better, his anger leaving him, the tightness in the cords at his neck relaxing, the burden of the past four years beginning to desert his shoulders.

Good-bye, Doc, he mused, you silly-looking dude-ass, you and that Diamondback popgun of yours, your needles and pins into my sensitive hide, that you always claim to have, that I'm the one who got. Good-bye, good luck; you turned out a disappointment to me, partner, but in a way you did me a favor, turning on me like you did. Not really turning on me, just not believing me as quickly as you could have busted the old camel's back. Others playing Doubting Thomas, he could take, he expected, but not his partner of four long years. Oh well, all good things come to an end.

Good-bye, Judith and that dumb apothecary wagon back o' your tail. A millstone around both their necks more often than it was any use. Good-bye, Chief Allan Pinkerton, Allan Pinchpenny, with all your dumb rules and regulations. General Principles, General Bullshit! In how many daydreams, bored by long hours in the saddle, his imagination stretching for something to amuse him, had he pictured himself collaring some no-good with a .44 in one hand and the rule book open in the other? Chief Pinchpenny. That reminded him, he had less than four dollars in his pocket left from the money lent him by Doc. Nearly fifty. The agency owed him twenty-six-fifty; he must remember to tell Wagner to give it to Doc when he sent in his resignation. He had other expenses due him as well, and pay. He'd get all of it sooner or later. Allan Pinkerton may have been tighter than a well-soaked spoke thrust into a wagon wheel, but the man was honest.

Tell me something, Raider, what are you fixin' to do for a living? The railroad? The army? Riverboat gambler? It's a free country, nobody can force you to run around the territories after bad guys to keep old lobo from the door. How's about heading back to the farm?

Hell no! There was gambling and there was gambling, but busting one's hump getting a crop down, working practically from dark to dark only to see it washed away or dried up and blown away was not for him. It had been, but never would be again.

He rode on, the sky lightening, the sun rising at his back, a most beautiful awakening of the world, the wondrous white disk absorbing the blackness, cooking it in its furnace, releasing it pale blue, the azure hue of a gnat-catcher's back. A sunrise to set an artist's heart thumping in his chest. The Davis Mountains came into sharp relief, the light flooding the plains, brightening the greens of the shrubs, the gold of the grass. Hunger overtook him. He had crossed over into Upton County by now, heading east, gaining the Middle Concho River. Pulling up, he searched his saddle-bags and found a couple of dried sourdough biscuits as hard as rocks, and very nearly as old, he decided, examining one, then the other. Some meal, no coffee, no way to boil it if there was, no bacon or salt pork or dried fruit. He soaked both biscuits in the river, then bit into one, munching it slowly, gingerly, lest he break a tooth getting it down his craw . . .

He was dying for some coffee, a pot brimful of Arbuckle's boiled half an hour, six-shooter java, strong enough to float a man's iron.

Up ahead where the Middle Concho gave out and the North Concho came wandering down from the northwest, roughly paralleling the Colorado, lay San Angelo, a distance of eighty miles or more. There he would stop for the night and make plans. A master plan for the future, where to go, to settle, what to do with his life. He'd wasted enough of it, time to sink his teeth into something worthwhile.

He finished the second biscuit and, filling his hat with water, set about scrubbing down the sorrel, ridding it of sweat and dust. Then he cinched the saddle back in place, mounted up, and went on.

His thoughts carried back to Barstow, to Doc and the others, but mostly Doc. The boys down from Denver were good sorts, for the most part, but he didn't know them like he knew Doc, had never had the chance to get to know them. To know someone you've got to be with him night and day, month after month, share things, a bottle, a trail, a case, the seat of a wagon for ten thousand dusty miles, danger, all kinds of experiences. In four years they had gotten deep inside each other's minds and hearts; proof of that was how well they worked together, anticipating one another's every move, knowing, not guessing, certain as to how the other would react in a given situation, even when they were miles apart. Like the time over near Lawton when he'd been bushwhacked by Red Knife, a Comanche subchief. Doc had been on his way to Amarillo, but partway there he had turned around, come back, and somehow gotten on the Indians' trail, gotten to him in the dead of night along the way, cut him loose, packed him out and away, claiming that he'd "sensed" he, Raider, was in danger.

He had downgraded that at the time, even to ridiculing it. Doc had known that Red Knife was in the area, known that he, Raider, and the sinister son of a bitch were blood enemies from way back in the game, that Red Knife would go fifty miles out of his way for a chance to grab him, a chance to straighten out accounts between them. Oh yes, Doc had had more to go on than "sensing." But when it came right down to it it had been his instincts only that had turned him around. Instincts? Intuition? Call it what you will, it was a talent that could only come from long association between two souls.

He'd like to believe that Doc would be totally lost without him. But of course he wouldn't be. Wagner would team him up with another man, another type much like himself. Raider's sort wasn't unique in the organization. It would be an ideal pairing. Their success over the years was all Wagner would need to lead him to such a move. Of course once they got together they'd argue over everything, squabble incessantly, go at it nose to nose and swinging, but as time went on they'd grow closer and closer. Until Doc had pushed this old boy far back in memory. Life, after all, was today and tomorrow, not yesterday, not for people like them.

He wondered if he and Doc would ever see one another again. Probably not, but if they were to, next year, five years, ten . . . Yes, in ten years; where? Anywhere, maybe up by Belfield, west of Dickenson, Stark County, North Dakota. Site of their first case, first journal; the Hampton brothers, three of them, four counting Dale, who'd turned out to be a half brother. They had gunned down a Northern Pacific track crew that had surprised them setting up a barrier to derail a train.

He and Doc had cleaned that one up in short order. Getting their partnership off and running; first case; first of how many? A hundred? More, lots more. God Almighty, how many pounds of lead had gone down gun barrels, how many gallons of blood spilled, how many lives taken, how many close calls? How many wounds? Both their bodies were covered with scars, afflicted with achings that never really went away, not completely. Wet weather, dampness woke up every one, something less than gentle reminders of the past.

He rode on, following the river, now and then meeting riders or wagons coming the other way, once at the crossroads near Campton sighting a stage heading south. Late in the afternoon he was within two hours' ride of San Angelo when a caravan of wagons appeared coming from the northwest, black dots in a chain crawling across the landscape.

It couldn't be . . .

Heeling his horse, he raced toward the moving line bringing the wagons into definition. It couldn't be, but it was, Colonel J. P. B. Hardy's World's Greatest Carnival. Featuring The Great Zemo, World's Most Fearless and Strongest Man.

Raider's head whirled. They had left Hobbs, but instead of heading down to Barstow had drawn a line through it on their list and were on their way directly to Sauer City, leaving Doc and the others sitting in Barstow, waiting.

Why? Why had Zemo elected to bypass Barstow? Carl Haskell? No, he couldn't know that Haskell had been picked up for the printer's murder. Had the snake-biter even suspected that, he'd have written off Sauer City as well. No, for whatever reason, Sauer City was to be the end of the line.

He slowed the horse. What was he doing? What did he care where they were heading, what their plan was? He was out of it, totally. To red hell with the whole mess, let Doc and the others deal with it, or not, whichever, he couldn't care spit. He dismissed it from his mind, pushing it out like a drunk out of a saloon.

Back it came, his hand sneaking to his forehead where Zemo had pounded him senseless. It had hurt, but what hurt even more had been his grin. He could still see it. It said it all: *I'm better than you, bigger, stronger, tougher. You can't dent me, you're crazy to try. You'll only make yourself look like a fool in front of her.*

Dolly Dee. She'd suckered him in from the first, playing friendly, cozying up to him, only because she'd been ordered to. Two-faced bitch! To hell with her, with all of them; to hell with the Pinks. To hell with Doc. No, not Doc . . .

He swung behind a grove of cottonwoods and watched the caravan through the gently moving branches. Never to hell with Doc. What would he and the others do, he wondered; sit and wait in Barstow until tomorrow, the day after at most. Then cut and run to Sauer City. The caravan would still be there; after all, their schedule coincided with Carl Haskell's for the printings. Probably they'd camp outside town, arriving early as they would, then make their grand entrance, like in Roswell. Set up and put on their show and take the unsuspecting bank president to the dump. Unless they were stopped. They would be, if big-mouth Turnbullshit didn't screw things up.

The line passed less than a mile away. Temptation coiled like a prairie rattler in his brain, coiled and prepared to strike. Follow them and, come darkness, sneak up and ascertain where Zemo slept, take him and run him off, maybe north to the law in China Springs. No, better into Sauer City, hand him over to Doc. It wouldn't be hard, work it the way Doc had run him away from Red Knife and his cutthroat buddies. He himself had rescued or captured people the same way a dozen times. It was best to wait and watch their tent or them lying on the ground in their roll. Wait for them to get up during the night to go take a leak. Let them, and grab them on the way back. Taking a man in his roll outside was a little harder, but not much, not when you had the gun and he could feel the muzzle against his temple.

Mounting, he hesitated. He could swing south, down toward Ozona on Howard's Creek, stay there the night, miles away from any foolish temptation. After all, what was in it for him to risk his neck? For what, to polish his somewhat tarnished image in her eyes? What did he care about her? What was she but a heavy-chested slut with no more feeling for him than a hound for a flea. Twenty-three years old and five husbands! What a waste of time . . .

He drew the sorrel right, intending to ford the river.

He even started down the bank. The sun was lowering, burning fiercely, reddening and sending long, soft shadows down from the peaks, dappling the plain, setting pink fire to the undersides of the clouds. He'd have to hurry to make Ozona by nightfall.

Fuck it! Swinging left, he began following the caravan. It wasn't Zemo or her, it was a familiar something beginning to gnaw at the back of his mind, harder, more tenaciously as the minutes dragged by, dropping into the past, into gone forever. A little ratlike creature, part habit, part sense of duty, all awareness of a job left unfinished. Worse, left for somebody else to finish.

He picked up sight of them less than a mile down the road, following the last wagon into the twilight. They stopped and camped near a hill a short walk from the river, setting out their fires, breaking out utensils and food, carrying on like an emigrant brood on the Oregon Trail. Raider circled the sight, coming up behind the hill, wrapping his reins around a boulder and climbing up to the top. Bellying down behind a bush, he watched the activity below. Presently somebody broke out a banjo, plinking into "There She Stands, a Lovely Creature." The song was taken up by a score of men and women, the fires flared, the flames building, then settling back into the coals. Supper was made. The smell of kidney beans in the pot wafted upward, mingling with those of coffee and some kind of stew. As the darkness gathered, the campfires put rosy glows on the faces of those drawn up around them, throwing their shadows back in a circle like a wagon wheel.

Raider was famished and the smells gradually became every bit as tantalizing as the coffee and bacon from the same pots and pans had been earlier outside Roswell. Only this time Judith and Doc were not behind him. There'd be no supper this night, unless he rode an hour or two farther into town, which wasn't the worst idea. The carnival wouldn't be back on the move again before sun-up.

He spotted Zemo coming up to the fire directly below, Dolly Dee beside him. The snakebiter crouched, coffee cup in hand, filling it from the pot, tasting it, burning his lip, reacting, bringing a loud guffaw from the others watching. Dolly Dee clapped him on the back and chided him. He took it good-naturedly, then began showing his lip to those around the fire, pretending he was hurt.

All in good fun, reflected Raider, watching. A good time was had by all, except Joe Gilbertson.

Still, that and the flimflam interested him not in the slightest; catching them was really all he cared about. Seeing them get what was coming to them, a neatly noosed length of three-quarter-inch Manila rope for the Great Zemo, a few summers behind bars for her and the others. A nice thick case journal filed away.

He heard a sound behind him, brush moving. Up on his forearms he turned to look back down. Footsteps. He went for the .45. Too late. His hand froze in midair, a rifle was pointing straight at him. The other man carried a burlap sack over his shoulder taut to the bottom of it. In his free hand was a snake stick, a small rope loop around one end. Both men grinned broadly at him.

"Well, well, Jace, see what we got here."

24

Doc was in a foul mood; his nature was such that he rarely failed to look for and find the bright side of even the gloomiest problem or circumstance, but this time he was unable to even initiate the search. He simply didn't have the heart. With Turnbull he had approached Wilton O. Talmadge, the president of the Barstow Bank, shortly after the eight—now seven— Pinkertons took their breakfast at the Wooden Spoon Café. Talmadge had heard the two of them out and promised his full cooperation. He obviously recognized one aspect of the situation which Horace F. Catterbury had studiously ignored, his obligation to the banking community as a whole.

"It 'pears to me that if we don't pull the plug on these shenanigans here and now, that bunch'll go on for years. Long after Sauer City. It's much too slick a swindle to shelve permanent after that. Count me in; all I ask is that you keep me up on everything that's goin' on."

Nothing was, up to two in the afternoon. The road from Hobbs to Barstow ran approximately one hundred miles almost directly south. If the carnival traveled a mere thirty-odd miles a day, camping and resting eight hours each night, they would have to arrive by late afternoon of the following day; if they picked up the pace, early the next morning. This assumed, to be sure, that Zemo planned to spend no more than one day in Hobbs, if that long. Talmadge planned to print two thousand ten-dollar banknotes on Thursday, two days hence. Common sense suggested that the snake-biter would want to reach Barstow and set up at least one day before. This had been his pattern so far. And, at least in Doc's view, he appeared to be the type who devised a plan and then stuck to it religiously. Unless something like an unscheduled explosion or attempted doublecross on the part of a printer forced changes.

Doc and the others sat in his hotel room discussing these and other relevant matters for the dozenth time, a sure sign of boredom and growing impatience. A change of subject was definitely in order, but the subject changed to would not have been Doc's choice.

"He'll be back," said Walter Tyndall, confidently. "You know Raider, he flies off the handle at the least little thing, blows off steam, cools down, settles down and . . ." He snapped his fingers. "There he is, back on the track, spoiling for more action."

"He won't be back," said Doc evenly. "Yes, I know him, and I say he's gone for good."

He raised his eyes from the floor and saw Turnbull standing by the window, holding the curtain back, looking down into the street. Then he returned to staring at the floor, looking through it, his mind crammed to bursting with the events of the past few days. And last night. It was a relief when the major didn't turn toward him and catch his eye. Had he done so he, Doc, would have been hard put to keep from starting up with him. Not that he could blame him for Raider's quitting. If anybody was at fault for that it was he himself. He'd seen it coming for a long time and had done next to nothing to prevent it. Probably because Raider had been threatening to quit for years; not when the situation in which the two of them found themselves became more than they could cope with. No, that sort he was not; he loved the action and the long odds. They nurtured something inside him, fed something into his blood that fired him up and brought out the best in him. No, it was Chicago that got to him, disappointed and discouraged him, Wagner and Allan Pinkerton's blasé attitude toward Raider's and his efforts, the lack of appreciation, the carping, the nitpicking, the red tape, the Chief's miserliness, his and his manager's inability to recognize that fighting crime in the wilds of the West was not like fighting it in any city. Out here the law was stretched thin; the vast dis-

tances between towns and settlements worked in every
suspect's favor. Pursuit was difficult, dangerous, often
impossible. Half of the cases assigned them had to be
dropped unsolved when the enemy got across the Mexican border before he could be stopped. They did the
best they could, better than any other team working
the territories, Doc was sure; it was just too tough a
row to "hoe up," as Raider put it.

Raider. Suddenly so many things were coming to
mind that he wished he'd said to him. Like good-bye
and good luck. Hope we meet again.

Damn! It was awful; it sat inside his stomach like a
mound of gall. It felt as if his right arm had been
ripped from his shoulder. Six men in the room and
still he couldn't recall feeling this lonely, this deprived
in years. Of what? Only the best friend he had in the
world. Wagner would assign him a new partner, unless
he himself quit. Should he? Were he to do so, it would
look like a sympathy play. Fairly foolish, a move everybody, officers and operatives alike, would chalk up to
impulse, to emotion rather than intelligence. A decision
made and very soon regretted. You don't quit your
job because somebody else quits his. Not as a rule.

Not that he wasn't tempted. A new partner. His
eyes roamed the room; one of these six? Not the
Fanchettes; Wagner didn't like pairing up brothers, too
much chance of both getting killed, a double-barreled
blow to the family. But Leon and Paul had made their
working together one of the stipulations for taking the
job. And Allan Pinkerton had made an exception. Only
because they were too good to risk missing out on.

Walter Tyndall? A good man, too. A trifle slow with
a decision and with a gun, but courageous, resourceful, easy to get along with. Cy Schwartz he didn't really
know, except that he had worked with Dom DePaolo
for longer than he himself and Raider had teamed.
It was unlikely Wagner would break them up.

Henderson Turnbull. He worked with everybody,
but nobody in particular. His personality appeared a
major obstacle to the major's teaming up permanently
with any other operative. Sneaking a second look at

him at the window, Doc grudgingly conceded that Turn-bull was everything he himself had claimed to Raider he was, all in all, a first-rate operative. He'd conducted himself admirably in Talmadge's office earlier in the day, making a very good impression on the banker, helping to win his confidence. When it came down to it, the man's faults were rather petty, certainly none could be cited as detrimental to the overall success of his career.

Nobody had anything like the trouble with him Raider had. As far as he personally was concerned he didn't dislike the major. But of course Wagner would never team them up. What he'd find for him would be another Raider.

As if there were another Raider. Certainly he'd never met one.

"I wonder where he's heading?" asked Dominic, shattering Doc's concentration. "Do you suppose he'll go back to Arkansas?"

"I don't know," said Doc. Moving to the mirror he began fussing with his disguise. "Anybody got a match?" He fished out a cheroot. Cy Schwartz lit it for him. "I'm going down and have a look at the local print shop; from the outside. Anybody feel like stretching his legs?"

"I'll come," said Turnbull, turning and smiling affably. Two bruises were forming on his face, on his right cheek and the point of his chin. And, mused Doc, nodding acceptance of his company, there had to be a bump the size of a hen's egg on the back of his head where he'd hit the wall.

25

Raider sat with his wrists bound behind his back against the pole inside Zemo's tent. The big man stood over him grinning triumphantly. The two roustabouts had been out hunting rattlers for the snakebiter when they'd spotted Raider's horse at the foot of the hill, and him at the top. Now they flanked their employer. The one carrying the rifle Raider had recognized at once as one of the men who had blocked his and Doc's escape from the dressing tent back in Albuquerque.

"You think graying your hair and mustache and clipping the ends off is enough to keep me from recognizing you?" asked Zemo.

"There was a lot more to it," said Raider wearily. "Wrinkles and powder, all washed off by now. The gray I got to grow out of."

"You should live long enough to." He laughed, the others joining him. "You surprise me, mister. How the hell did you ever track us all the way down here? You must have followed us to Hobbs . . ."

"He's a snoop, Heinz, he's trained good as a redskin. All nose," said the man with the rifle, a muscular individual with a churn-sized neck and the glazed look of the exceptionally stupid. "So Alfred says, right, Alfred?"

"Oh, he's a snoop all right," said Zemo. "The little girl found that out back in Albuquerque." Kneeling, he searched Raider's eyes. "You one of John Sherman's* boys? Or the Secret Service? What, tell me . . ."

"Nothing that grand. I'm just the nosy sort."

Zemo slapped him hard, igniting red-and-purple bursts in his brain. "Give me a straight answer."

---

* Treasury Secretary in the administration of Rutherford B. Hayes.

"You do that again, I'll kill you."

He did it again. The other cheek. More red-and-purple bursts, bigger.

"Once more, what's your line?"

"I'm nothing. I got no line. That's the God's truth."

"You're something, partner. Private? A Pinkerton maybe?"

Dolly Dee came in, took one look at Raider, recognized him, and covered a gasp with her hand.

"Good God in Heaven, what's he doing here?"

"Ssssh, he's about to tell us," said Alfred, grinning.

Coming forward, she bent over Raider, running her fingers through his hair gently. He twisted free of her touch.

"I don't think he likes you anymore," said Zemo. "You know how fickle men are. Okay, so you're a Pinkerton."

"I didn't say that. I'm not. Okay, okay, I was, but I quit."

"Oh, will you listen to this?"

"It's the bald truth. I couldn't care less what you're up to."

"So how come you're spying on us?" asked Alfred.

Zemo rose to his feet. "If you don't mind, I'll ask the questions. What's your name, fella?"

"John O'Toole," said Dolly Dee. "At least that's what he called himself to me."

Zemo nodded. "Good enough. Okay, John O'Toole, where's that well-dressed friend of yours?"

"Back in Roswell. As far as I know he's heading back to Denver."

"Do tell? Just ran up the white flag, right? After the house blew, is that it?"

"Right."

"You're a damned liar." He drew his hand back a third time, but Dolly grabbed him by the wrist, fingers and thumb reaching barely halfway around it, Raider noted. People shouldn't grow so big, especially bad ones. It was downright indecent.

"Let me talk to him," she said.

"Hey, what's going on with you people? You trying

to crab my act or something? Back off, little girl. Now, John O'Toole, I'm going to give you one last chance. Open up and tell us what's going on."

Raider sighed. "Okay. The Secret Service more or less gave up on you, and the governor of New Mexico called us in. We got to Albuquerque too late to stop you there. We followed you down to Roswell and set a trap. That is, we tried to. We were there when the printer made up a batch of new banknotes for Catterbury. The trouble was we couldn't pinpoint anything going wrong, not there, not after. So we figured all we could do was to keep a sharp eye out for any new notes."

"How were you supposed to tell the difference between his and ours?"

"Imperfect signatures."

"What 'imperfect' signatures? We've got two artists with us who have to be the most talented forgers in North America, maybe in the world."

"You mentioned that house blowing up," said Raider. "What did that have to do with you?"

"Did I say anything about a house blowing up?" He stared at first one, then the other roustabout, then Dolly Dee. The two responded with mystified looks, both shaking their heads. She turned away.

"You say your partner gave up on us after Roswell. He disappoints easily, doesn't he?"

"What else could he do? There was nothing to grab hold of. Nothing either o' us could see."

"You know something, John O'Toole? When you lie, your eyes start up into your head, not much, just enough to give you away. Isn't that so, little girl?"

"What are you going to do with him?" she asked.

"Drop him into the deepest gully we can find. A simple accident. His horse threw him and he broke his neck."

"That's stupid."

"Oh?"

"If he's lying . . ."

"If?"

"Let me finish. Say he is, that means his partner and

Lord knows how many others are hot after us. Him we could use. He's lots more valuable to us alive than dead."

"What would you like me to do, break him in as a ticket taker? Give him Franklin's job? No, little girl, we can't start taking on excess baggage. Hostages we don't need. My guess is his friends are right behind him. Which wipes out Sauer City. Up to now they've got nothing to go on but suspicions. Nothing solid; that much I think he's telling the truth about. I say we quit while we're ahead."

"And go where?"

"Anywhere."

She shook her head. "You kill him, Heinz, and there's no place we can go where we won't be found sooner or later."

"How about Mexico?"

"Do you want to spend the rest of your life down there? I don't."

"Little girl, you go where I say you go."

"You go to hell!" Bristling, her anger surfacing instantaneously, she pivoted and marched out, pushing the two roustabouts aside, passing between them.

The unnamed one with the rifle cocked it and lifted it slowly, grinning down the barrel at Raider.

"Say the word, boss, an' I'll blow his head off."

"Just hold it. Goddamn woman; stubborn as a damned mule." He reflected a moment. Alfred started to say something, but Zemo held up his hand, stopping him. "She may have a point, though, I mean about using him as a hostage, an ace up the sleeve we only pull out if we have to. John O'Toole, answer me this, how'd you like to live?"

"What do you think?"

"Okay. You'll live until your boy shows up. If he doesn't show, we'll figure out something we can do with you. If he does, we'll have us a poker game, with you up my sleeve. If he likes you, if he feels for you, if he's smart, he'll back off and stay backed off. He'll leave us alone. Or he dies and you do, too. Alfred, Jace, you know something? I just had a thought. I believe we should go right ahead with Sauer City."

"Wouldn't that be risky?" asked Alfred.

"Not too. What it would do is bring this boy's friend and anybody he's got with him out into the open. Him I'd recognize as easily as this one. Even disguised. Which he'll be if he's smart."

"What if he's got a whole army with him?" asked Alfred.

"We run. They don't have anything on us, why chase us? What it boils down to is Sauer City. We pick the apple or we pass it up. I say we pick."

Jace emitted a low whistle. "Thet promises a pile o' money, don't it, boss?"

"A fortune. More money than Deming and Albuquerque combined, according to you-know-who. Enough with what we've already got to get us all through the next ten years."

He droned on. Raider listened and reflected; the man was as greedy as they came. Sauer City was too big, too tempting to overlook. His greed was mixed with an equal portion of ego, actually. He'd outfoxed the Secret Service, he'd outfoxed the Pinkertons—at least he believed he had. He'd outfox them a second and last time.

He was on fairly solid ground. If Doc and the others rousted him out *before* he got into circulation, if they were so shortsighted as to attempt to do so, all they'd have to nail him with would be Joe Gilbertson's murder. A smart lawyer might get him off with a couple years, even out from under altogether. And with his money Zemo could afford a very smart lawyer.

Carl Haskell would take an oath that the snakebiter had broken the printer's neck. But he hadn't actually seen him do it. He'd had more sense than to risk being seen witnessing such an act. Haskell appeared to be a fairly brittle individual. A smart defense attorney could cut him into strips on the witness stand.

On the other hand if, as Raider surmised, Doc waited until *after* Zemo got into circulation, enabling him, at least theoretically, to catch everybody in his net, there could be a slip-up. There had been in Roswell.

He speculated as to the whereabouts of the elusive lead plate. At the moment, it was probably down at the bottom of Zemo's trunk, until a second opportunity to take Catterbury presented itself at some future date. The plate was not something the snakebiter would readily dispose of. But if he was true to his word and went ahead with his plans for Sauer City, the chink in his armor, in the armor of the entire scheme would be the sleight-of-hand during the printing. If Doc was as smart as he gave him credit for being, he'd grab the Sauer City lead plate before it got down into the press, into its temporary hiding place. With the plate he'd get the printer. What then? Perhaps alter the plate ever so slightly, straighten one of seventy or eighty swirling lines. An expert would have to do it, of course, but the bank president would be able to help Doc with that.

Once the plate was altered, it would be given back to the printer, who by then would be scared out of his boots. All too eager to cooperate in exchange for a reprimand as against three years behind bars as an accomplice. Once the plate was in Zemo's hands he would see to its being transferred to two copper plates, whereupon *he* would go to press. Hopefully, Doc wouldn't wait until then to close in on him.

Where? The printer would know. If he didn't, Zemo himself could be shadowed, which he had to expect, however. Still, one way or another, Doc would catch him with the goods. Good man, good men with him.

Sure. Only what was all of it to him? What was he doing here trussed up like a Thanksgiving turkey? What had ever possessed him to follow the carnival and climb the hill? Would he ever learn! Was it possible he might stay out of the grave long enough to make some kind of effort in that direction?

He was not completely persuaded that Zemo would buy Dolly Dee's advice to keep him alive. So it was with no little relief that he heard the snakebiter instruct Alfred: "First thing tomorrow take him over to old man Reagan's. He'll keep an eye on him for us. See that he's kept tied."

"You bet, boss. Do you think—"

Raider cut in: "Can I have something to eat?"

"Sure," said Zemo. "Jace, tell one of the women to get something together for him."

"Much obliged."

"You're welcome. Aren't you going to thank me for your life?"

"Oh yeah, that too."

26

Dawn broke gray and misty, the color and condition of Raider's insides as he came awake. It was the aching in his too tightly tied wrists and ankles that opened his eyes. His hands and feet prickled furiously, the circulation all but completely cut off from them.

Alfred double-rode him on his borrowed sorrel about two miles to a farm that, at first sight, appeared deserted. It was not; as they neared it he spied a slender ribbon of smoke issuing from the wooden chimney into the mist hanging wraithlike over the lush farmland. The house was the sorriest-looking apology for human habitation he had ever seen. Old man Reagan, whoever he was, would have done himself well by moving out and into a hole in the ground, before the roof caved in. Most of the windows were shattered, the upper hinge on the front door missing, the front stoop planking and the railing rotted and broken. It was a house that looked as if the first winter wind down from Oklahoma would pick it up and kite it clear to the Gulf.

The grounds around were thick with weeds. The barn appeared ready to collapse, and only the posts of the corral fence were still standing, the fence itself vanished down to the last rail. Most people took care of their property, some neglected it shamefully. A few systematically destroyed it through neglect. Such was the case in this instance, the occupant being too attentive to other matters to care. He was hard at work over a still, mumbling to himself as he tightened the copper worm in place. The sting in the air in the fetid confinement of the room made Raider's eyes water. As, he noted, it did Alfred's. If possible the place was even more disreputable and slovenly-looking inside than out.

The still stood in the fireplace, a simple Georgia copper cooker, its furnace fueled by the last of the corral fence rails, the two ends poking out six feet onto the floor being pushed in as the oppposite ends burned away. A bedrock platform above the firebox prevented the bottom of the still from coming in contact with the fire itself. This was important, as Raider knew; never burn or even scorch your whiskey. All heating took place around the sides of the still, the area, save for the flue, completely enclosed.

A still was not a complicated mechanism, but its construction was tricky. Everything had to fit neatly or it would leak. Smooth, good-quality copper had to be used; sheet iron or valley tin often burned the beer. All the parts were cut from three thirty- by sixty-inch sheets, the still, the condenser walls, the cap, cap arm, slop arm, washers . . . the works.

The still stood cooking away merrily, sending the steam down the cap arm to the worm, twenty feet of copper tubing coiled to a height of two feet standing inside a barrel filled with cold water. In the worm, the steam issuing from the cap arm condensed into liquid. It flowed through the worm out of the lower end, sticking out of the barrel through a tightly sealed hole. From there it dropped into a funnel filled with coals to remove any residue before the alcohol passed down the neck of the funnel into the jug. Dozens of jugs stood about the floor.

Working a still was a demanding job. Not ten minutes passed without something needing tending to, the worm monitored to make sure the drip rate was steady, the firebox fed and stirred, the cooked meal readied and mixed and stirred, the raw rye added, and a good deal more that Raider knew nothing about, necessities and refinements of the art. All these things considered, it was evident that the old man spent a lot of time at his work. To this the condition of his property and his clothes and person testified eloquently.

He wore bib overalls that any self-respecting tramp would have discarded years ago. They badly needed washing, needed soaking in kerosene, needed burning even more. The right shoulder strap had parted, the ends hanging down; the left held securely. He wore no shirt. He had not shaved in weeks, his salt-and-pepper beard running wild over most of his dirty face. His hair, also black and white, hung in a tangle a foot down his back. He reeked of body odor and worse. He stood very close to six feet tall, but could not have weighed more than a hundred pounds with a good-sized sad iron in each pocket. In every respect, he was a disaster disguised as a man, uniquely suited to his immediate surroundings.

"Pop," said Alfred. "This is John O'Toole. He's a bad sort, nothing but trouble. Heinz wants you to look after him. Just for a few days, probably till the end of the week."

"Right you are, soldier!" Reagan drew himself up out of his stoop and saluted smartly, soundlessly clicking his bare heels together.

"Feed him, give him water, treat him kindly. Just don't let him get away." Alfred handed the old man Raider's .45. "Use this on him if you have to. Keep him tied day and night. And keep your eye on him. He's a Pinkerton detective."

"Do tell!"

"In the flesh."

"My my . . ."

That was all of that. Away went Alfred on Raider's horse. Glancing about the room Raider spied an octagon-barreled Hawken with a shiny copper-plated stock hanging over the fireplace. Reagan watched him, one eye closed, the other gleaming like a hawk's spotting a hare.

"That there's Sally. I brung her out from Georgia in forty-four. What was your name again, son?"

"John O'Toole."

By now Raider was getting used to the man's smell and to the acrid air in the room. The mist had turned to rain, plopping down, pocking the dry ground, setting the weeds glistening. Raider began planning. If he could get away, even on foot, he could make the Hubbard Hills to the north, lose himself behind them, steal a horse, and get back to Doc and the others.

No. Why should he? Better he keep heading north, get himself well out of the line of action and stay out. To hell with the satisfaction of seeing Zemo and his people caught, protecting his own hide came far-out-in-front first!

"Where do you find corn in this part o' Texas?" he asked. "I always thought it was cotton, peanuts, and sorghum around here. Far as that goes, nobody grows corn anyplace in Texas."

Reagan winked and grinned. Moving to the kitchen door he pulled it wide. Corn was piled three quarters of the way to the ceiling.

"Mister, iff'n a man's gotta mind to grow hisself corn, he can raise it outta solid rock, up from a wet creek bottom, most anyplace. Corn be hardy stuff, a fair 'mount o' sile, 'nuf water, plenty o' sunshine an' watch them stalks shoot up. Oh, this ain't the best, not by a long shot. 'Tain't pure white like good ol' Holcomb Prolific, which'll give you three full quarts to the bushel. But it does right fine by my taste."

Raider politely declined a sample. "How come you know Zemo?" he asked.

"Heinz? Oh, I knows him 'bout as good as I knows you. Only met him once't. He's close friends with my boy. My boy works with the carnival. All over the West. He likes it. It's not a job a work fer all his life, o' course. He's only doin' it to save money so's he can go to school."

"What does he want to do?"

"Engravin.' You know, drawin' on metal, copper, an' such. Like to see some o' his work? What he teached hisself?"

"Sure."

Reagan got a cigar box out of a table drawer, opening it, revealing two mezzotints, both landscape scenes, simple, but skillfully executed, at least to Raider's uncritical eye.

"Good work. He sure enough has talent."

"You bet. I'm right proud o' my boy Franklin."

"Did you say Franklin?"

"My son, my onliest son. His maw died yars back of

the pee-new-monya. Franklin's all I got in this world; all he's got is me," he added proudly.

"Mr. Reagan, what does Franklin look like?"

"Oh, he's right good-lookin'. Tall, sharp dark eyes . . . like mine."

"Like a hawk."

"That's right."

"What is his job with the carnival?"

"Ever'thin'. Ever'body does ever'thin' with a bunch like that, roustabout, barker, stickin' up han'bills, takin' tickets."

"Franklin." Raider described his face in detail, the face of the man who passed him in to see Semena, Queen of the Nile, the face of the man emerging from the room across the hall from his own in Mrs. Struck's rooming house.

"Tha's my boy, my pride an' joy," said Reagan, beaming. "You know him real good?"

"Mr. Reagan, I hate like hell to have to be the one to tell you, but Franklin, well, I'm afraid he had an accident. He's dead."

The old man's proud smile vanished, his jaw going slack, his eyes rounding.

"Yo'r a liar, 'tain't so! It cain't be . . ."

"I'm afraid it is."

Raider told him what had happened. He picked his words carefully and delivered them in a matter-of-fact tone. Don't sell him, he told himself, just let him judge the facts.

Reagan made his judgment. Lowering himself slowly onto a stool he clapped his hands on his knees, staring straight ahead out the door, his eyes glistening with tears. Then he sneaked one hand under his nose, sniffling.

"You couldn' be mistook?" Raider shook his head. "You wouldn' lie to a ol' man, wouldja? No, of course you wouldn'. Nobody'd be thet heartless."

"Like I told you, it was an accident, but that other boy, the printer gettin' his neck busted, that was Heinz deliberate. He killed him to get that plate. He's a dangerous man, Artis, he's got a vile temper and he's in this business so deep he'll stop at nothin'. When it comes around time I'm no more use to him for a hostage, he'll kill me in two shakes."

"On account he's afeerd yo're gonna kill him."

"No. All he's afraid of is gettin' caught. Look at it this way, your boy got involved in something over his head. I'm not saying it was his fault or wasn't, but he got mixed up and now he's dead. More people are gonna die if somebody doesn't stop that son of a bitch. You, Artis, are the only man alive in a position to pull the plug on him."

"Let you go?" He shook his head. "Oh no, I couldn't do that. That there Alfred or somebody'd come back here an' find you flied the coop they'd bust my skinny neck. For sairtain."

"No, they wouldn't. Not if we make 'em think I overpowered you. You untie me, give me back my gun, I leave. You keep your eyes peeled. When you see any o' them coming, you just lie down on the floor and pretend you're just waking up from being clobbered. They won't waste time with you, they'll accept what they see. They'll light out after me. You'll be off the hook. Hell, Artis, you'll never be on it."

Reagan rubbed his chin thoughtfully. "I don't know. Purely. My brain's too doggone fuddled. All I can think on is my poor boy, poor young innercent."

"That kid printer was even younger, no more than sixteen or seventeen. Green as grass. What kind of son of a bitch goes around bustin' children's necks, you tell me . . . Look, if you really want to make it look good, untie me and I'll tap you on the head. Not hard, just enough to raise a bump; you know, something to show, something . . ."

Raider's glance had wandered to the open door. Out of the sheet of rain a horse and rider materialized.

Alfred.

27

Major Henderson Turnbull was growing increasingly edgy as time in Barstow went on. As was everyone else. Sitting in one of the company's rooms talking, at dinner, at drinking, even down at the stable checking their horses for want of something better to do to kill time, Doc sensed the others' eyes boring into him questioningly.

At six o'clock on the eve of their third night in Barstow he dropped the other shoe. They had assembled on the front porch of the hotel and were aimlessly watching traffic moving up and down the main street.

"Let's pack up and get out of here," Doc said abruptly to Dom DePaolo. "They're bypassing Barstow; they've got to be. Heading straight for Sauer City."

Heads nodded, there was murmured agreement. Turnbull agreed, but at the same time posed a question.

"But as far as that goes, why would they? Is it possible this Zemo may have found out that the bank and office equipment salesman disclosed their itinerary?"

"That I doubt," said Doc, generating all the conviction he could in his tone. "How could he possibly know Haskell was picked up? Besides, if that were the case they'd jettison Sauer City as well as Barstow."

Turnbull frowned. "Who's to say they haven't?"

Doc started to respond, but instead let the question sink in. Then he nodded slowly. "What you mean is their not showing up here doesn't automatically mean they're heading there. I accept that. Which means we've got to make sure. Dom, why don't you and Cy stay behind us. Until, let's make it, tomorrow noon. If they've been delayed or they're merely taking their own sweet time they'll still have to be in by then. The printing's tomorrow."

"That's logical," said Turnbull. "But you still can't be absolutely sure." He was speedily warming to his role of devil's advocate. "Dom and Cy could leave here at noon and the carnival show up an hour later."

"Look," said Doc, "we can deep-think this thing from now until doomsday. But if we did, we'd be playing right into Zemo's hands. I suggest we vote on it. My own feeling is that we have to gamble a little. I say we leave now and ride all night. Dom and Cy, you hang back until tomorrow noon. And catch up with us in Sauer City. Everybody in favor, kindly signify."

The ayes had it. Turnbull shrugged.

"Does anybody have any idea how far to Sauer City?" asked Walter Tyndall.

Nobody did. Raider would know, wherever he was, Doc thought.

They checked with the stableman.

"Close to a hundred miles."

Tyndall whistled and Leon Fanchette sighed heavily. Doc shook his head.

"I hope this doesn't turn into a wild-goose chase," observed Paul Fanchette, suddenly wearied by the prospect of such a ride. "If we get there and have to turn around and come back . . ."

"We can avoid that," said Doc. "We'll send a telegram up to Hobbs. Ask the clerk which direction the carnival took when it left town. Down to here would have to be almost dead south; to Sauer City is southeast. More east than south, even."

"That makes sense," said the major, then covered his face with a dubious look. "*If* they left Hobbs at all."

"What do you mean 'if'?" asked Cy.

"It could be they never went into the town. Remember, Weatherbee, you told us they weren't going to Hobbs to perform, just to replace the material and equipment that had been destroyed when that rooming house blew up. It could be they camped outside Hobbs and sent someone in to do their shopping. In which case . . ."

"We won't know one way or the other until the clerk up there tells us, will we, Major?"

"I expect not."

Doc nodded. "Let's get over to Western Union."

Alfred came tramping in, depositing small puddles on the bare floor, growling, complaining.

"This place stinks even more in the rain than dry," he muttered. "If that's possible."

Reagan shrugged. "What you doin' back here?"

"Never mind. *I* got to watch him." Divesting himself of his poncho, he flung it into a corner. Pulling a chair up to a solid oak table, he sat, mopping his face with his bandana.

"Get out them playin' cards o' yours, why don'tcha?"

The old man produced a worn deck of Dougherty's Climax playing cards. Raider sat with his back to the open door watching the two of them.

"Old man," said Alfred, "give me back his gun." Reagan did so. "I wouldn't want you to hurt yourself with it."

"What the hell you talkin' about? I can handle me any gun made."

"Sure. O'Toole, you play poker?"

"Sure."

"Good. Anything to kill time around this stinkin' dump. I'm gonna free your hands. I'm gonna tie your legs and chest to that chair you're sitting on. You try anything funny you're dead, got it?" Raider nodded. Alfred handed the .45 back to the old man a second time. "Cover him while I truss him up. Stand back, gimme room."

Alfred untied Raider's wrists, sat him down in his own chair and, securing additional rope from the old man, bound the Pinkerton to the chair, ankles and chest under his arms. This accomplished, he sat down opposite him.

"Got any money?" he asked.

"A couple bucks."

"Shit. To hell with it, we can play for matches. Anything to pass the time, eh?"

"How much time we got to pass?"

"Till Jace shows up."

"What happens then?"

Alfred smiled. "You'll see. High card deals. Stud, okay?"

"Whatever you like." Reagen fetched a box of Red Top Safety matches, obligingly counting out thirty five to each man.

"Can I play, too?" he asked in a pleading tone.

"Why not?"

Reagan counted out his supply and pulled a chair up to the end of the table, a jubilant smile stretching his unwashed features.

Raider glanced at the open door. Alfred had tethered the sorrel to the gate post. It stood patiently, blanket and saddle in place, the rain spattering its flanks. Alfred dealt, the cards coming to rest in turn in front of each man. Raider played with little attention to the game, now and again casting a furtive eye toward his captor, who quickly became deeply engrossed. A serious card player, decided Raider and, as it turned out, a poor one, as well as a sore loser.

"JESUS!" Alfred slammed his hand down. "Kings and queens and the son of a bitch comes up with three stinking treys!"

"Beginner's luck," said Reagan, chortling.

"Just shut up and deal."

Raider turned the situation over and over, studying every facet, every possible result of any action he might take. With his hands free, he could handle Alfred, although he would have to knock him out first shot; there was no way, chair-bound as he was, he could slug with him. The problem was the old man; he still had the .45, returned to him and since shoved into a tool loop in the side of his overalls. He, Raider, couldn't reach the gun, nor could he edge his chair closer to the right-hand corner of the table to permit him to. Not without raising Alfred's suspicions. The longer he examined his plight, the clearer it became that he would have to knock both out, free himself, grab his gun from Reagan, his belt and holster from Alfred, and get out.

"Wake up, will you?" snapped Alfred irritably.

"Deal." He was down to five matches and reaching into the box to replenish his supply. A fourth-rate poker player if Raider ever saw one, impulsive, thoughtless, inexperienced; three "virtues" no serious player had the slightest acquaintance with.

Raider shuffled and dealt one down, one up, dealing himself the ten of spades, Reagan to his right the jack.

"Open for five," said the old man happily.

"You can't, goddamnit!" snapped Alfred. "Three's the limit, pay attention, can't you?"

"He's right, Artis," said Raider.

Alfred lowered his face, snapping his hole card up with his thumbnail, reading and rereading it in annoyance. He hadn't been doing well, he was not about to do any better. The pot was fed, made right. Raider dealt Alfred a second up card, the deuce of spades to go with his seven of diamonds.

"Son of a bitch!"

The deck in his right, Raider lowered his left as far as he could, tensing, bringing it up, driving it full into the man's face, at the same time dropping the deck, reaching down the table with his right, pulling up the end, slamming Reagen with it, dumping him over backwards.

Alfred had collapsed in the still, toppling it and the barrel, sending moonshine sloshing about. Raider strained both hands to reach the knot at the back of his chair, but could not. Cursing, he threw himself, chair and all, sideways, slamming against the underside of the table, shattering the back and very nearly his shoulder, freeing his chest bonds. Quickly he began untying his ankles, his fingers working feverishly. Alfred was groaning, moving feebly in among the wreckage of the still. Reagan, panting like a drowning man, was struggling to extricate himself from under the table. Raider snatched his belt from around Alfred's waist, retrieved the .45 from where it had landed on the floor, and, strapping on and holstering the gun, slammed his hat on and ran out the door.

Sloshing through the quagmire he got to the horse, untied it, and threw himself up on its back. Over the hammering of the storm he could hear activity back inside the house and, wheeling about, was starting off when a loud outcry turned his attention back to the doorway.

"HOLD IT, YOU SON OF A BITCH!"

There stood Alfred, holding the Hawken pointed straight at him, the old man behind him, peering over his shoulder. Raider groaned inwardly and, doubling over, heeled the horse as hard as he could, starting off, turning and sneaking a second look back.

Alfred fired. The rifle blew, a crimson explosion filling the upper half of the doorway, ripping his face from his head, dropping the two of them where they stood.

"Jesus!" Swallowing fit to crack his windpipe, Raider reined up hard, coming to a halt in a splatter of mud, turning in his saddle for a good look.

Alfred lay in the mud; behind him Reagen was struggling to his feet, badly shaken, but apparently unhurt. Raider hesitated. Alfred was dead; should he go back and see to the old man?

No need, he was back up on his feet, a little dazed-looking but able to function, leaning over Alfred, examining him, shaking his head.

Raider sighed and resumed riding, heading down the narrow road, moving at an easy gait, sparing the horse. The storm was beginning to let up, the sky brightening overhead.

He headed toward the Hubbard Hills, an area he was familiar with, having taken part in a shootout there two years earlier. Hidden cuts, caves, and natural fortresses afforded excellent protection were anyone to pick up his trail. A glance behind him assured him nobody had. In the hills he could rest the horse and himself until nightfall, then set out for wherever he pleased. Any place that would separate him from the action to come.

He closed his eyes and saw again the blinding flash, the Hawken exploding. What a way to die. Hang it proudly, Artis, just don't bother to rod it out. It didn't surprise him. If a man couldn't be bothered washing his face or his feet, like as not he wouldn't trouble himself to clean a rifle that served him as an object of admiration only. Nearly five feet of lethal wallop relegated to dredging up recollections of better days.

Ahead loomed the Hubbard Hills, green and glistening in the still-bright light of day, restored to the heavens with the departure of the storm. Two miles and he would be up among them. Pulling up, he surveyed the scene and·at once heard hoofbeats off to his right. A lone rider was coming up fast, threatening to cut him off. He went for the .45, but the onrushing stranger already had his own iron out and was firing.

Raider booted his horse, lowering his profile. Closer and closer came the hills, and the man shooting up on his right. A slug whined by Raider's head, another crossed an inch above his shoulderblades. He returned both. A third and fourth missed him by a wide margin. And a fifth.

The sixth struck the sorrel full in the rump, tumbling it in a pile, tossing its rider ten feet ahead of it, thumping to rest in the mud. Rolling over, scrambling toward the fallen horse to crouch low behind it, he got off two wild shots, getting two in return, the fall and his landing giving his attacker time to reload.

Now he was up to the fallen horse, dropping his forearm against its motionless flank, steadying his hand to aim, when a third shot slammed into the .45, knocking it out of his grip. The man came barreling up, waving his gun, grinning, yelling:

"Give it up, Pink!"

Jace.

28

Miles Atwood, president, guiding hand and grand panjandrum of the Sauer City People's Bank, bore not the slightest physical resemblance to Horace F. Catterbury. Where Catterbury was small and thin—wasted-looking—Atwood was one hundred pounds overweight, most of it equally divided between his belly and his neck, in which his chins were buried. He was taller, wider, louder, and healthier-looking than Catterbury as well. But to hear Atwood speak, the nasal twang issuing from his face, the extraordinary self-confidence of the man, Doc, lowering his head and closing his eyes briefly, would swear that he was listening to Catterbury.

"Let them come, gentlemen!" boomed Atwood to Doc and the major, sitting in his office, each clasping a dusty glass of Tinker's Rye. "They can sit by and twiddle their thumbs for all I care. I have no intention of going to press. I'll wait them out if it takes the rest of the year!"

"Mr. Atwood," interposed Turnbull. "The only way we can trap this bunch is by proceeding as planned."

"No, thank you! Gentlemen, I have my depositors to think of. You can scarcely expect me to jeopardize their savings, open my door to a flood of counterfeit notes . . ."

On and on he declaimed; shades of Catterbury, reflected Doc. He was tired, his rear end was sore from the long night ride. Tired, sore, hungry, discouraged, unhappy with life in general, with Miles Atwood in particular. The man was proving as stubborn as Raider, by far the stubbornest human he, Doc, had ever encountered.

Where, he wondered, had Rade gotten to? Was he

still in Texas? Had he headed north? He was partial to the Dakotas, to Fargo and the surrounding area.

Turnbull was not so easily discouraged. He continued working on Atwood, cleverly stroking the man's ego, inflating it.

"You'd be the man of the hour, center stage. A bonafide hero to every banker in the West. And there'd be no risk, absolutely none."

Atwood dismissed this with both hands. Doc didn't like hearing such flat-out assurance, but he refrained from commenting. Stretching things a bit there really wasn't any risk, now that they knew that a lead plate would be slipped into the press. At the printing they could collar the printer the instant he lifted it out, then back him into a corner and bully him into cooperating.

Atwood showed signs of wavering, a nod, a brightening of the eye. Doc let Turnbull move in for the kill. In his most persuasive tone, the major pointed out the advantages of working with them. Atwood listened and pondered and tapped his empty glass on the edge of his desk. He was moved to the brink, but suddenly he pulled back.

"No. I can't. It's out of the question. You say there's no risk? Nonsense, of course there is. Even a little is too much. No, I'm sorry, gentlemen, count me out."

Turnbull lifted his hands slowly in capitulation.

"As a matter of fact," the banker went on, "you two have put the fear of Almighty God in me. I'm getting those plates out of here tonight. What am I saying? Right now!"

"Mr. Atwood . . ." began Doc, "that would be very unwise."

"Nonsense, I have the perfect hiding place."

"Better than your vault?" asked Turnbull, mystified.

"Much better." Atwood stood up and, coming around his desk, opened his door partway. He winked slyly. "On second thought, I'll take only one out. Either one is worthless without the other. If I keep them separate, one in the vault, one elsewhere . . ." He waved a finger high victoriously. "Problem solved! Hazel, will you come in here a minute, please?"

Moving to the bookcase behind his desk he picked up a toy steam engine set between Harrison's *Principles of Banking* and Mulcahy and Strom's *History of the Bank of England*. Removing the plug from the engine's boiler, he brought out a small key. Hazel appeared in the doorway, bringing with her a whiff of jasmine, a quizzical expression on her pretty face, a casual glance at Doc, one considerably less casual at Turnbull.

"Hazel, go into the vault and get me the five-dollar plates, please."

"Yes, sir."

She was back moments later, moments occupied by Atwood with working up a paragraph or two designed to lock all blame for any mishaps firmly onto the collective shoulders of the Pinkertons. The plates were wrapped in blue velvet. She set them on the blotter in front of the banker and handed him the key.

"Thank you, my dear."

Turnbull and Doc locked eyes briefly. The girl withdrew, her taffeta skirt rustling. She closed the door. Restoring the key to the steam engine, Atwood set it to one side and, shooting his cuffs in the manner of a riverboat three-card-monte professional, seized the corners of the cloth and unfolded it deftly.

Horror gripped his face. A gurgling noise climbed up his throat and out his gaping mouth.

"Great Caesar's ghost!" he exclaimed in the voice of one confronted by the Angel of Death.

Two metal plates were revealed—both blank.

Doc's brain spun like a runaway wheel. Leave it to Zemo! It wasn't to be the printer this time. No need. He already had his man, *inside* the bank, bought and paid for. Or about to be. No need for any lead plate, either; the real thing would do nicely, thank you. Atwood sat dumbstruck, his fat face threatening to slip from his head altogether, his pink mouth working wordlessly. The major had risen from his chair and was moving to him, gripping the banker's forearm, placing his other arm around his shoulders. As if, mused Doc, to prevent his toppling over face first in a dead faint.

"My God, my God, my God . . ." whispered Atwood hoarsely. "I don't believe it."

"Calm yourself, Mr. Atwood," said Turnbull. "It's all right; we'll take care of this. We'll find them. They're still in town, they have to be. We can—"

"Mr. Atwood," interrupted Doc. "Obviously somebody in your employ has stolen them. We're going to have to question everyone. There's no point in wasting time, you may as well start marching them in."

"Yes, yes, of course. Everybody's here except . . ." The major and Doc leaned forward. "Orville . . . Orville Casey."

"Who and where is Orville Casey?" asked Doc.

"He was one of my cashiers."

"Was?"

"He quit his job last week."

"Excellent!" burst out Turnbull. "He's our man."

"Probably," said Doc.

"Definitely," said the major.

"It can't be. I'd trust him with my life." Atwood was beginning to tremble, his cheeks whitening perceptibly. "He was with me for seven years. He sat right where you are." He pointed at Doc. "Told me he had to quit, had to go home, down to Corpus Christi. His mother's taken quite ill; there's nobody else to take care of her. Orville's always been very fond of his mother. He writes to her regularly. I can't believe he stole my plates . . ."

"We'll see," said Doc.

"When exactly did he quit?" asked Turnbull.

"Let me see . . . last Friday. He's got to be long gone by now. He told me he was leaving right away."

"I doubt he's left," said Doc. "My guess is he's hiding out until he can collect his share." He didn't believe a word; he only hoped that Atwood might.

"You realize what this means?" sputtered the fat man.

Doc nodded. "At this very moment they could be printing up your banknotes. By tonight they could be papering the county with them; at least starting to."

The life seemed to seep out of the banker, his shoulders sagging. His whitened cheeks were rapidly turning gray, ashen. He resembled a man who had been struck from behind by the flat of a two-headed axe and was about to collapse.

"Mr. Atwood," said Doc. "There appears to be nothing to be gained by questioning your employees. Not at the moment, at any rate."

"I say we call in the law. Between Fred LaFarge and his men and you and yours you can turn this town upside down, find Orville, and get those plates back!"

Turnbull shook his head. "I'm sorry to say I don't think he still has your plates."

"Mr. Turnbull is right," said Doc. "There's no reason for him to hang onto them. The carnival's due in. I would imagine he's ridden out to meet Zemo to hand them over."

Turnbull nodded. "They're a little hot for Orville to be handling." He stood up. "Mr. Atwood, getting all worked up over this business won't help any."

"We have the rest of the day," said Doc. "We know it's the carnival people. The minute they show up, we'll round them up."

"And what if they don't show up? Why should they bother if they already have my plates? Why? You tell me!"

Doc had no answer for that. Nor did Turnbull. The best either could do was attempt to reassure the man.

In this they failed completely.

29

Sauer City was a three-going-on-four-church town, beter than twice the size of Roswell, large enough to absorb Barstow, attach it to one end or the other with little perceptible change in its overall arrangement of buildings. It formed the hub of a thriving area devoted to general farming, livestock, and cash grain, a prosperous place and a natural magnet to settlers crossing the Mississippi River, Arkansas, and Louisiana in quest of a better life.

It was a town ripe for the plucking; Atwood's five-dollar banknote plates stolen and put to work could turn out twenty thousand in unauthorized currency in three hours. The necessary signatures could be forged and the money thrust into circulation, bringing to the "pluckers" gold and silver in abundance, and all but bringing down the Sauer City People's Bank with a thud that would be heard from one end of central Texas to the other.

For all his bombast, his mulishness and self-serving posture, Miles Atwood was intelligent. And a thoroughly knowledgeable banking man. He had to be; he was a success and had been since the granting of his bank's charter nineteen years earlier. He was also, suddenly, a very frightened individual. His concern was well founded, completely helpless as he was to deal with the swindle threatening him. He could not call in his banknotes already circulating; many had been held in reserve and only recently put into service. They looked brand-new and they were. How was he or anyone in his employ to differentiate between his notes and Zemo's? By the signatures? Hardly a foolproof method. No method at all actually. And so it was that Atwood found himself in the position of the fisherman in the leaking boat in the middle of a vast sea. Uncertain as to precisely *when* his boat would sink and take him to his doom, but entirely persuaded that it would.

To Doc's and Turnbull's surprise, the banker was to prove something of a prophet. His suggestion that the carnival might not even arrive in Sauer City appeared more and more valid as the day wore on. There was no sign of so much as a single wagon, its bonnet artistically proclaiming Colonel Hardy's pride, an exotic animal, or a spangled performer.

The seven Pinkertons had gathered in the Muskrat, a somewhat dingy-looking watering hole up the street and around the corner from the bank, there to discuss the latest turn in the case. Doc and Turnbull had left Miles Atwood in a state of near collapse, with Hazel summoned a second time standing over him fanning him with the contents of his outgoing box.

"I only hope he doesn't do something hare-brained," said the major morosely, fondling a beaker of Paulsen's Beer, early lunch in a glass. "Like close his doors."

"That wouldn't affect Zemo," observed Doc. "All it would do is cause a run on Atwood's cages when he reopens, which eventually he'll have to do." He shook his head. "You have to hand it to that snake-biter; he's really hit on a way to hamstring a bank. Nothing as crude and laborious as turning fives into fifties or duplicating tens with counterfeits filled with misspellings and smeared swirls. No, he either duplicates your plates or pilfers them. Then marches into action and destroys you."

"We've got this Orville Casey's description to a tee," said Walter Tyndall. "Why don't we break up and comb the town?"

"A waste of boot leather," said Doc. Turnbull nodded. "Only a lunatic would stick around. My guess is he's off someplace hooking up with Zemo. Zemo's already collected a fortune; he could buy those plates for a flat fee."

"That's the deal I'd make," said Domenic.

Doc pounded the table, jiggling the contents of several glasses and the half-filled bottle of Taos Lightning sitting in the center. "We've got to find the carnival. Spread out in an ever-widening circle around this town and hunt and hunt and hunt! We know they came from Hobbs to the northwest. It would make sense to concentrate on that slice of the compass. If we get lucky and locate them, we'll take them then and there. I for one am fed up with playing this thing cleverly."

"All well and good," said Turnbull. "But if we do take them we'd better hope we find the lead plate from Roswell, Atwood's plates, that cigar box full of fives you and the plowboy spotted back in Albuquerque, something. Something incriminating." Elevating his glass of beer he sent half the contents down his throat. "I've been thinking, charging Zemo with that printer's murder is fine, but if the salesman lets us down in the witness chair . . . I don't know, Weatherbee, I just wish we could catch the lot red-handed."

"We're not going to in here." Doc pushed his chair back, tapping his derby tighter on his head. "Let's start looking."

Raider sat on the floor, his back against the wall, a twenty-inch stick passed over the crooks of his arms, locking them behind him, his wrists and ankles tightly bound. His right hand was sore where Jace had knocked the .45 free of his grip. Jace had brought him from the scene of the action over unfamiliar interconnected roads to this house, a solidly built three-story clapboard dwelling located like Artis Reagan's dilapidated home out in the middle of the back of beyond.

The room was about fifteen feet square, with a long table set against one wall where two forgers sat hard at working plying their nefarious talent, preparing five-dollar banknotes of the Sauer City People's Bank for distribution. They sat with their backs to Raider, bent over, scrawling the same two names over and over under the light of two Nile-green shaded banquet lamps set equidistant apart. They worked slowly, laboriously, in silence, tilting their heads one way, then the other, examining their handiwork, blowing the signatures dry, adding each note to the growing stacks left and right of them. Off in one corner sat a Merry Sunshine Heater sending forth warmth to dispel the dampness left in the air by the storm. Pictures adorned the walls, landscapes mounted in four-inch frames finished in ivory enamel with tinted edges and gold-tipped ornaments, and a wooden-framed portrait of an elderly sort sporting fierce-looking mustaches and sideburns. A mohair rug too small for the floor occupied its center and a rocking chair sat by the heater. A tranquil, cozy scene to anyone entering the room. To Raider not unlikely the last scene his eyes would ever behold.

The door creaked, opened, and Zemo came back into the room. Ignoring his prisoner, he stood behind each of his forgers in turn, examining their efforts, nodding approval, pulling out his watch and announcing that it was getting on to seven o'clock.

It was going to be a long night, mused Raider wearily. Would he ever see the sunrise, he wondered. Zemo came over to him and, crouching, leered.

"Mr. John O'Toole, I think you're entitled to know that this whole picture has changed. I bought the idea of hanging on to you, keeping you alive to use as a hostage, if the need ever cropped up. Now, whatever crops up, you're not going to be any hostage. No sir, now you're a dead man."

Dolly Dee appeared in the doorway, her hands against the frame as she leaned in, catching the last sentence and frowning.

"I'm going to watch you die. Slowly, Mr. John O'Toole, very slowly, painfully. I didn't like you back in Albuquerque, I liked you even less back where we camped. Now, after what you caused to happen to poor Alfred, I hate you worse than the Lord hated Esau."

"You gonna quote me scripture, Heinz?"

Zemo stiffened and scowled at mention of his Christian name.

"That's your name, isn't it? Oh, we know all about you, friend, all about St. Louis, your four years inside, that killing back in Roswell." A grimace tightened his face. "Did you have to break the poor bastard's neck?"

"You're not helping yourself any, Mr. Wisemouth."

Raider laughed brittlely. "What have I got to lose?"

"Maybe for starters, every tooth in your head!"

Zemo made a fist the size of a twelve-pound stone axe and drew it back well behind his right ear.

"Don't do it, Heinz," said Dolly Dee icily behind him.

Zemo turned. "Are you trying to tell me what to do again, little girl?"

"Don't be stupid. Whatever he's done he's still worth more to you in one big piece than a lot of little ones."

"So you keep saying." Zemo stood up; Raider sighed inside. The snakebiter crossed to the door, seizing her by the elbow, steering her outside, and closing the door.

It was the second time she had saved his hide in less than forty eight hours. For humanitarian reasons? Or because she'd developed a fondness for him? *Why* wasn't important, what mattered was that she had.

All the same, there'd be no stopping Zemo when the job was wrapped up and he could turn his full attention on Mr. John O'Toole. How did things stand at the moment? Doc and Turnbull and the others had to have reached Sauer City by this time. Though what good that would do him looked to be none whatsoever. This house could be two miles from town or twenty; coming to it with Jace he had lost all sense of direction. Doc and the rest would no doubt be out looking for the carnival; they'd have the job of their lives finding it. If Zemo were smart, and he had yet to prove himself anything but, he'd have long since sent the members of his troupe off in sixteen different directions, keeping a skeleton staff on tap, his forgers, a handful of passers, guns, enough people to get the finished product out to the others scattered all over central Texas.

The only way Doc would locate this house would be to go from door to door in a widening circle. A four-year job, at least. In addition to which, the place had to be an armed camp; any attack would be greeted by all the lead Zemo had to throw. The Pinkertons would need local assistance; a posse fifty strong would do nicely.

Unfortunately, as matters looked even under the most favorable light, it would never come to a showdown. How could it? By morning Zemo would be in business; in two days Sauer City and the surrounding area would be flooded with his banknotes. Gold and silver would pour into his trunk until the cow dried up. At which time Colonel J. P. B. Hardy's World's Greatest Carnival would fade into the landscape like the mists of morning.

Leaving him face down dead under a pile of cowshit in some sodbuster's backyard. What a way to leave! What an ignominious closeout to his illustrious career! If anybody ever found his body it would be the sort of demise that Turnbull and every other Pinkerton would tell about with smiles on their faces. Dead in a pile of shit, that was Raider.

Everybody but Doc. He wouldn't think it funny; he'd kick himself the rest of his days for failing to show up in time to save him.

As if he could . . .

The seconds of his life ticked soundlessly away. The two forgers, continuing to act as if he wasn't even in the room, finished their work, putting their pens down one after the other, stretching, relaxing, the taller, darker of the two rubbing his eyes. Both turned off their lamps, pushed back their chairs, squared their stacks of banknotes, and went out the door with them.

The house stood in silence, save for the occasional clomping of heavy feet across the floor above. Now and then a door would close, or voices could be heard, faintly, muffled. The day was dying, the lowering sun sending broad, almost horizontal shadows across the floor through the two windows beyond the corner occupied by the heater. Raider tugged at his bonds; it was useless. A full-grown bear couldn't have broken free. He watched the shadows level and the window glass darken.

Presently a horse came galloping up, the front door opened and closed; voices, anger, shouting. Zemo. He'd been told something that apparently upset him. Within seconds he began carrying on like a man who had taken leave of his senses. Then gradually he simmered down, moving with whoever had brought him the bad news to a room out of range of Raider's hearing.

Steps, a light tread. The door opened. It was Dolly Dee. She came in, quietly closing the door behind her, her forefinger going to her lips, signaling silence. In her other hand she carried a tin plate heaped with beans, steaming, delicious-looking, a fork half buried in them. She came to him, kneeling.

"Take this," she whispered, glancing anxiously over her shoulder back at the closed door.

It was a white bone-handled penknife less than three inches long.

"Thanks," he said, his voice tinged with surprise. "You don't happen to have a gun, do you?"

"I'll find one."

"You're something else, you know that?"

"What do you mean?" She began feeding him the beans. He answered with his mouth full. They were hot but tasty going down, cooked just right.

"I mean you. You sucker me into this mess, now you turn around and try to help me get out."

"Try is right."

"How come?"

She sighed. "Him." She nodded toward the door. "Money is one thing, count me in anytime there's a chance to make some fast and easy. But killing is something else."

"Who's the latest victim?"

"What's the difference? I . . . well, I like you, John. I'd hate to see you hurt . . . badly."

"Like my neck broken. I appreciate your concern. I do. What was all the to-do about?"

She grinned, then made a face she would have made if she'd been a little girl caught with her fingers in the jam jar.

"There's been a terrible mess-up. You know those two who were in here forging the names on the banknotes? Well, they made a mistake; it seems they were copying the names from a wrong real note."

"Wrong?"

"Counterfeit."

"You're kidding!"

"Sssssh. It's crazy, but one of the men gave them one of the Sauer City bank's notes to use as a model. Only it was a fake. Whoever forged the president's and cashier's names used a pen point with a real stubby point. It turns out the real names are done with a very fine point, extra fine. Much finer than any other bank's."

"So all that work those two did turns out to be for nothing."

She nodded. "He's throwing away every note, printing up all new ones. They got to start all over with the right pen points. He's furious."

"I heard. How much more time will it take?"

She shrugged. "Plenty. They'll be back in here working most of the night, I shouldn't wonder. Starting in soon as the printing's done. It was terrible, I thought he was going to strangle Ben."

"Ben?"

"Watters; he came back from . . . well, he was the one came and told him."

She was nearly done feeding him, scraping the beans that were left to one side of the plate to make one last forkful. Out of the stillness came the sound of hoofbeats approaching the front door.

"Now who can that be?" she asked.

"Sounds heavy for a horse. Could be a mule."

The front door opened. A heavy tread up the steps, across the stoop, and into the hall. Now two people, coming closer, down the hallway outside.

Voices became audible. "You got no business coming here!" snapped Zemo.

"I plumb had to."

Artis Reagan.

"Well, what do you want? Spit it out, then get out and stay out. Stay away, go back to that dump and stay there until the day after tomorrow. We'll have cleared out by then."

"It's 'bout my boy Franklin."

The irritability went out of Zemo's voice, his tone becoming suspicious, worried. "What about him?"

"I hear tell he's been kilt."

"Who says?"

"Don' matter who. I jest wants ter know iff'n it's so."

"It's bullshit, pure and simple."

"Is that the truth? Cross your heart hope to die?"

"Artis, would I lie to you?"

"Then where is he? Here? I wants to see him."

"He's gone. He's working over by Holcomb."

"He's all ri', he ain't hurt none."

"He's fine, why shouldn't he be?"

"I hear tell they was a explosion, a accident, and he was kilt. I been worried plumb outta my haid. I shore am relieve ta hear nothin's happened. Maybe I'll jest mosey on o'er ter Holcomb and look him up. 'Tain't fur, on'y a hour er so . . ."

"No, wait . . . Okay, okay, there was an accident."

"Oh dear God!"

"Now don't go getting all unraveled. Look, I'll tell you all about it, but not now. You caught me at a very bad time. Go back to your place. The day after tomorrow I promise I'll drop by and . . ."

"Did you kill mah boy?"

"Are you crazy? Why in hell would I do a thing like that? You're upset, You're not thinking straight . . ."

Reagan was crying now, sobbing loudly. Raider and the girl stared at each other transfixed. Zemo was no longer getting through to the old man. Losing his temper, he bodied him down the hallway and out the door, slamming and locking it. Outside Reagan continued to carry on, wailing pitifully. A full two minutes elapsed before he stopped pounding on the door, got on his mule, and rode away.

Zemo meanwhile had gone upstairs. Soon a steady thumping sound could be heard overhead. The press.

Dolly Dee stood up. "I'll get you a gun. Get away fast as you can; you'll find a horse in the barn."

"What about you?"

"Don't worry about me, I can take care of myself. Always have."

She went out. The press continued thumping monotonously. She came back shortly, carrying a two-shot derringer. Christ, he thought, a riverboat gambler's pop-gun.

"Don't look so disappointed," she said. "It's better than nothing, isn't it?"

"DOLLY!"

She stiffened, recovered, and began thrusting the weapon inside Raider's shirt. She never made it. The door flew open. Red-faced and raging, Zemo came pounding in.

"WHAT THE HELL . . . GODDAMN SON OF A BITCH, I TURN MY BACK ON YOU TWO SEC-ONDS . . . GIVE ME THAT!" Wrenching the derringer from her, he hurled it through the window, the glass shattering loudly. "BITCH!"

She was petrified with fear, the color drained from her cheeks, her eyes enormous, her lower lip quivering. Raider watched aghast, unable to believe what he was seeing. Grabbing her by the hair, Zemo jerked her to her feet, then, without another sound. without a moment's hesitation, threw his left arm around her head and snapped her neck like a twig.

The sound was sickening. She went limp as rags, sinking to her knees, her head lolling to one side. But she did not fall over; he picked her up before she could do so, holding her on the point of his hip, like a sack of meal, arms and legs hanging down loosely. Scowling fiercely at Raider, cursing, he stalked out .

30

There was no direct train line connecting Barstow and Sauer City. The Texas and Pacific reached Barstow from Van Horn, but beyond Barstow veered northeast for Odessa, rather than east for Sauer City and points close by. Corpus Christi, Orville Casey's presumed destination, presented a similar problem. It was situated more than two hundred and fifty miles south of Sauer City. It would take Casey a full week to cover the distance on horseback. Doc had more or less determined that the cashier was in the process of doing just that, that he had handed over Atwood's plates, gotten payment, and was on his way.

The Pinkertons had ended the day exhausted following a futile search for the carnival, assisted by Sheriff LaFarge and nine deputies. Doc and the others now sat at dinner in the Bluebonnet Café in a secluded corner, grumbling discontentedly over their steaks, washing down sinew and gristle and fat with bitter coffee, and generally disporting themselves like the vanquished survivors of a distinctly one-sided battle.

"The man's got to be a damned fool," remarked Walter Tyndall, dexterously separating the meat that was left him around an unusually possessive T-bone. "Atwood tells you his mother is down in Corpus Christi, he's close as skin to her, and he makes no bones about heading down there. Stupid!"

"On second thought, it seems to me he took pains to lay it on fairly thick," said Doc. "Too thick. He could be heading for Mexico, for Oklahoma . . ."

"He still represents our last hope," murmured Turnbull. The major, noted Doc, had become uncharacteristically subdued, as if he were accepting defeat. It was unlike the man, to be sure, but hardly an impractical posture in the face of things. "No hope at all, if you ask me."

"I wish we knew a little bit more about Mr. Casey," said Dominic.

"Amen," said Doc.

It was a wish that was to be granted within the minute, a favor on the part of the fates who had massed such a massive offensive against them. The front door opened and in walked Miles Atwood. He looked frightful, as if he had died, been interred and dug up to wander about in a daze. Bewildered, crushed, utterly defeated. Spying Doc and Turnbull he waved feebly and came toward them.

Both rose to greet him, shaking hands, the major introducing him to the others at the table.

"I've been looking all over for you," said the banker. "It dawned on me leaving the bank late this afternoon. Orville Casey has a ladyfriend; he never mentioned her, not to me, not to anyone so far as I know. All he talked about in the way of a relationship was his mother. But I happened to see a letter from the lady about three months ago and when one of our other cashiers made fun of Orville about it—it, well, it, the envelope smelled of lilac—Orville got as red as a beet."

Doc and Turnbull leaned toward Atwood, the major licking his lips in anticipation.

"Did you happen to see her name?" he asked.

"Priscilla Swanson. From Colbyville."

"Where's that?" asked Doc.

"About forty miles from here, north. A little corner of a town, no more than thirty people. The thing is, I don't believe Orville knows any of us spotted her name and the return address."

"And you think he may have headed there," said Cy Schwartz.

"Who knows? If all that talk about his mother's illness and all his anxiety was so much hokum . . . Mister, I'd give my right arm to find him, the double-dealing scoundrel. After all I did for him over the years, reputable position, good salary. I can't imagine what got into him . . ."

"Money, Mr. Atwood," said Turnbull. "It 'gets into' a lot of people. Good people, responsible, reliable people."

Atwood nodded. "The root of all evil."

"I'm glad you told us," said Doc.

"Do you think it might help?"

"We'll see."

"What will you do?"

Doc broke his eyes away from the banker's, which had been riveted on him appealingly.

"Mr. Atwood, it boils down to a string of 'ifs.' If he's headed there he probably won't stay long, not with his pockets full of money. But if we move fast, maybe we can catch up with him before he gets too far. We'll telegraph the sheriff, tell him as much as he needs to know, in confidence, and request he arrest Orville and hold him. If he gets him behind bars we can ask him the necessary questions via telegram, to save time. If he knows where Zemo and his people are, he'll no doubt tell us. The man is an amateur; he's gotten in well over his head. Once he's apprehended and he sees everything's lost he should welcome a helping hand up and out of his trouble. If. If, if, if . . . what I'm saying is none of us should get his hopes up."

"Or down," added Turnbull.

Atwood beamed. "Yes. Of course. Thank you, gentlemen. Thank you both. Thank you all. Good evening." Doffing his hat, he wheeled about and fled the Bluebonnet.

31

Raider sat leaning against the wall in shock. It hadn't happened. Seven seconds; snap and she was dead.

Upstairs the press stopped its thumping; the run was finished. The two forgers would be coming back in, the two lamps relit, the work of duplicating the banknote signatures resumed. Copying an authentic note this time. He felt the penknife in his fist; working it into position, opening it, cutting himself free wouldn't be hard. Just as long as he was careful not to drop the knife. With the stick thrust in front of his biceps he'd have a devil of a time trying to retrieve it.

The question was *when* to get out? At the moment time looked to be discouragingly short. It might make sense to stick it out for another two or three hours, for as long as it took the two to finish their forging and leave him alone. The only trouble with that was it brought the whole crew that much closer to distributing the completed product to their passers.

His decision was made for him; the two men came in carrying stacks of banknotes, grumbling in low tones, disgruntled looks furrowing their faces. Taking their places they lit their lamps, changed their pen points, consulted the authentic note under a six-inch magnifying glass and, dipping into their inkwells, went to work.

The door opened a second time. In came Jace grinning his stupid grin, swaggering like the town bully.

"Hi-yah, Snoop."

"Beat it, you bastard. You got some gall, gunnin' down my horse like you did. That's the lowest o' the low . . ."

"Stopped you, though, didn't I? I just dropped in to tell you what we're fixin' to do with you. We're gonna run you up the stairs to this lil' ol' room on the top floor, strip you down nekkid, tie you back up agin an' close the door. Only 'afore we closes it we'll be dumpin' a sack in thar with you. You recollect thet thar sack you seen me luggin' the night Alfred an' me surprised you up on the hill? Thet thar's a snake sack. With six foot o' rattler in it. Hungry, mean, jus' dyin' to get his fangs inta somebody." His grin broadened. "Inta you. He cain't hardly miss a spot iff'n you ain't wearin' nawthin' but rope, ain't thet so?"

"You bastards got to have your fun, don't you? Some buncha crackbrains."

"We shor 'nuff is gonna have our fun; we'll be a'standin' in the doorway watchin'. You'll be watchin' too, Snoop."

"That snake bites me it'll die in ten seconds," said Raider.

One of the forgers laughed. Both turned back to their work.

"Be seein' ya," said Jace, straightening up. "Don' go noplace now." He laughed. "Get it? Go noplace . . . Ha, ha, ha, ha, ha . . ."

And he was gone, trailing his merriment after him.

"Either o' you boys got the time o' day?" asked Raider.

Again they pretended not to hear.

"I asked . . ."

"We heard. We're not supposed to talk to you," said one. "Zemos's orders."

"Just tell me what time it is and I promise I won't ask anything else."

"Getting on to nine-thirty."

They worked steadily for three hours by Raider's estimate, tirelessly, finishing at last, stretching and rubbing their eyes as before, and leaving with their stacks. The moment they were out the door he swiveled the knife in his hand, got it into the V between his thumb and forefinger, and flipped it open with his thumbnail. Then, angling it, he began sawing the rope. In seconds he had parted it and, divesting his wrists and ankles of it, he began working the numbness out of his wrists, getting up and crossing to the open window as he did so. Opening it farther, to its limit, he tossed out the pieces of rope. Leaning out as far as he could, he looked down. No light showed in the windows above. No lights anywhere on this side of the house. Twisting his body as he climbed out, he slowly let himself down six inches to solid ground. Crouching, he waited and listened, the little knife opened in his hand. Then, realizing how useless it would be as a weapon, he slipped it into his shirt pocket, thinking as he did so that it was all he had left of her. Small souvenir of a relationship doomed from the beginning.

The sky was awash with stars; the moon shone full, painting the way to the barn as bright as day. A pale yellow light from a rear window flooded the ground. Better he circle wide, he thought, keep well out of the sight line of anyone who might casually glance out the window.

He circled, coming into knee-high weeds, brushing softly through them, reaching the barn, slipping inside through the partially opened door. Looking back at the house through the open rear window he could see several men gathered around a table studiously examining banknotes.

He started to open the door all the way to permit him to lead a horse out. The hinges creaked loudly, the sound assaulting his ears, causing him to flinch and tense. Jesus! As it shattered the stillness, a stallion in a stall somewhere in the darkness behind him began whinnying loudly. A quick glance at the window froze the blood in his veins. All six men had heard and were on their feet. The back door opened, but even before the first one came out, out of nowhere a man came lunging into the barn, all but bowling him over.

Zemo!

Raider threw himself to one side to avoid contact, but in the moonlight flooding the floor of the barn with the door wide, the big man saw him, recognized him, came at him swinging . . .

Once before, Raider had gone around with the snake-biter; recollection of his patent inability to dent any part of the bastard came back to him. Now Zemo was swinging wildly, cursing, his friends boiling out the back door, coming to a stop, grouping, watching the two of them. Raider lurched to his right out of range of the huge, flailing fists. In the barn doorway Raider let go a left, packing everything he had back of it, catching Zemo from behind in the kidney. He roared like a stricken bull, swinging about, eyes blazing, fists driving at his tormentor, a right catching Raider in the shoulder, sending him staggering back. Christ it hurt! Like a piledriver smashing; a miracle he hadn't fractured it . . .

The onlookers were cheering now. Others, drawn by the noise, were filling the upstairs windows, throwing them open, leaning out.

Raider was never to be quite sure exactly what happened then during the hectic few seconds that followed. So much so quickly. Riders, seemingly fifty of them, thundering up, coming in from all sides, surrounding the house, the one-sided fight. Guns out, firing in the air, orders barked and bellowed, windows slamming shut, glass breaking and, centering it all, Zemo, head lowered, charging, eyes bulging, steaming with hate, saliva slathering out of one corner of his twisted mouth. Raider backed off, clutching his injured shoulder, no longer that sure it wasn't broken. Twisting about, he started to run. Out shot Zemo's foot, tripping him, sending him sprawling, his cheek hammering the ground. He lay gasping, gathering himself together, then rolled over, blanching, stunned by the sight that met his eyes. Hovering over him the snakebiter clutched a pitchfork, lifting it high to plunge it into his face. Roaring triumphantly he started it down . . .

Shots filled the air. A slug plowed into Zemo's left rib cage, hitting from so close so hard it spun him around. The fork loosened from his grasp and rattled harmless to the ground at Raider's feet. He glanced to his right. Turnbull stood crouched fifteen feet away, his mouth turned up at the corners in a grin, his .44 smoking. Disregarding the weapon, Zemo started for him, snarling, his arms high, apelike, his fingers open, bent, clawing the air.

Raider looked on fascinated as Turnbull pulled off a second shot, the muzzle aimed squarely at Zemo's heart. Only the bullet never left the barrel, his trigger squeezing halfway only, the recoil spring, something, jamming.

"RADE, GET AWAY!" snapped Turnbull. "GET..."

Zemo landed on him, hands at his throat, thumbs under the soft part of his jaw, pushing upward, fingers squeezing, as slugs plowed into him from all sides. Turnbull's knees buckled, his neck snapping . . . Raider groaned, rolling over, coming up on hands and knees, shaking his head, to rid his brain of the awful sight, the sound.

Turnbull lay in a crumpled pile, dead. Zemo dead, blood welling out of him, imprinting his chest and sides with crimson flowers.

And as quickly as it had begun, the battle was over.

32

Raider sat on the ground, bathed in moonlight, glowering, boiling under his breath, his knees drawn up, forearms draped over them, unable to tear his eyes from the blanket-shrouded corpse lying fifteen feet away. Opposite him sat Doc polishing his Diamond .38 vigorously with a square of muslin.

"The son of a bitch," growled Raider. "Of all the stinkin', dirty, rotten . . ."

"Will you cut that out!" snapped Doc. "The man saved your life, the least you might do is show a little compassion."

"He did it a-purpose!"

"You're ridiculous, you know that? Simpleminded. A one-track simple mind, that's you."

"Fifty guys come ridin' in . . ."

"Thirty-five. Sheriff Lafarge and twenty-seven men and the seven of us."

"Thirty-five. How come he's got to be the one to save me? And croak doin' it?"

"You miss the point, numbskull. He didn't save *you,* he saved one of the good guys. You just happened to be it; he didn't plan it that way."

Raider jerked his eyes from the body and fastened them on his partner. His tone turned abruptly milder, self-consciously subdued. "Any way you look at it, it's a goddamn dirty trick."

"Nonsense, it's merely fate slapping you on the conscience for your childish attitude toward the man."

"How about his attitude toward me?"

"Rade, will you forget it?"

"I didn't move a hair, Doc. I sat there like I was chained to the ground. I coulda jumped Zemo . . ."

"If you had, you would have caught half a dozen slugs. He himself must have caught fifteen."

"I froze . . . I plumb froze."

"Lucky you."

"Has he got kinfolk up in Michigan, you think? He must have. God forbid a missus, young-uns . . . I got to wire Wagner first thing in the mornin' and find out. Then wire them I'm comin' up." He turned his head, and for a fleeting instant Doc imagined he saws tears gleaming in his eyes, but never having seen them before he could not be sure.

"Aren't you the least bit curious how we managed to find this place?"

Raider shrugged. The sheriff and his men and the other Pinkertons were milling about, having finished rounding up the carnival people. A buckboard had been brought up, a body loaded on it, then Zemo's, and now two men were picking up the major's body to place it in the bed.

Raider watched them, biting his lower lip, picking up a nonexistent pebble at his feet and tossing it down irritably.

"You musta got lucky."

"Luck like you've never seen before in your life. Not to mention timing. We'd all turned in for the night. Really. I actually had one leg in bed when a knock came at my door."

"You mean you gave it up for the night?"

"What else could we do?"

"Fine buncha buddies."

"Come off it, we had no idea you were here."

"You shoulda figured . . ."

"You should have made your future plans clear!"

Doc went on to say that they had telegraphed Colbyville only to be informed that Priscilla Swanson was no longer living there. With nowhere else to turn, Doc and the others had returned to the hotel. Ten minutes later one of the sheriff's deputies appeared at Doc's door. A man had shown up at LaFarge's office demanding he swear out a warrant for one Heinz Werner

Brauchitz on a charge of complicity in murder. Doc had jumped into his clothes and run down to the office.

"Artis Reagan," said Raider.

"You know him?"

"Hell yes, we're old poker-playin' buddies."

"Then you know what he looks like. What he smells like. That's good, I wouldn't be able to find words to describe him. He came in on a mule."

Raider cut in, nodding emphatically, explaining that Reagan had come to the house, that Zemo had brushed him off, had thrown him out. When the old man had stopped crying and ridden away, he had no doubt lost his temper. He had shown up expecting an explanation, patience, sympathy. His curt dismissal couldn't have sat very well.

"He figured Zemo knew more about Franklin's death than he was telling. When LaFarge got wind of it, naturally he got word over to us." Doc grinned. "How many times does this make it?"

"Times what? What are you talkin' about?"

"How many times have I saved your life, seven, eight?"

"*He* saved my life, Doc." Raider jerked a thumb over his aching shoulder at the buckboard moving slowly off toward Sauer City. "And died doin' it."

"Good grief, are we back on that?"

"You make it out as nothin', don't you?"

Doc got up, dusting off his trousers, throwing up his hands. "Get Dom and Walter over here. Run through it for all of them." He started off, stopped, turned back. "Oh, one other thing. Something you ought to know. Now you've retired there's a form you're supposed to fill out. YD-62. You're required to list everything you've been issued, everything missing, lost, or stolen. It's for accounting."

"Fuck them, I can't be bothered."

"You'd better be if you want to collect your pay and your expense money. Everybody leaving the agency fills one out."

"They'd better not try holdin' out on me. Not if Wagner and the old man wanta keep their goddamn teeth!"

"Regulations are regulations, Rade. It looks to me like staying on is one heck of a lot easier than quitting. Less complicated."

Raider threw away his temper and began loudly expounding on the unfairness of the Pinkerton National Detective Agency's policies, Chicago's callous mistreatment and indifference toward hard-working operatives, rules and regulations and other related matters. One after another, the quiet conversations going on around him ceased as his voice grew louder and louder.

Six days later the two sat at a table in the Muskrat, separated by two pints of beer. Raider abused his brain, struggling to summon up all the information demanded by Form YD-62. Doc was also occupied, completing the journal for Case No. 2451. Dom DePaolo and his five surviving associates had since departed for Denver. Major Henderson Turnbull had been interred in the Methodist Cemetery. Wagner had responded to Raider's query regarding his family with word that Turnbull had been alone in the world.

Doc's hand was wrapped around his Columbian vulcanized rubber fountain pen mounted with fine gold-filled bands and taper cap:

Final Report—July 22nd

DECEASED:

Suspect ALFRED WITHERS
Age: 24
Place of birth: Unknown
    Death accidentally self-inflicted in the act of firing rifle with residue lodged in barrel. Date of death: July 14th.

                    Interment: Methodist Cemetery,
                                Sauer City, Texas

Suspect DOLLY DEE BOWLES
Age: 23
Place of birth: Unknown
    Murdered by Heinz Werner Brauchitz 15th July.

Accused broke decedent's neck. Death instantaneous.

> Interment: Methodist Cemetery,
> Sauer City, Texas

Suspect ORVILLE THOMAS CASEY
Age: 26
Place of birth: Corpus Christi, Texas
  Shot in both lungs on or about 13th of July. Remains buried in shallow grave behind barn on Pedersen property.

> Interment: Holy Name Cemetery,
> Corpus Christi, Texas

Suspect JASON HILLYARD
Age: 21
Place of birth: Shackleford County, Texas
  Accidentally bitten by rattlesnake shortly before or during action resulting in capture and arrest of Brauchitz gang.

> Interment: Pine Grove Cemetery,
> Moran, Texas

Suspect HEINZ WERNER BRAUCHITZ
Age: 40
Place of birth: Stuttgart, Germany
  Died of total of sixteen wounds inflicted by Pinkerton operatives and sheriff's deputies. Date of death: July 16th

  Suspect accused of murders of
> Joseph Mark Gilbertson
> Dolly Dee Bowles
> Orville Thomas Casey
> Interment: Pine Grove Cemetery,
> Moran, Texas

Five-dollar banknote plates, obverse and reverse, recovered and held for presentation as material evidence. Owner Miles Atwood, president Sauer City People's Bank, apprised.

Lead plate bearing impressions of obverse and reverse plates of ten-dollar banknotes, property Horace F. Catterbury, president Roswell Farmers and Merchants Bank, recovered and held for presentation as material evidence. Mr. Catterbury so apprised.

Copper plates, obverse and reverse of five-dollar banknotes issued to T. D. Morgan Territorial Bank, Albuquerque, New Mexico, confiscated. To be held for presentation as material evidence. Mr. Morgan so apprised. Plates believed to be duplicates made from impressions on lead plates present whereabouts of which undetermined.

A bank in Deming and, surprisingly, two additional banks' plate copies were also recovered, banks in St. Johns and Clifton, Arizona.

Ninety-two thousand dollars, mostly in silver and gold pieces, with the exception of four thousand two hundred and thirty dollars in banknotes recovered. All forwarded to the Denver office. Distribution to be directed by William Pinkerton.

Thirty-one suspects arrested, including fourteen at the Pedersen house. List of names not yet completed. Upon completion list will be forwarded for filing. All photographs will also be forwarded shortly.

Eight horses appropriated from gang seeking to hold up the Eastern Railway Company of New Mexico Clovis–Barstow, Texas train sixty-three miles north of Barstow. Horses given in charge to Sheriff Fred LaFarge of Sauer City, including all gear. Incident written up separately, pages 46–48.

Surviving suspects bound over for trial, circuit court, Sauer City. Messrs. Atwood, Catterbury, Morgan, Hightower, Wills, and Dierckenschmidt informed as to date and circumstances. All to appear as witnesses.

Confiscated carnival equipment and rolling stock

being held by Sheriff LaFarge until authorities determine disposition thereof.

Case closed.

Doc signed his name with a flourish and proffered the pen to Raider.

"You sign."

"Why should I bother?"

"It's your case, you wrapped it up, didn't you?"

"You and fifty other guys wrapped it up."

"Thirty-four other guys."

"Yeah."

Raider signed, then shoved his own paper, Form YD-62, toward Doc.

"That's the best I can do with that."

Doc scanned the form. "You haven't filled in half the blanks, not a third."

"Screw it."

Raider stood up and put on his hat.

"Where are you going?"

"North, south, east . . . who knows. Maybe up to Wichita Falls first. I know a lady up there. Pinky Something."

"Mister, you are unbelievable! The most bull-headed human on the face of the earth. You make up your mind, even though you're dead wrong, and you stick to it through the fires of hell, don't you?"

Raider finished his beer, licked his lips, and hammered the table with his glass.

"You bet."

Doc shoved the paper back at him. "Fill this out properly or don't expect any money. That's the law, Allan Pinkerton's." Capping his pen, he jammed it down into Raider's breast pocket. "Oh, one other thing." He brought out a telegram, unfolding it. "I just got this about an hour ago. We've been reassigned. Cheyenne."

"*You've* been."

"You're going to make me travel nearly nine hundred miles up there all by my lonesome?"

"I'm not makin' you nothin'. You wanta go, go. Good-bye, Doc." He extended his hand.

"Save it. I'm not shaking it."

"You sore? How come? I MEAN WHERE DO YOU GET OFF BEIN' SORE AT ME!"

Other patrons stopped talking and eyed the pair curiously. The bartender wiping down his mahogany frowned.

"Good-bye," said Doc.

"No good luck?"

"Good-bye, good luck, good-bye, good-bye, good-bye! Get out if you're going!"

"I'M GOIN'! I'M GOIN'!"

Snatching back Form YD-62, Raider walked off, stomping slightly, as if he were letting his annoyance out his heels. Pushing through the batwing doors he vanished from sight.

Doc sat back grinning. He'd give him ten minutes, time to saddle up his new horse and ride out the north road in the direction of Wichita Falls. Then he'd walk across the street to the sheriff's office and lodge a complaint.

A man simply could not be permitted to get away with stealing another's property.

That Columbian vulcan rubber fountain pen mounted with fine gold-filled bands and taper cap was fitted with a solid gold sixteen-carat point. Price: three dollars and seventy-five cents. Not much, just enough to support a charge of petty larceny and overnight in jail.